ANNE BONNY

—⊰ ALSO *by* CHLOE GARTNER ⊱—

❈❈❈❈❈❈❈❈❈

THE INFIDELS

DRUMS OF KHARTOUM

THE WOMAN FROM THE GLEN

MISTRESS OF THE HIGHLANDS

ANNE BONNY

by

CHLOE GARTNER

William Morrow
and Company,
Inc.
New York
1977

Printed in the United States of America.

1   2   3   4   5   6   7   8   9   10

Library of Congress Cataloging in Publication Data

Gartner, Chloe.
    Anne Bonny.

    1. Radcliffe, Anne Bonny, b. 1700—Fiction.
I. Title.
PZ4.G243An   [PS3513.A7415]   813'.5'2   77-3182
ISBN 0-688-03208-7

BOOK DESIGN   CARL WEISS

When I was a child I wanted to grow up to be a pirate like Anne Bonny. When I told Ronald this he said, "Why don't you write a novel based on her?" So this book is for him, for Sistie and Stan, Kristin and Robin, all of whom insisted I write it; and for Marianne McCleary, who went with me to Charleston and Jamaica in search of Anne's past.

I am grateful to all of them and to the librarians of the Portola Valley, California, library for their endless pursuit of books through inter-library loan; to Mr. Clinton V. Black, Government Archivist, Spanish Town, Jamaica, and to the West Indies Library, Kingston, Jamaica.

CONTENTS

((7))

It is better to swim in the sea below

Than to hang in the air and feed the crow,

Said jolly Ned Teach of Bristol.

PROLOGUE

MARY HAS ESCAPED the hangman. The others swing in chains
on Deadman's Cay. Their faces grimace with decay. Their
trousers are stained by their emptied bowels. "There's nothing like hanging to cure a fellow of blind gut," Ned Teach
used to say.

I am appealing for another reprieve.

Reprieve after reprieve, but never a pardon. Often I
wonder if Fate and Governor Lawes are playing me out like
a fish, the more easily to pull me in, so soon I, too, will
dangle at the end of a rope.

Another petition must be submitted. "Put down everything," I am told, "so the petitioner can choose the facts that

will most aia your case. Begin at the time when you were a child and put down everything you remember."

"Everything?"

"Even the most salacious facts, the better to make you seem repentant."

I sit in the hills high above Kingston. The air is never still. The wind in the trees sounds like surf. John Crow soars on the air currents, dipping so low I can see his evil beak and red head. Smoke from the fields of dead cane drifts across the plain into the blue mountains. A bank of white clouds borders the sea. In the harbor there are ships: pinks, brigs, schooners, sloops, and a man-of-war. One of the brigs is hoisting sail. I remember the sound of the capstan, the rattle of anchor chain, the crack of canvas as it fills.

Was I ever a child?

I

ANNE

My earliest memory is the smell of the sea and the taste of salt on my lips.

"And so it should be," my father said. "I held you in my arms when we left Ireland so together we should see the last of its green shores and the first graying of England. You were but two years old. You cannot remember, Annie."

"I do remember." I touched my tongue to my lips as if the taste of salt were still there.

My father smiled down at me and patted my wind-tumbled hair. "I'll not be questioning it if you say so, for you're a strange wee girl. Not like a child at all. You're so much in my company and the company of men you've grown old before your time. First thing I am knowing you'll be wanting to marry. Who shall it be, beauty? Some young clerk aiming to be a lawyer like myself or a grand gentleman with a country estate?"

We were standing on the riverbank gazing upon the Pool with its forest of masts. The sails were reefed and the merchantmen anchored side by side, but I saw how they tugged at their lines as if they would be free. It was my favorite spot in all London. I would have stayed there all day filling my eyes and my mind and my heart with the sight of those ships.

"I shall marry a seaman."

"Ho, ho, a seaman, is it? To be wed to a seaman is as bad as being widowed, Annie. A few days ashore and away he goes again for three years or more. You'd not be liking that."

"I'll go with him."

Overhead the kites and gulls circled. The river roared through the arches of the bridge. The watermills clanked and the watermen shouted as they shot the bridge. Far down the river lay Greenwich and beyond Greenwich the mouth of the sea.

"I shouldn't wonder but what you would, now. And speaking of going, beauty, we must push along. I've much to do to wind up my affairs before we sail."

I tugged at his hand. "Wait! Point it out to me again. Which is our ship? The one on which we sail?"

I knew which it was but every day I must have it pointed out to me.

"That one, do you not see, where the paintmen are putting new rose into the cheeks of the figurehead and prettying her gown."

"She looks like mother."

My father cocked his head and squinted at the figurehead. "Um. Not so beautiful, Annie. Not so soft."

"Not by far."

We made our way through the narrow streets to his offices near St. Catherine's Docks. I walked close to him, clinging to his hand. I hated the streets in early morning before the dead—those who had drunk themselves to death or starved, the abandoned babies, scrawny and ugly as fledglings—had been carted away, just as I hated them in the early dark of winter when fog and thieves slunk through the passageways.

"But to be sure, beauty, we cannot spend all our time out and about at midday with the grand folk, or cavorting in Covent Garden eating China oranges no matter how sweetly the new mown grass smells."

I did not tell my father for fear of injuring his feelings that I would have liked to spend my time at home with my mother even though it meant doing needlework and listening to the prattle of ladies at gossip. I loved my beautiful, lively young mother. I wanted to ape everything she did: wear a silken gown, carry a fan, welcome my father home in the evening with kisses.

Instead I went every day to his offices dressed in the clothes of a boy. I was called Andrew and was introduced as a young relative apprenticed to learn the law. It puzzled me and I never quite knew who I was.

Only once I asked my father about this pretense. He had sighed heavily. "I knew one day you would be asking, beauty, but it's not yet time to be answering. 'Tis but the sins of the fathers and me own hot blood and the pious, narrow minds of the accursed Sweeneys."

I had no idea what he meant or who the accursed Sweeneys were, but he looked so downcast I did not question him further. I had learned there is a time to keep silence and a time to speak. I accepted my world more or less philosophically and when I was not looking out the window at the busy river—and I never tired of that—I ran errands, filled the coal scuttles, learned to make my letters and numbers, and studied Greek, Latin, and French. I learned quickly and well for I had a lively curiosity about everything. I even learned a bit about the law.

But soon all this would be changed. We were going to the New World, to the Carolinas, where, my father said, the winds were warm and the earth blossomed underfoot.

"Away from the cesspit of London where law is a travesty and justice can be bought and sold for a ha'penny." Father's voice boomed out as if he were in the courts instead of our cozy sitting room. Then he winked at my mother. "Besides, my darling Pegeen, the accursed Sweeneys'll not be following us to the New World. 'Tis too far for their forked tongues that belabor me and their serpentish ways that are set on my ruin. There I'll no more be Patrick William McCormack but plain William Cormac, gentleman at law, with wife, Margaret, and daughter, Anne. William Cormac. Are you learning to like the sound of it, Pegeen?"

My mother tilted her head to one side and tapped her pink lips with her fan as she considered. She nodded. "It sounds a gentleman's name."

"'Tis a pity the Sweeneys'll not be knowing the favor they've done us, buying themselves free of me. They were generous, that I'll not deny."

"Pooh!" Mother tossed her head so her curls bounced.

"Pooh all you wish, Pegeen, but generous they were in truth, and you know the truth is sacred to me. 'Tis a grand free place, Charles Town. It has welcomed dissenters—Irish, Scots, Dutch, and Huguenots, displaced men like myself. Men with any learning are in short supply and there are opportunities for a man with wit and wisdom. And you know, as I know myself, I have both.

"Charles Town and I will grow old and rich together. You'll never be needing to lift a hand, my darling. You'll have redmen and black for slaves, or indentured folk from England if your preference of color is white. Within five years you'll be a grand lady and we'll have a fortune.

"Lawyers, unfortunately, are forbidden to charge a fee. The law, they say in Charles Town, being the right of any man. *You* may say 'tis damn foolishness, but we'll bide by it. Who could object if true justice prevails? Never mind, there are more ways than one to spin a sixpence.

"If I cannot grow rich practicing law I'll find another way. Merchants, too, are in short supply. A merchant with a knowledge of the law—he could turn a trick or two, eh? A merchant with his own warehouse, his own ships? Ho, ho!

"Then, when the money is pouring in like a golden tide, a plantation of our own, slaves to work the fields, a grand house, and a rich marriage for Annie." He bent over and kissed my mother. "How does that sound to you, my darling? Are you sorry the Sweeneys drove us out? Are you sorry I came to your bed?"

"Never!" Mother smiled. I loved her smile. It made her look as if she had just eaten a comfit. "Just to think!"

From the moment we boarded the ship everything was real and familiar to me: the shrill whistle of the boatswain which pierced my heart as well as my ears; the stave the men sang as they drove the capstan round (*"Good St. Anne is gone to sea. I, Boys, Oh, Boys"*), the anchor dripping at the bow; the shiver along the keel as the ship began to move.

I stood between my parents and watched the land glide past. Men in small boats bobbing in the ship's wake waved and called. Gulls followed us, white-breasted against the silvery sky.

We rounded Greenwich Reach. The ropes began to sing. The sails cracked as the wind filled them. The gray sea came up to meet us. Slowly England sank into the water. The rabble of gulls swang back to land crying farewell in their hoarse voices. I waved to them and I, too, called farewell.

Never since have I been so passionately in love as I was in love with the sea and that ship. I loved the ever-changing water, the creak of the timbers, the sound of the wind, the smell of tar and brine, even the days we were becalmed scarcely a week out of England.

The thick fog muffled all sounds. I could not see the water but I heard it, lapping at the hull, speaking to me. The life went out of the sails. They hung flattened, sagging like dead things. The pennants drooped. The ship twisted, rocked, drifted. Every half hour a cannon was fired off the bow to warn other ships. I mention this because it was while we were becalmed that mother fell ill.

Soon our cabin was as stuffy and foul smelling as the air rising from the hold where the poor folk and criminals bided. I hated going to our cabin even to sleep. Father loathed it, too. I knew from the way his nose went pinched whenever he entered to urge mother to come out on deck.

"The air would be the curing of you, my darling. Here you breathe your own vomit and prolong your sickness."

Mother moaned and retched again, soiling her pillow.

One morning a gale wind snapped at the sails with a crack like the cannon. The fog disappeared and white horses raced across the sea. Waves broke over the deck leaving a glistening of salt and flopping silver fish.

Our chests and baskets slid across the cabin, crashing into one another. The floor became a wall before the ship righted itself, then slowly keeled over in the other direction. It delighted me, but mother grew sicker.

Father and the other gentlemen aboard crowded into the saloon talking of business and the colonies. I was on my own with the admonition to look sharp and not fall overboard. I had no intention of falling overboard. Grown-ups are fools when it comes to giving advice to children.

When I was not clinging to the rail, watching the rise and fall of the sea, I watched the sailors, the things they did with ropes and sails. I knew if I was allowed I could manage as well as any of them. I liked their rough talk and bitter laughter. I envied their striped trousers and tarred pigtails, and the way their bare toes curled to cling to the deck. I admired the way they ran up the riggings and I wished I could join the maintop man, for he could see farther than any of them.

One day after father left the cabin and mother was sleeping pale and still, I rummaged through the luggage to find the suit of boy's clothes I had worn in London.

Now instead of the wind wrapping my petticoats about my legs and filling my skirts as if they were sails, I could move with the ease of the sailors.

No one took any notice of me. The hands were aft swabbing the decks with vinegar to keep down the sickness. It wasn't keeping down mother's sickness or that in the hold. I had heard the gentlemen talking about the fever raging there and taking wagers on how soon the first death would occur.

I chose a mizzen shroud and started up. I had not expected the rope to hurt my hands and I wished I had taken off my shoes so I could wrap my toes around the ropes the way the sailors did. Up, up, slowly, steadily, pausing at each new height to look over my shoulder, straight down into the sea before the ship tilted back, flattening me against the shroud. I had nearly reached the crosstree when the seaman called Clym looked up. His mouth fell open and he shook his swab like a club.

"Comee down 'ere, you young divil, afore the sea has you."

The ribbon that held my hair came loose and sailed out to sea like a narrow-winged bluebird. My hair blew into my face, blinding me.

"God save me, it's the lass!" He knocked over his bucket of vinegar and seawater in his haste to get to me. The ropes shook under his weight and I had to cling so tightly my fingers began to bleed.

He pinned me with his great hairy arms. To my surprise he was trembling. Below the captain strode up and down shouting orders and pausing to gesture at us. The gentlemen came out of the saloon and father staggered with shock at the sight of me. He kept mopping his face with his handkerchief and crossing himself. I thought him a fool, much as I loved him.

"Now, lookee, do as Clym tells you, see. Slow and steady

((21))

and below we go. If you miss footing you'll not fall for I'm covering you, see."

"I won't miss."

"You say you won't but it's work coming down. What in the divil's own name were you a-doing, anyways?"

"I wanted to go to the very most top."

"And I wager you'd have done. But it takes a steady head and a strong stomach. Many a sturdy fellow's turned giddy aloft and lost his poor miserable life. But there, save our breath."

"Are *you* afraid?"

"Afeared for you. I've a lass at home as bold as yourself. I'd hide her if ever I caught her a-doing what you were. Now, swingee clear into the cap'n's arms."

I thought the captain was going to beat me. He held me roughly for a moment, then grunted and handed me over to father. Father, too, was trembling when he embraced me. Men pretend to be brave, but they aren't when they are faced with danger. It was a wonder he didn't swoon the way mother was always doing.

"Beauty, beauty, what if you'd been lost? 'Twould have killed me. I'd never have drawn another happy breath."

I endured his embrace. The other gentlemen shook their heads.

"She'll be one to reckon with when she comes of age. You have our pity, Cormac."

Clym was rewarded and I was ordered to remain in our cabin.

"I'll be sick if I do."

"God forbid!" Father flung up his hands and rolled his eyes. "Then stay close by, beauty, or the captain'll be casting us off in a small boat with nothing but moldy biscuit and a jug of sour wine."

I pretended to believe him.

The next few days I spent listening to the gentlemen's

conversations, watching them play cards. Father won, lost, cried endearments to the cards, won again, and laughed in triumph. He said I was his good luck charm. The card games were augmented by a great deal of brandy and soon the men forgot me. Then I slipped away to lean against the bulwarks where clouds of spray laved my face. Always, Clym was nearby, shaking his finger, nodding, grinning, revealing his broken, blackened teeth, tipping me a wink.

He once carved a jointed doll for me. I had never been given much time to play with dolls in my guise of Andrew so I didn't care much for them. But Clym was so pleased with himself that I smiled and curtsied. Making a sailor costume for it kept me busy for a day. I used one of father's handkerchiefs for a shirt, a bit of red ribbon for his cap, and I cut the flowered lining from a cape to make trousers as jolly as Clym's own.

Clym laughed when I showed him.

"I meant it for a lassie like yourself, but any lout could see you'd prefer a sailor lad. Here, shipmate, let me fix Jack's hair proper." He took the doll and carved away the curls, shaping and shaving the wood until Jack had a sailor's pug. "He's a reg'lar seaman now and could climb the rigging with the best of us."

"I could as well if I was allowed."

Clym cocked an eye at me. "Don't go trying that again, mind. Be good, Mistress Annie, and I'll carve a titchy skiff for Jack to sail."

"I mean to have a ship of my own one day."

"I never heard tell of a ship captained by a female, but if any do, it'll be yourself. And you know who'll be the first to sign her papers?" He tapped his shirt front with his tarry finger. "Clym here, that's who."

"I'll make you quartermaster, but mark you, I'll be captain and climb the rigging whenever I wish and you'll not be stopping me."

At Madeira while the ship replenished its stores and re-filled its watercasks father and I rambled on the golden-green hillsides. We bought baskets of fresh fruit for mother but she was too ill to eat it and turned her head away from its fragrance.

A few days later we picked up the trade winds. The water changed from gray to sapphire and the skies were like blue porcelain. But every day bodies were carried up from below and cast into the sea. One body was not properly weighted and as the captain said, ". . . in sure and certain hope of resurrection . . ." it reappeared like a gray headless fish. All day it followed the ship, rolling in the wake.

At night father whispered to me, "Say your prayers well, beauty, that tomorrow it will not be your mother we cast over."

Mother was almost transparent, her arms and hands flesh-less claws. She neither answered nor opened her eyes when father spoke to her. Father paced the deck, his face haggard with worry. He told the captain he doubted mother would live to reach the Carolinas. I think I worried about her, too, but I am not sure. Sometime during those weeks she had ceased to be my lovely mother who dispensed kisses and comfits to father and me, and become instead a corpselike stranger.

The captain chewed his fat lips for a moment. "There's a woman in the hold who has some rough knowledge of nurs-ing. They tell me it's because of her we've had so few deaths."

"Few! Ha!"

The captain ignored the interruption. "Mayhap—but, she's a convict. She dirked her lover during a quarrel."

Father laughed mirthlessly. "As a lawyer I've had some dealings with criminals, Captain. 'Tis the cutpurses in the alleys of London who are more dangerous than a female whose passions caused her to do murder. Have her up!"

I hated Clara—for that was her name—at first sight. She saw my scowl, then she tossed her head and gave a sneering laugh. It was plain she had no liking for me either.

But she went to work fetching buckets of water, heaving them over the side of the ship by a line, and scrubbing the cabin. She washed the soiled bedding and hung it to dry in the sunny, salty wind. She emptied the slops every morning, held a pannikin when mother was ill, and smoked a pipe three times a day to cleanse the room and sweeten the air. I thought it worsened it.

She made me wash my pantaloons and hose. "It'll do those pinky hands no harm and I've enough to do without washing up after a spoiled brat."

"You aren't to speak to me in that way."

"Who's to stop me?"

"My father."

It was Clara who discovered that father's handkerchief and my cape had been cut to make clothes for Jack.

"You're a wicked brat, you are, destroying what cost your father good money. If it was for me to do I'd whip you every day to keep you in line. But your father worships the pot you piss in, so I'll keep mum. But I'll have no nonsense from you. I'll have my eye on you even when I sleep, and don't you go forgetting it."

I hated her.

We were in calm water now. Flying fish and dolphins accompanied the ship, flashing in the air like a sparkle of jewels. The air and wind were warm, the sunrises and sunsets golden, and by night the powder of stars lay so low I was sure the maintop man could gather them.

A hammock was slung on deck for mother and father carried her to it every day. Color returned to her skin and her eyes lost their opaque glaze. Clara forced her to eat, sometimes no more than a spoonful of broth, a little dried fruit, or a sip of the wine we had taken on at Madeira.

But the deaths continued in the hold.

((25))

Once the maintop called a ship astern. Everyone crowded to the ship's side to see the distant white sails. I heard a mutter of fear among the gentlemen that it might be pirates, but it went on its way and disappeared against the white clouds piled along the horizon.

We were on short rations now. The barrels of meat had spoiled, the bread was full of worms, and the water was murky stuff that smelled too bad even to wash in.

At last Clym pointed out a bird.

"We'll be sighting land soon. You'll smell it long afore it comes in sight. You'll be a-seeing signs, too. Flotsam, garbage, signs of man, see. Then one day, there'll it be. Low in the water, 'cause the Carolinas are half water theirselves. The ship'll buck against the land swell as if her doesn't want to come to anchor. A ship's a free thing and it's no liking for a-being tethered like a dog."

It was all as Clym said. The birds came out to meet us. Logs and sacking, bits of cloth, bottles and rotting vegetation drifted past. The wind took on a subtle aroma of greenery and spice.

One morning when I went on deck we were passing between thickly forested islands. Beyond like a faint line drawn with a paint brush was Charles Town.

Then it all happened too fast. The round-mouthed cannons at the Guard House fired a salute. Men hailed us from the landing. Boys ran along the seawall waving like windmills. The sails dropped like the folded wings of birds come to rest. The anchor plummeted into the water. We went ashore in a small boat, surrounded by our boxes and baskets and chests.

These past months I had thought I loved only the sea. Now my love veered round like the wind and I was committed to a new passion. The moment I set foot ashore I loved that land. I close my eyes and see it as I saw it then. The milky-blue harbor, water splashing against the seawall, the noisy, bustling waterfront with its taverns and warehouses and markets. Seamen, Indians, blacks, and the militia with their scarlet mountings. Pastel houses ornamented with iron-work. Wide orderly streets, so different from London's tangle of ill-smelling lanes. Dazzling sunlight and purple shadows. The scent of mud and gardens steaming in the heat. Palmetto leaves rattling in the wind, the oaks shawled with moss, yellow blossoming trees, and beyond town, the dark and mysterious forest.

I longed to break free from Clara's hand and race ahead the sooner to see it all. But Clara had me in a grip of iron. I might as well have been manacled. For Clara was still with us. Father had bought her indenture.

I had stamped my foot and screamed when he told me. "Why? Why? *Why?*"

"We'll be needing servants, beauty. She's a strong, capable young woman and she saved your mother's life."

"I don't care. I hate her! I wish she were dead!"

"There now, Annie, it's a wicked tongue you have in your mouth. We should be grateful to Clara."

Grateful! Clara had a way of looking at me as if she could read my mind. I think she wished me dead as well.

I see no reason to recapitulate all that happened in the next few years. Every damned petition submitted so far has told and retold it in tiresome detail, as if extolling my family also extolled me.

My judges must know our lives as well as they know their own. They know how my father made a fortune, that we had one of the few brick houses in Charles Town—though I am told they are using more brick these days—about our plantation in the Goose Creek area, about our slaves and servants, my tutors, our horses and hunting dogs, the boat that carried us to and from the plantation, and our lavish entertaining.

They know mother never quite recovered from the voyage and had long bouts of illness that kept her to her bed. The year the hurricane took the roof off the house in Charles Town we summered at the plantation against everyone's advice, while the house in town was being repaired. There mother became a victim of lowland fever. She survived it, God knows how, but every year it returned, determined to claim her its victim.

More and more, Clara assumed the role of housekeeper. More and more I resented her, mother's dependence on her, the friendship that grew between them, and Clara's all-knowing, all-seeing eyes.

The judges have heard I was a wilful, spoiled, bad-tempered seed though I was given every opportunity to be otherwise. No advantage was denied me.

I learned to dance, to play the harpsichord, to speak French, to sail, shoot, ride, and manage money. When the public school opened I would have no more of tutors but attended classes there. The truth was I longed for the competition of other children. Not their friendship. I had no need of friends. I was self-sufficient. But I longed to show off. I longed to be challenged for it pushed me to further heights.

The school rued the day it accepted me as a pupil. I asked questions the teachers could not answer. I blackened the eyes of the boys who made the mistake of teasing me. In turn, I teased the girls until they cried, then jeered and mocked their tears.

All that wearied me soon enough and I took to running about the waterfront with a gang who spent their days fishing from the seawall, running errands for the tavern doxies, picking the pockets of drunken seamen, pinching unguarded goods from the warehouses, and in general preparing themselves for a bad end. I even stole from my own father and thought it a great joke.

Most often I was in the company of my father. He had grown so accustomed to having me at his side that he said he could not do without me. He still had plans for arranging a wealthy marriage, and he was determined I should know how to handle our affairs.

"I've seen too many husbands squander the fortunes their brides brought with them. I haven't worked like a cursed slave to have some careless young blood toss away your inheritance on the bottle or dice. Not that I think you'd allow it. 'Twill take an iron jackboot to manage you, beauty. But you should know what business is all about and how it is conducted."

So I sat by his side in the warehouse offices going over prices and taxes and accounts. Often I was Andrew again, in buckskin breeches and my hair tied in a pug, to be rowed out to the ships, for the seamen and pirates had no liking for a woman aboard. "And a beauty like you, Annie, would distract us from the business at hand." I was Andrew, too, in the waterfront taverns where every merchant in Charles Town conducted some portion of their affairs.

Doxies conduct their affairs there as well, and it doesn't take long to understand what the seamen expect of them or what they expect of the seamen. I was so curious as to what it was all about that I forced one of the gang I ran with to take down his breeches and show me his parts. After that he was eager to demonstrate their use. I pushed him off the seawall. He needed a wash anyway.

It was in the taverns and on the ships and in my father's warehouse that I fell in with pirates. So indirectly my own father led to my downfall.

I don't have to tell my judges that much of our trading was with pirates. This was not only in Charles Town but also up and down the coast as far north as New England. Pirate crews were recruited openly in New York. The Quakers in Philadelphia winked at them, and the governor's own daughter was married to a member of Captain Avery's crew. The governor of Jamaica supplied Jennings with the ships to attack the Spanish Plate fleet. Henry Morgan was once governor of Jamaica and used to sit in the streets of Port Royal with a keg of rum, threatening to shoot anyone who would not drink with him.

It is only since the Brethren have become an inconvenience to the merchants who have gone crying to government that they are being hounded and hanged.

In Charles Town pirates were not only tolerated but also encouraged. The bodies that had hung in chains at the mouth of the harbor were removed lest they embarrass our business associates. The pirates brought money into the country—gold doubloons, pillar dollars, pieces of eight, silver cobs. They harried the rival Spanish shipping. They sold their stolen goods more cheaply than we could buy it from England. For everything sent to the colonies had first to be shipped to England, taxed, and shipped back to us. Everyone knows Home Government are determined to bleed the Colonists until they are too poor to call their souls their own. It's a tax here and a tax there, and the devil to pay if you buy so much as a peppercorn from the Spanish, French, or Dutch.

The pirates not only sold life's necessities such as rum, sugar, molasses, naval supplies, cotton, dyestuff, and tobacco; they supplied us with luxuries. Velvet, linens, lace, fowling pieces, pistols, wine, candlesticks, baubles, spices, furnishings grander than our crude homemade benches. The lace at my father's throat, the brocade of my mother's gown, our damask curtains, my gold-damascened fowling piece, were all bought from pirates.

They were entertained in the best homes, accepted as gentlemen of blood rather than gentlemen of fortune. Some of them had retired and become respected citizens, even holding office.

((30))

Of course we could not have kept them away if they had been unwelcome. The militia was on the frontier trying to put down the Indian uprising and only a handful of old men, past fighting age, held the Guard House.

But my judges know all this. What they do not know is why I became a pirate myself. I am weary of the whitewash that has been flung upon my past. I shall put down everything.

CHAPTER

CLARA

MY DOWNFALL, as my petitioners choose to call it, began with Captain Benjamin Hornigold.

It was early autumn. There had been a week of chilly weather and rain squalls in Charles Town. Fever season had passed and we moved back to the plantation. No sooner had we settled in than the clouds dispersed, the winds died, and the weather turned unseasonably warm. The days were sticky and breathless, cooling only after the sun had set. In the evening white mists drifted along the waterways and across the rice paddies. Every morning a molten sun, red as a blood orange, rose and burned off the mist and blazed down on us.

In spite of the weather the ducks and wild geese were flying from the north, honking at dawn as they rose from the marshes where they had fed. They were so many we could hear the sound of their wings.

I was out with my fowling pieces every morning, knee-deep in ground mist, and seldom returned before evening. Often I had to go some distance to find my kill because every year there was less forest. The trees were being cut and shipped to England to be used as spars for the Royal Navy, and as the forest went, the animals retreated.

My father told me I should take a slave with me because the forests these days were the hiding place of Indian scouts, deserters from the militia, and refugees from the Indian-raided areas. But I preferred my own company to that of a reluctant slave who would hear Indians where there were none, and start at every shadow, frightening the game. Our Indian gamekeeper had taught me all he knew about tracking, and although I was only fifteen I was as tall and strong as a lad, and capable of carrying my own weapons and powder.

On this particular day I had bagged a turkey and three ducks but nothing else. The day was so hot all the game had gone to cover. I returned home early, left my bag with Gillah in the kitchen, and went to the house.

The petitions have neglected to describe the plantation house, though my judges know they've described everything else. Father did himself proud when he built that house. It rose three stories with galleries surrounding each floor and Grecian pillars supporting the galleries. The cypress had weathered to a silvery-gray, and wisteria vines festooned the galleries like garlands. The doors and windows were jalousied. The drawing room opened onto a garden that sloped down to the river. The hallways formed a cross except on the second floor where there was a ballroom the full length of the house.

I can still see mother and father dancing there. They always outshone their guests, always knew the latest dances and the most complicated movements of the minuet. Our entertainments were famous. My father was my favorite partner. The floor cleared when he led me on it to perform an

Irish country jig or a hornpipe. I was as tall as he was and had his golden-red hair and high coloring. It was said we made a handsome couple.

Sometimes of an evening when there were no guests, I would play for mother and father and they would dance alone across the grand length of the ballroom, gazing into one another's eyes, forgetting even my presence.

The kitchen, the coolhouse, the smokehouse, the stable, and servant quarters formed a U in back. There was a vine-covered breezeway between the kitchen and the house but that door was for servants. I went around to the front and stopped to kick the mud off my boots and glower at a coach standing at our door.

For a moment I considered turning right around and going back to the cypress swamp. But it was late afternoon and bold as I was, I didn't like being there when the mists began to rise. Not even the dogs who were busily watering the coach wheels would go there at dusk without whimpering and slinking along with their tails between their legs. Things lurked there that frightened them. Things I couldn't see to shoot in that gloaming light.

Things lurked in the house, too. The damned Mackays. It wasn't enough they lived next door in Charles Town. Their plantation adjoined ours and in town or country, Mrs. Mackay and her milksop son called three times a week. My mother had the brains of a titling when it came to choosing friends. Like Clara. Who ever heard of making friends with an indentured servant and letting her run the house as if she were mistress of it? I used to wonder why my father tolerated it, but his Pegeen could do no wrong. He doted on her and he carried her off to bed every night as eagerly as if he were a bridegroom.

He doted on the Mackays, too, so much so that he had affianced me to Colin Mackay without so much as asking my leave.

I wished the devil would carry off Colin Mackay with his round pale eyes and pudgy cheeks. So far I had managed to put off the wedding. Most of the girls I had shoved into mud puddles at school had married at thirteen or fourteen and were bulging with their second pregnancy. Their husbands were squeezing my hands when we danced and ogling my breasts and asking where I went to hunt and if they could meet me there. As if I wanted their secondhand caresses!

The dogs bounded in ahead of me as I deliberately clumped into the house and banged the door so the slats rattled. I put my gun in the rack and started for the stairs. I could hear mother's voice through the jalousied door, sweet and bell-like and empty as a bell. I stopped to listen.

"There's Anne now, Colin. I was right not to send you to meet her. You must help us convince her it's unsafe to go into the forest alone these days. She thinks she's invulnerable."

"Lucifer's dog!" I said. Then I jumped, for Clara was behind me. She had a way of appearing as silently as if she were a ghost.

"You're to change out of those clothes before you go in."

"The devil I will. If Mrs. Mackay doesn't like buckskin breeches she can go back to her own drawing room."

I had intended to change. It was hot in the house and I was sweating under the buckskin. I had a new dress of some French silk father had bought off a one-eyed pirate. It was so low-cut the curve of my breasts and the hollow between them showed. It would have been amusing to see Colin trying to keep his eyes off them, turning red and gulping. But now I was damned if I would.

"You'll disgrace your mother. It will sorrow her."

"And she'll swoon. Then you can revive her, Clara, and she'll tell you how kind you are. The way you suck up to one another it's a wonder to me you aren't lovers."

Clara raised her hand as if to strike me. But of course she didn't dare. "You're a foul-mouthed bitch and it's a wonder to *me* your father doesn't turn you out on the streets where you belong."

"The day he did he'd come running after me, begging me to return." As soon as I said it I had a grue.

For a moment I hesitated, my hand on the door, wondering if I should change after all. Then I felt Clara's eyes burning into my back and I tossed my head and slammed into the drawing room.

Anyone but thickheaded parents could see Colin Mackay didn't like me any better than I liked him. From the time we were children I had terrified him. I had taken away his toys, teased him, put sand down his neck, pushed him into the river, loosened the buckle on his saddle so when he tried to mount he fell in the dust, and more than once shot off his hat. Once I even shot a buckle off his boot but that was foolhardy. Even an expert shot can make a mistake. I could have lamed him.

I was half a head taller and I could ride better, shoot better, speak better French, dance better (he always managed to stumble over his own feet), even fence better, though it scandalized his mother that I had learned how to duel. Mr. Mackay said I had a better head for business.

"And a muckle fine thing it is! Colin with his head in his books and his mind full of Latin would be ruined in a season if left to himself. You'll have to counsel him, lass."

I thought it wasn't only business I'd have to counsel him in. He hadn't been under my skirts yet though he had every right to be since we were affianced. André Prudeau told me all Colin's friends ragged him for being so backward. But André Prudeau bragged he had already got with child one of their slave girls. It wasn't anything to brag about in my opinion. The girl was probably afraid of a beating if she resisted.

"Colin claims to be as hot-blooded as any of us but he

wants to wait until he's wed. I ask you, Anne, what sort of man is this you're to marry? You'll need me to keep you satisfied."

"Don't sit around being celibate waiting for me to call on you, André." This was a jest. We all knew André chased every petticoat he saw.

I, too, enjoyed ragging Colin. Only the day before I had been hunting and had climbed a tree to eat my bread. While I sat, hidden by leaves, who should come through the woods but Colin. He gave a quick look around to see if he was alone, then unbuttoned himself and began to piss against that very tree.

I burst into laughter and he looked up at me, red-faced as a boiled crawdad and just as slack-jawed. He looked as if he wanted to tuck himself back into his breeches and bolt to safety, but he might as well have tried to stop the Cooper River from flowing. He pissed on and on.

"You're a mighty man in some ways, Colin," I called. "Who would have though such a tiny mollywart could produce such a noble stream?"

He gave a last spurt, covered himself, and fumbled at his buttons. He got them all wrong and had to start over.

"I tell you, Colin, you should tug at it every day to make it grow larger or it'll never make the dear babies your mamma is set on your producing. Perhaps the sight of these will make it grow."

I swung down to a lower branch sending a shower of leaves onto his head. He jumped back as if he thought I'd hurtle to the ground. I opened my shirt to the waist revealing my breasts.

I'd be a fool if I didn't know I had a fine pair, pink and firm and well-shaped as pears. André Prudeau and Tom Drummond would give anything to get their hands on them. But Colin gave a strangled gasp and crashed through the underbrush as if the devil were on his heels.

I was surprised that after that episode he had the courage

to call, but no doubt his mother had bedeviled him into it. He certainly would never have told her of our encounter.

As I entered the drawing room now my shirt was half-unbuttoned and I bulged beneath it. My breeches fit so tightly I knew my woman's shape and the split of my buttocks were outlined. Colin sat down hastily and crossed his legs, his face flaming. I looked at him sideways.

"I had expected to see you hunting again today, Colin. I waited for you at the tree where we met yesterday."

"I was busy."

Mother frowned as if there were something going on which she didn't understand. "I thought you would wear your new taffeta today. Buckskins are unsuitable in a drawing room. Especially when a young gentleman is present."

"Surely Colin knows ladies are divided in half just as men are, though our cleavage is more complete for their convenience." I was sorry as soon as I spoke. Mother went white. I put my arms around her. "I'm sorry, mother. Please, don't swoon. I've learned bad ways following father around the docks."

Colin glared at his boots and Mrs. Mackay laughed nervously. "You speak plainly, Anne, but truth is often plain. The Puritans have infected us with their false modesty. Heaven knows there was no room for modesty on the ship coming from Scotland. We were kept below decks, crowded in together, never alone, no privacy for our—our functions." Mrs. Mackay launched into her favorite subject. They had been bound for a Scots colony on the Darien Peninsula when a storm had disabled their ship. It had limped up the coast to Charles Town but was too low in the water to cross the bar. Mr. Mackay had brought his wife and infant son ashore in a boat with fourteen others. "And just in time, by God's grace. The next night a storm broke the ship apart, drowning all who had remained behind." She always paused at this point to wipe her eyes. "Mr. Mackay elected to remain here and he has done well. Aye, very well."

I decided to go change. Anything to avoid the next portion of Mrs. Mackay's reminiscing, which I knew by heart. The woman was a parrot. She even looked like a parrot with her red hair piled in a crest atop her head and her bright green gown.

In my room I stripped off my clothes and stood naked by the window letting the southwest breeze cool me. Why did I deliberately distress my mother and always be sorry too late? It was as if two different souls inhabited my body, one good and one evil. Often I wished to injure her because I was jealous of the time Clara spent in her company. "Clara has been like a sister to me," mother would protest.

Clara might be like a sister but a sister with a wicked tongue who carried tales of my doings—God knew how she learned of them—and added to mother's distress.

This time it was the fault of that damned Colin who tempted me to shock him. But the other times I didn't understand.

I moved from the window to the long, gilt-framed mirror that father had bought from Captain Hornigold. The pirate had taken it from a Dutch ship on its way to Surinam. With that mirror I needed no man to tell me I was too beautiful to be wasted on Colin. There wasn't a young man in all Charles Town who wouldn't be glad to claim me.

Not that I wanted any of them. Conceited young fops, petticoat chasers, sobersides like Colin, young plungers like Tom Drummond who was already poxed by some whore. I had let young Kendall have his way with me for he was less objectionable than the others. But he had cried afterward and offered to marry me. Cried, for Lucifer's sake!

The man I did want was Captain Hornigold. Never mind he was a pirate and older than my father. He was tall and burned black by the sun and wind, and he smelled of the sea.

He wore a gold hoop in his ear and rings on his fingers and thumbs—stolen, every one of them—and a gold bracelet heavy as a slave's manacle studded with green stones that he said matched my eyes. His eyes had a lusty twinkle as if he were bedding in his imagination every woman he met.

One day when he had delivered some goods at the warehouse my father had been called out of the office. Hornigold and I exchanged glances in silence, then he said, "Damn my blood, lass, I wouldn't mind a gallop with you. Nor am I thinking you'd object. Though how the devil we'd manage it, I don't know."

"I'll manage it."

That startled him, then he laughed and slapped his thigh, "By God, I knew you were a saucy wench the first time I sighted you. When?"

"I don't know. I'll just appear."

"You expect me to take that answer?"

"If you want me enough."

He jerked me to my feet and pressed his cracked, rough lips on my mouth. None of my childish swains had ever kissed me that way. I liked it and learned quickly how to respond.

But I had not managed to meet him. The next day mother had decided to move back to the plantation and there was the usual confusion of packing, deciding which furnishings to take, and leaving the house in a bachelor state for my father.

We had been been here almost a week and I was frantic to find an excuse to get back to Charles Town before he sailed. I might as well live before I was buried alive with Colin.

As I dressed I flirted with my reflection in the mirror, imagining it to be Captain Hornigold. I wore my white satin petticoat embroidered with green pea pods and pink blossoms on a deeper green vine. I had worked the pattern myself, the more carefully because Clara had sneered at vegetables as a decoration. The stiff silk of my dress rustled like palmetto leaves as it cascaded over my head. Hornigold's bracelet wasn't the only thing that matched my eyes. The silk that changed from soft green to softer gold as I moved matched them perfectly, and they changed color in the same way. I wished he could see me dressed like this. He'd never be satisfied with tavern doxies again.

Some spirit, evil or benign, must have been in attendance at that moment. For father and Mr. Mackay came from Charles Town unexpectedly that evening. As they walked up the path from the river landing, Captain Hornigold was between them.

He was dressed like a gentleman in burgundy velvet with lace at his throat and a gold-inlaid cutlass flashing at his side.

I was at the harpsichord playing one of Shakespeare's songs. Just as I sang, *"One foot on sea and one on shore . . ."* I saw the men coming. My heart started beating in my throat and I knew how mother must have felt just before she swooned.

Colin said, "She's going to faint."

I took a great gulp of air, wishing I hadn't laced my bodice so tightly—that's what vanity did—and snapped, "The devil I am!"

I picked up my skirts and ran to meet them, and flung myself into father's arms.

"Beauty, beauty, you'll be ruining those silk slippers running through the grass. Don't tell me you've been missing your old father. I've been gone but two days."

"I always miss you." I was aware of Captain Hornigold's mocking amusement, but even his mockery could not disguise the admiration in his eyes.

"See who I've brought, beauty. The captain himself! Here now, don't go curtseying and spoiling the hem of that silk on the grass. Save your curtsies and greetings for when we reach the house."

When we reached the drawing room there were introductions and explanations. The last of Captain Hornigold's cargo had been sold and the ship was being careened in an inlet up river. "And it is an honor he's doing us, coming to dine. We want a grand spread, Pegeen, my darling. No light supper for such an honored guest. I'll give the orders to Clara myself so there'll be no mistake."

Mr. Mackay greeted his own family then gave me a hearty kiss on each cheek. "On my soul, lass, you are bonnier every time I set eyes on you. But you've a hard heart beneath that green silk, to make my lad wait. Or is it that you like whetting a man's appetite, eh?"

I liked Mr. Mackay. If Colin had had half the spirit of his father I wouldn't have been so reluctant and wouldn't have ended up the prisoner that I am today. "It's Colin who is guilty of waiting, do you not know? He thinks if he holds off long enough you'll allow him to go to Edinburgh to study medicine. He wants that more than he wants a wife."

Colin looked astonished that I knew so much about him.

"He can think again. I'm handing him a fortune in rice and indigo and he wants to go about bleeding folk and sawing off their rotting limbs. You are not to encourage him to become a leech, lass." He turned to the pirate. "What do you say, Captain? Isn't my lad blessed to have such a beauty waiting for him?"

Captain Hornigold cocked a critical eye. "Her beauty I'll not deny. But there's a saying in Jamaica, marriage has teeth and bites hard. I hold to that. In my profession—which I admit is not the best—I've yet to meet a female who is faithful in word or deed, with all due respect to the ladies present. They are inconstant as the wind and Jezebels at heart. Doesn't the Bible say, 'All wickedness is but little to the wickedness of a woman'?"

Mrs. Mackay waved her fan reprovingly. "The Bible says a great deal that can be taken with salt, Captain Hornigold.

As for inconstancy, *I* have never been inconstant in my life."

More's the pity, I thought.

"Perhaps your good man has never given you the opportunity, m'lady."

Mr. Mackay shook a finger at me. "Are you a Jezebel at heart, lass?"

Mother said, "Anne would be the greatest Jezebel of them all, given the chance. Poor Colin. You'll have to keep her on tight rein."

Captain Hornigold laughed. "You might as well try to rein the tide, Master Colin. Beat her if you must, but let her run free."

Hornigold told me later that my eyes turned yellow as a cat's. "Lucifer's dog! I'll not be criticized or listen to a lot of rotten advice given to Colin. If you all think so poorly of me I'll dine in my room." I started for the door, my skirt a hurricane of crashing taffeta. As I passed him the pirate reached out and grasped my arm and held me fast.

"Come back, Jezebel, for your own mother called you that. My advice to your intended was for your own happiness. You'd not like to be reined, would you now? It would be your ruination." I could see he was remembering the kiss a few days before. "Tell me, do you have nine lives like the cat whose eyes you stole?'"

"I hope so, for I mean to live forever. Faithless, inconstant, and wicked."

I had intended nothing of the sort. I had promised myself that if I was to marry Colin I would die at the earliest opportunity. Captain Hornigold laughed and released me.

"By God, I believe you will."

Again, I think the fates were listening for I have been all three since that day.

I remember every detail of that meal: the small pink

shrimp cooked with okra and onion; oysters baked in their shells; the ducks I had shot dressed with apples and raisins; pilau; ham; fish poached in wine; wild gingerroot chutney; sour cream tarts. The jalousies rattling in the evening wind; the reflection of the candles in the hurricane lamps winking in the green stones of Hornigold's bracelet; and my own headiness that was not caused by wine but by the vibrations passing between Hornigold and me. I wondered everyone did not feel them.

Perhaps they did. Colin watched us across the expanse of mahogany table and Clara, moving in and out of the room, supervising the servants, also watched. The woman was a damned witch.

He talked as he chewed, telling about the days when he had sailed with Captain Jennings and marauded the Spanish Plate Fleet, and about the earthquake at Port Royal.

"Luck was with us. The first shock broke our anchor cable and we rode out the tidal wave. They say Lucifer watches over his own, and a good thing it is. The sea's a tough master, but it's my home and I can't rest without its rocking me. That's not to say I won't sleep sound under your roof, sir."

"You're sleeping here?" I exclaimed, my mind already going to work on the possibility.

"Do you think I'd be sending him back to town after nightfall, beauty? Clara's prepared the east chamber for him."

I made the mistake of looking at Clara and found her appraising me.

Then brandy was served and the ladies were excused. As the door closed Mr. Mackay was saying, "Those sights you've seen in Port Royal, now, Captain. Perhaps you'd enlighten us on some of the refinements of wickedness we don't see in Charles Town."

Soon shouts of laughter reached our ears. I fumed at the unfairness of not being able to listen in.

The men took a long time over their brandy. Twilight turned to darkness. Mother and Mrs. Mackay yawned behind their fans. I paced the floor.

At last they emerged and the Mackays departed with two of our servants carrying torches and running before their carriage. Captain Hornigold was shown to his room and mother and I went upstairs on father's arms. Father lingered at my door.

"Beauty, Dougie Mackay is after me again to set the date for you and Colin. He wants the lad tied down before he talks his mother into letting him go off to Edinburgh. You're getting no younger, Annie, and the longer you wait the more difficult it is to settle down."

"Oh, Lucifer's bitch!"

"There you go using tavern language. Time and again I have told you to watch your tongue, just as I've told you 'tis a good match I've made for you. You heed me no more than if I were the wind. Your wild Irish ways will be your undoing, beauty."

"And who taught me those ways but yourself?"

"I admit the accusation but I also gave you over to the best tutors and dancing masters. But, no. 'Tis to the public school you would go and don't think it didn't come to my notice that half the time 'twas not in school you were but roamings the docks with lads already wanted for thievery and worse. Now you're making eyes at Hornigold. I saw it, Annie. I know that hot look. You've inherited my randy nature. My soul, Annie, I'll not be sleeping easy at night 'til you're wed, for the devil knows what will happen to you otherwise."

"If I were a man I could go to sea."

"But you're not a man, beauty, as anyone can see. It's not only Colin but also old Mackay himself can't keep his eyes off your charms."

"That mooncalf Colin wouldn't know what to do if I stood naked before him."

Father chuckled. "And how would you be knowing that? If Colin's been at you the better for both and the more important to set the date or half the society of Charles Town will be counting on their fingers, eh?"

"He has not been at me, father. All right. I'll set a date for you and Mr. Mackay. But I'm doing it against my will, and don't you forget it."

"And don't you be threatening me, beauty. The day will come when I'll have no more patience with your ways. Where will you be then, I ask you?"

"No worse off than I'll be married to Colin."

"You're a fool, Annie." He sighed and started for his bedroom, his shoulders sagging. In a flash I knew what a trial I was and I was sorry. "I love you, father."

He tossed me a kiss and a smile.

I rubbed myself with scent before I put on my prettiest night dress. It seemed a pity to cover myself for I have a fine figure, but even pirates might consider it improper to appear naked. Only a few days before a whore had been beaten nigh to death for removing all her clothes before a customer. She was fined for exposure, the man let off with a reprimand. Sometimes I think we have strange morals. It is all right to expose your breasts—indeed, in the French Court it is the fashion not only to show them but also to rouge them —yet the woman who shows an ankle is ruined.

It took a long time for the house to grow quiet. Just when I would think all was safe a board would creak. I was never sure whether someone was still abroad or if it was only the wood cooling. At last I opened my door. The hall was empty except for the striped moonlight filtered through the shutters.

Captain Hornigold was leaning against his pillows, naked, smoking his pipe. He laughed soundlessly as I entered and held out his arms. "You were the devil's own time coming, Jezebel."

He was rough and savage as an animal. There is no saying which of us was the more passion-swept. At last he extinguished the candle and took up his pipe again and I lay in the curve of his arm. After a while he chuckled.

"I was thinking of you in bed with your Colin. He won't be the one who holds the reins and does the mounting. Where did you learn to rouse a man like that?"

"Here. With you."

"Stow the flattery."

"I wouldn't bother with flattery. Until now it's been child's play, over in an instant, leaving me hot and restless."

"Damn my blood! So I'm your first real man! Ho, I'm still a bit of a dog, eh, old as I am." A new thought struck him. "Do you know how to prevent conception, Jezebel?"

"No."

He groaned. "You young bitch, you'll have us in Execution Dock. Lookee, you must learn about such things if you're to be my woman."

"Am I to be that?"

"Whenever I'm in Charles Town."

"Then I'm damned if I'll marry Colin."

"It's a fool's match. You'd castrate him. You could be a frightening female. Now hear me, if you find yourself pregnant there's a doxie on the waterfront called Tilda Redhose. Don't laugh, it's the name she chooses to go by and her hose *are* red. You go to her as soon as you suspect you're caught. Don't wait, for that makes it the more dangerous. I don't want to come back and find they've forced you into marriage with Colin or are hiding you with a bulging belly. You'd be no fun for me then and there's no place for brats in my profession. Understand?"

"Yes."

"Good." He put aside his pipe. "And now, as we've stolen the horse we may as well ride it."

The hallway was a chiaroscuro of moonlight and dawn when I returned to my room. I stopped just inside my door and gave a cry. Clara was standing there in her night robe, her mouth twisted with scorn.

"What the devil are you doing here?"

"Waiting to confirm my suspicions. You've been with that pirate the night through, haven't you?"

"What if I have?"

"I wanted to know."

"Now you know and the devil take you. Get out of my room, you sneaking bitch."

"I'm going. But I warn you, you'd best look careful or you'll be producing a bastard like yourself."

I jerked her around. "What's that you called me?"

"Bastard. Bastard! *Bastard!* That's what you are."

I struck her across the lips.

She blotted the blood with her sleeve. "I know what you do not. Your mother told me everything. She was a serving maid in your father's household and he got her with child. You. His in-laws hounded him out of Ireland, then out of England. Paid him good money to clear out. But they aren't married. His wife, the Sweeney woman, is still alive. So you're no better than I am and a bastard beside. You and your fancy ways and Frenchy speech and silken dresses. You, a serving maid's bastard, a sow's ear, and you behave like one, giving yourself to murdering pirates and the devil knows who else."

I grabbed her shoulders and shoved her out the door and locked it after her. Then I stood in the middle of the floor shaking with anger and fatigue.

The Sweeney woman. The accursed Sweeneys. Myself dressed as a boy and passed off as a young relative. All the winks and nods and innuendos suddenly made sense.

What a fool my mother had been to tell Clara. The bitch could blackmail her, ruin her socially, ruin my father's business. The Mackays wouldn't be after me to marry Colin if they knew. The pity was, they wouldn't know unless Clara

((48))

told them and I felt certain she would not. She loved my mother too much to injure her. She carried the keys to our household and was mistress of it in all but name. Our mutual dislike had not lessened over the years, but mother stood between us.

I went to bed and closed my eyes against the dawn. It was almost midday before I awakened. I knew before I opened my eyes it was another hot day with heat haze low in the sky. There was no wind, the moss hung motionless on the oaks. The house was deathly quiet. The maid who brought my breakfast said father and Captain Hornigold had returned to Charles Town and that mother was in bed with a bout of fever.

I hated the house when mother was ill. There was little enough to entertain us when she was well. I decided to go hunting again, partially to escape Clara, partially because if I could bag some doves mother might be tempted to eat.

As I passed the cookhouse I thought I'd ask Gillah how to prevent having babies, though for all I knew it might be too late. Gillah had buried her first husband in the yellow fever epidemic and three since with lowland fever. She was married to her fifth but she had no children. It never occurred to me she might be barren. Almost every woman I knew gave birth frequently. My mother's sterility was laid to her frailty. It wasn't lack of father's trying.

The cookhouse with its huge brick fireplace and array of blackened pots was stifling. Gillah knelt by the fire stirring in a pot. She smiled when I came in and wiped her hands on her apron before she got up and curtsied.

"I making rice water for ma'am. It cool the fever."

"Gillah, how do I keep from having babies?"

She rolled her eyes toward the door to make sure no one else was there. "Why you want to know?"

"I'm to be married soon and I don't want a lot of babies hanging on my skirts."

((49))

"You be a no-good mother. Riding around on horses, man-style, wearing britches, shooting around like you off your head."

"So tell me."

"It not my place."

"Mother and Mrs. Mackay won't tell me. They want me to have babies."

"It your duty."

"Gillah, please! You know I love you and you love me."

"Umph. White don't love black nor otherwise. Buy and sell and order 'round 'sall whites do. Work themselves to death 'sall blacks do. Maybe you different. Maybe not."

"You know I'm different. I'd never let father sell you. Not that he'd want to. You're the finest cook in the Carolinas. Everyone says so."

"They never says so to me. All right then. You count the days of the moon."

"The *moon*?"

Gillah groaned. "God, give me patience. Come, sit here on the step and I tell you. But don't you tell ma'am 'bout my mouth."

We sat on the stone steps, cool to our bottoms. I hugged my knees and prepared to listen. I remember thinking what a strange day it was, not like fall except that the trees were bare and the kitchen garden dead.

Gillah looked at the sky and sniffed. "Weather like this breed trouble."

"What kind of trouble? Hurricanes?"

"I dunno." She gave me a hard look. Her eyes were round and button-black. "You been with a man?" I nodded. "Master Colin? That who?"

"No."

"Oh, Lord. When your flux?"

"I just had it a couple of days ago."

"That all right then. I don't want to go poking no hooks

up you. Case you died I'd get beat and sold off. Now listen here to me."

My head was soon whirling with counting days, linen sheaths, cotton packing, stones, ointments of herbs, and magic incantations.

"But which way is best, Gillah?"

"*No* way best. Maybe some work, maybe not. Just have to trust God don't want *you* having children. Umph. Here come that one."

"That one" was Clara. She came down the covered breezeway carrying the silver tray on which mother's meals were served when she was ill. Her skirts brushed me as she passed but I might as well have been a doorstop sitting there for all the notice she took. Gillah poured the rice broth into a bowl and added a sprinkling of red pepper. Clara never even thanked her, but swept out again and went to the house.

"That one," Gillah said sitting down again, "always smelling 'round, poking in the pots. What she think? I dunno how to cook? All my life I cook. Soon as I could stand by my mama's side, stir the soup, turn the spit, pound the sugar, grind the salt, powder the pepper. Her!"

"I hate her."

Gillah nodded. "You and her—the path of your stars, they cross. When they come to same place at same time, everybody watch out."

"Are you seeing the future, Gillah?"

She didn't answer for a moment. "I don't want to see it."

"What do you mean?"

"A feeling. You—you got dark clouds coming and going like hurricanes. And men, my God, men crowding 'round you."

"Does that mean I'll have lots of lovers?"

"And water. Water everywhere. God, I not see so much water since I a child coming from Barbados."

"There's water everywhere in Carolina."

"This foreign parts. Not Carolina." She stood up. "I don't like it."

I didn't like it either. It was nonsense, of course, but it made me nervous. I thanked her for her advice but she didn't answer. She was back kneeling on the hearth. I helped myself to some bread and cheese and sausage and went away.

No wind stirred in the forest. No covey of birds started in alarm. No serpent glided away from me. Nor was there any sound but the whine of mosquitoes and that damned mourning dove. The smell of hot black mud was heavy on the air and there was an eerie breathlessness about the place.

It struck me I was a fool to be wandering around when the entire forest seemed to be awaiting danger. Even my dogs had slunk back home without my noticing their going. I decided to follow them and felt as if I couldn't get out of there quickly enough.

A sound close by made my hackles rise. I stood stock still expecting a Yamasee to scalp me or carry me off as a slave. For a moment nothing happened, then the sound came again, a whining, sighing moan, like an animal in pain.

I peered into the undergrowth and met the terrified eyes of a black lying in a hollow of oozing mud. His face was shrunken as a skull but his belly was bloated with hunger. His leg was broken and he had lain there long enough for the stink of infection to be rank in that still air.

"Are you a runaway?"

He nodded.

"Where from?"

"Up country. Cruel mon."

I didn't think he was lying. There are some masters who consider their slaves less than animals and more expendable. None of our slaves has ever run away but not everyone is as tenderhearted as father.

I tossed him my swag of food. "Eat it slowly or you'll be

sick. Don't try to get away. I'll be back with a litter and take you to our plantation. My father isn't cruel."

He leaned on his elbow, watching me warily, fingering the knot of the bandanna, but waiting for me to go.

He had eaten when I came back with the stable boys and a hammock. Already he looked better, but the smell of the leg and the flies and mosquitoes crawling over it made me doubt we could save it.

Swallowing my pride I hunted out Clara and told her to go see to the slave.

"It's not my place to take care of blacks. Let like take care of like."

"It's your place if I tell you to do it. You're the only one who'll know whether the leg can be saved, though it chokes me to admit it. The blacks would saw it off without a thought. It needs a thorough wash with carbolic. One of the boys can do that but you supervise it."

"It's against the law to harbor a runaway slave. He should be returned to his master."

"I found him and I'm keeping him if he lives and I expect you to see that he does."

"It's not fitting."

We stared each other down and she went. She liked administering medicines and caring for the sick. It's a pity she couldn't have been a surgeon.

She had her revenge. Late that afternoon she said mother wanted to see me.

It always astonished me that such a slip of a woman could have produced a tall, large-boned Amazon like myself. Today she looked especially small, shivering under a mound of comforters. Fever glazed her eyes and burned in her cheeks. I knelt by the bed and kissed her forehead and took her thin, dry hand in mine.

Tears welled up in her eyes and spilled down her cheeks. For some reason I thought she was dying and wanted to say good-bye. I began to sob but managed to ask if I should send for father.

"No, no. Not until I've talked to you. Perhaps he need not know." I never knew whether the bouts of fever left her so weak she had no voice or if she dramatized. Whichever it was, she whispered as if with great effort. "Clara said—Clara told me—"

Of course, it would be Clara. My sobs dried in my throat.

"About the slave? Damn it, there's no point in crippling a man because she thinks herself too fine to look after him." The bewilderment in her eyes told me she had no notion what I was talking about.

"Clara told me you lay with Captain Hornigold. How could you do such a thing? A filthy pirate! A thief! A murderer!" Her tears choked her.

"Damn that woman's tongue!"

"She said it's not the first time you've sinned. Is it true, Anne? Clara wouldn't lie to me, would she? Would she, Anne?"

I should have lied. She might have believed me. Instead, "She wouldn't lie to you, mother. She didn't lie. It's true. I don't care what he is. I intend to be with him whenever he's in port and there's no use trying to stop me." I began to pace the room, wishing I could get my hands on Clara. "Why shouldn't I? What do you expect, affiancing me to a clod like Colin. I want a real man before I settle down with that mollysop."

"If you carry on like this Colin won't have you. You'll have to go live on the waterfront with the other trulls." I had never seen her so angry and whispered anger is frightening.

I was angry, too. "Then I'll go, if you wish it. Better a trull than Colin Mackay's tit-horse. What do you expect of a bastard? That she behave like a lady? Oh, yes, mother, Clara told me about the Sweeneys. The accursed Sweeneys.

Clara tells everything she knows, the better to make trouble. You were stupid to trust her."

Mother's sobs rose to a scream. She beat the bed with her thin white fists and threw herself back and forth. I left her to her frenzy.

Clara was coming from the cookhouse carrying mother's tray with a bowl of steaming pilau. I barred her way.

"You damned bitch! Carrying tales to my sick mother."

"Not tales. Truths."

"I'll tear out your tongue!"

Gillah came to the door of the kitchen, her hands kneading her apron. I sensed rather than saw her apprehension.

Clara tried to pass. Still I barred her way, feeling my hatred burning in my guts. "I'm not finished with you yet, you bitch."

"Perhaps this will finish you!" She flung the pilau into my face.

The stuff was boiling. I screamed and clawed it off my face. Then I jerked out the knife I wore thrust in the belt of my hunting clothes and lunged at her. I felt it enter her soft belly. Too late I realized what I had done. I pulled it back and flung it from me as if it, too, were scalding.

Clara staggered. The tray of dishes crashed about her. She clutched her wound, staring in surprise at the blood on her hands. Then she crumpled and fell.

Gillah threw her apron over her head and wailed. A green lizard darted across the walk and the palmetto tree at the cookhouse door rattled suddenly with the first wind I had felt all day. I knelt and tried to feel Clara's pulse. Her eyes were open as if she were watching me, but she saw nothing.

"Gillah, stop that caterwauling! Send a boy to town for father. At once! Do you hear me?" I went to her, pulled the apron off her head and shook her. "Gillah! Gillah! Do you hear?"

She nodded and broke away and ran to the quarters. I

went to my room. I jumped at my reflection in the gilt-framed mirror. The person there was a stranger I had never seen before.

It astonished me how easy it was to kill someone. I wasn't sorry Clara was dead, but I was sorry I had been the one to kill her. I wondered how I would tell mother.

Then I remembered she had been taking food to mother. I decided I should do it though I wasn't sure mother would want to see me.

Everything was still. Flies buzzed over the body, walking on sticky feet through the blood. Gillah wasn't in the cookhouse. There wasn't a slave in sight. When there's trouble they go to earth like animals and it takes a whip to drive them into the open. They weren't needed now and I let them be.

The fire had burned down but the coals glowed hot and the caldron of pilau bubbled like lava. I fetched the tray that had dented when it had been dropped, filled an earthenware bowl, cut some pone, and went back to the house.

Mother was asleep. I left the food by her bed where she could reach it when she awakened. Then I took a sheet from the linen chest and covered Clara. Then I fetched food for myself. It may seem strange to my judges that I could think of eating but they should remember I had given my bread to the runaway slave and I was ravenous. It had been a long day. The sun had set and it was dark under the trees. I ate alone by the light of a single candle in the huge dining room where the night before—it seemed a century ago—Captain Hornigold had sat by my side.

Once I went to mother's room. She was still sleeping. I felt her head. She was cooler. The fever had broken. I took away the tray. I thought, tomorrow everything will be all right.

It was stupid to think that considering Clara was dead and I had killed her, but it was as if a great burden had been lifted from me.

It was midnight before father came, Mr. Mackay with him. When I saw the torch on the bow of the boat blinking like a firefly as it passed the tree-lined bank, I nearly wept with relief.

Father took me in his arms and held me until I stopped trembling. Then he led me to a chair and he and Mr. Mackay stood before me. The candle flame kept bending and turning to smoke in the wind.

"Now, beauty, what in the name of all the saints has happened. That boy, wild-eyed and tangle-tongued as a madman could babble about nothing but runaway slaves and a quarrel between you and Clara. Dougie and I could make head nor tail of it. When we tried to question him he closed his mouth like an oyster and would say nothing."

Truth has many facets. I could not tell my father about Captain Hornigold in front of Mr. Mackay, but neither could I hide the fact that I had killed Clara. I chose my words carefully—God knows I had had the evening to rehearse—and my hesitation seemed to them nothing more than feminine emotion.

"Clara and I quarreled over a slave. You know she has—had—medical knowledge. I saw no need to lose a good black because she objected to his color. To revenge herself—she has always hated me, father—she told mother things that upset her. When I called Clara for it she threw scalding pilau all over me. You can see the marks."

"I thought you looked uncommonly red. You must see to it, beauty. It's blistering."

"I was damned angry at the bitch and meant to frighten her. I don't know how it happened. I didn't know what I was doing."

"I never liked the female," Mr. Mackay said. "She'd a leery way of peeking at a soul. Mrs. Mackay said she'd got your lady under her thumb right properly."

"Um, yes, she did in a way, Dougie, but she had saved Pegeen's life once." He turned to me. "Does Pegeen know?"

"She was asleep the last time I looked in. The fever's broken—" Suddenly an awful fright took hold of me.

"I'd better see her."

Mr. Mackay patted my shoulder. "Don't fret, Annie. There's not a court in the Carolinas would condemn you for doing away with a troublemaking indentured criminal. Didn't she stab her lover back in London? Well, then, she's perished by the sword."

His words were small comfort. I kept remembering the way the knife went into her, the spurt of warm blood, her look of surprise.

"The weather's changing and a good thing," Mr. Mackay continued. "That unseasonal heat always causes trouble."

Only that morning Gillah had said the same thing.

Upstairs father began shouting for me. Mr. Mackay and I exchanged alarmed looks, but before we could reach the door father stumbled into the room, wild-faced, trembling. The candle fell from his hand, rolled across the floor, and went out. He collapsed, weeping as I've never seen a man weep before.

"She's dead. Pegeen's dead."

Mr. Mackay and I went upstairs. She was lying as she had been lying when I took the tray to her. She was quite cold. Mr. Mackay said she had been dead for hours.

The heat broke and an icy gale harried us the day mother and Clara were buried. The priest's cassock bellied like a sail and the holy water was blown back on him instead of landing on the coffins. As they were lowered the rain came, drumming on the cedar boxes, stinging our faces. Father had to be restrained from flinging himself into the grave.

The funeral feast was subdued. Our friends and neighbors didn't know how to treat the murderess in their midst. The Mackays stood by me. Mrs. Mackay busied herself in the corners with the women, telling them what a mischief-maker

Clara was. She hinted Clara had taken possession of mother's mind by witchcraft, possibly even poisoned her. I almost began to believe it myself.

Colin was not the milksop I thought him. He never left my side. Once he squeezed my hand and whispered, "Outface them, Anne. You can do it."

"Oh, I'll outface them but not because I think I'm blameless, Colin. Which reminds me, there's something I should say to you. You probably don't want to saddle yourself with a murderess so I'll release you. Father will understand and yours will probably be relieved."

"Nonsense. Of course we'll be married. I think you need my protection." He looked so stiff and solemn and determined I nearly laughed.

Father and I moved back to Charles Town. I was glad to leave the plantation and get father away from mother's grave. He visited it every day, spending long hours there, returning home to drink himself into a stupor.

The night before we left the furniture was draped with sheets except for the chairs we sat in. Everything was packed away. Wind rattled the jalousies and rain hissed on the fire. Father dozed, his head sunk on his chest, a nearly emptied bottle on the table beside him. Suddenly he roused himself.

"All right, beauty, let's be telling the true tale. There's none to listen but your old father. Your hearing is two days hence and I should know the truth if I'm to save you."

"Mr. Mackay said they won't convict me."

"You never know what a man representing justice will do, beauty. Some of them pursue it too keenly."

"I thought justice was what you admired."

"Not when it's my own daughter. Come, beauty. Tell me."

So I told him, beginning with Captain Hornigold. He didn't speak until I had finished. Then he sighed heavily. "Beauty, beauty, the sorrow you've brought me! Whoring with pirates, carving up serving maids, causing the death of Pegeen."

"I had nothing to do with that. It was the fever and that damned Clara."

"It was tales of your doing. But how could you help yourself? It was my doing as well. The sins of the fathers. . . . You were begot in sin and it's tainted your life."

"Then what Clara said was true?"

"Every word of it. I loved your mother and I did not love my wife. Not that I wasn't a good man to her, doing my wedded duty and not finding it too painful. I made my own way, helped provide for her, though she had a fortune of her own. Many's the man would have thrown your mother in the street when he found she was with child. But not Billy Cormac! Thereby was my downfall. I could no more give up Pegeen than I could give up breathing. The Sweeneys would have no part of my arrangements. They made life so hot in Cork I had to leave, then they pursued me, panting like hounds, to London.

"But a man goes where his heart is. You were a beauty even as a babe, Annie, and I loved you as I loved your mother. I love you still, though you've brought sorrow down on us. You must mend your way or you'll end up in dock. We must keep the Hornigold business from the Mackays. God, beauty, couldn't you have cooled yourself with Colin instead?" He peered at me with bloodshot eyes. "No, you could not. It's the very devil himself you want."

"You brought him home."

"Not to service my daughter like a damned stud, just because she's in heat."

"What would the Mackays say if they knew you and mother had never been married?"

He poured another drink and tossed it off, spilling half it down his shirt. "That must be kept from them, too. A man who marries for money, and it was for that reason I married the Sweeney female, repents the rest of his life. Every copper of Sweeney money I squandered was thrown up to me as if I'd stolen it off a dead man's eyes. I'd give a pretty if they could see the fortune I've made for myself, though God forbid they should ever set foot ashore in Carolina."

"Yet you are forcing me to marry Colin for money. So you can knock down the wall between the warehouses, so you can join the plantations. Isn't that marrying for money? Money for you and Mr. Mackay? Don't you think I'll spend my life repenting? You know Colin wants to go to Edinburgh to study medicine. You know I want—" I stopped because I didn't know what I wanted. "You know I don't want him."

He was silent, staring into the fire. "I never thought of it in that way, beauty. Perhaps it would bring nothing but grief. I'll speak to Dougie, but it must be done properly. You speak to Colin. Tell him to press his mother. She's the one to work on. With her tongue she could topple the walls of Jericho."

He rose unsteadily to his feet. "Help me to my bed, Annie. We must rise early tomorrow and take up our lives again, leaving Pegeen to the worms and the rain."

CHAPTER

JAMES BONNY

WHEN COLIN AND I parted as he sailed for Edinburgh, we were friendlier than we had ever been. He knew I had helped in gaining his heart's desire, but he did not know how glad I was to be rid of him.

Thanks to his testimony and that of his parents, I was not charged with murder. My blistered skin was one evidence of Clara's temper. The Mackays testified that she was a foul-mouthed, spying mischief-maker intent upon blackmailing her employers and benefactors. The court decided that an indentured criminal was no great loss to Charles Town.

Time did not lessen father's grief. He was a broken man. He had no appetite for anything but drink and no will to work. He disappeared for days at a time and would be found drunk, half-frozen and half-starved, weeping on mother's grave.

With Mr. Mackay's aid I kept the business going. I donned

my buckskins, tied my hair in a pug, and rowed out to the ships to deal with the merchantmen and pirates as Andrew Cormac, William's son.

In the evenings, after father had drunk himself into unconsciousness, I went, still in my breeches, to the pot shops and the company of men who had neither grief nor conscience. More than once a doxie mistook me for what I pretended to be and offered "a special price" for the use of her body. Once I fought a duel but my opponent was too drunk to keep his feet and so comical that the duel ended in laughter instead of disaster.

When Hornigold was in port I was his. If father knew he shut his eyes to it. I was in love with him and had asked if we could not be married. God knows why I wanted such respectability, if being married to a pirate could be called that.

He laughed at my proposal. "You're too much for me, Anne. You know yourself before a year'd passed you'd be hunting down a younger, lustier man and I'd dirk you both from jealousy."

I denied it and sulked and pleaded to no avail. It was my sixteenth birthday and I said he should do what I wanted as a gift. This only made him laugh the more. He put his gold bracelet with the green stones on my arm, kissed me, and told me to get dressed and come to the waterfront with him.

"There's a young pimp newly come to town who does smuggling on the side. I've some goods I want him to handle for me. I can't sell it here. I took it from a Charles Town ship and the owners would recognize it."

That is how I met James Bonny who my petitioners would have my judges believe led me into piracy. Nothing could be further from the truth. Neither James Bonny nor Captain Hornigold "led me into piracy," nor did I become a fugitive from Charles Town for any reason other than my own folly.

When Hornigold and I entered the tavern Bonny was sitting alone in a corner staring morosely into a tankard of ale. His suit was velvet and his shirt edged with Belgian lace, and his eyes were that shade of blue one sees on a fine day in the Indies. If his hair had been clean and properly barbered it would have fallen in curls. He had that diffident air that makes a woman feel as protective as a mother. He didn't look like a pimp or a smuggler, but like a boyish, half-starved angel.

Hornigold called for rum and pipes for us, snapped the stems, filled and lighted them, before he got down to business.

James Bonny had scarcely acknowledged my presence other than to flush and lower his eyes when Hornigold presented me. This piqued me because I was accustomed to being noticed, but at the same time I found his shyness charming. While he and Hornigold talked I studied him, thinking how he could be improved and made into a handsome, respectable-looking fellow.

He was not unaware of my gaze. Suddenly he interrupted Hornigold and turned to me. "Why the devil are you staring? Do I have a louse in my hair?"

Hornigold bristled. "Here, you don't speak to a lady as if she were a tart. You're sitting with one of the richest belles in Charles Town. If you can't speak civilly I'll have your tongue."

"Oh, let him be, Hornigold. It's plain fine clothes don't make a gentleman."

Bonny flushed but he managed to sneer as well. "If you're such class what are you doing in the company of thieves?"

"I choose my company without worrying about how it earns its wage. Captain Hornigold does business with my father and even a pirate may have the manners of a gentleman."

"Enough of this palaver. Let's get on with business so I

can get Anne back home." Hornigold wound up his arrangements and we left James Bonny sitting in the corner. I didn't say good-night.

"I'm surprised you trust that churlish dog," I said when we were in the street.

"I trust him because he's so afraid of me he won't dare to cheat. He comes cheap, too. Aside from that fine suit he hasn't a groat to his name. He was starving when Tilda Redhose took pity on him. Why the devil she did I'll never know. She has as much use for a pimp as a mouse has for a cat. But that pathetic, hang-dog type always finds a woman to take pity on him and to leech off of until she comes to her senses and throws him out."

"Some women are fools."

"Now mark me, Anne. I told Bonny to pay you the money. You keep it for me until my return. I saw you could handle him, and knowing you're my woman, he won't hold back."

"So you're really off tomorrow? How long will you be gone?"

"Watch out, Anne, that's a wifely tone. I'll be gone until I return and don't you try to anchor me. A man might as well put his ship on a reef as to marry." He laughed and picked me up and swung me around. "Not even to the best gallop I ever had and the richest belle in Charles Town."

Someone opened a window and emptied a chamber pot on us but we got out of the way in time. We went quietly after that, and there was no sleep until he left in the black predawn to catch the tide.

The next few nights after father had drunk himself into oblivion I went back to the tavern looking for James Bonny. The fifth night I found him sitting in the same corner, staring into a tankard, just as before. I sat down opposite him without asking his leave or being invited. He didn't greet me or call for rum. I had to order for myself.

"You've been away," I said.

He gave a short nod. "Doing the business for your friend. I was coming round to your warehouse tomorrow."

"If you have the money you may as well give it to me."

He looked warily around the tavern. "It's not safe to be seen passing money here. You'd never get home with it."

That was true. "Then I'll see you tomorrow."

"I said so."

I puffed away at my pipe. He looked better seen through a cloud of smoke. A few days of wind and sun had brought color to his fair skin. His sailor's dress became him better than his velvet suit. It made him look more rugged, more of a man. He was handsome, for all he was a churl.

"Damn all! Do you always stare at a man like that?"

"Until I've seen what I want of him."

"What do you want besides Hornigold's pay?"

"I'm not sure." I was thinking what Hornigold had said about the pathetic hang-dog type and wondering why Bonny interested me. Partially I was still half-angry at Hornigold for laughing at my offer of marriage, but more than that, I wanted to break down Bonny's ill manners. I wondered if he were equally rude in bed.

So we continued to stare, though he spent more time staring into his tankard and avoiding my eyes. I ordered more rum and asked if he'd join me.

"Are you paying?"

"I am."

"Then I'll join you."

Leeching off me already, I thought. By Lucifer's dog, before I'm done you'll be the one who's paying. "Where do you come from?"

"Bristol."

"How did you get here?"

"I was conscripted into the navy."

"Where did you jump ship?"

"Are you calling me a deserter?"

"It's plain you're no navy jack."

"In the Indies."

"And now you're living by your wits?"

"It's the way I've always lived. I've no rich father to pay for my rum."

"My rich father doesn't know he's paying for our rum. He's lying dead-drunk in his bed."

The resentment faded from his eyes to be replaced by surprise. Score for me, I thought. I put down my pipe, drained off my rum, and stood up. "I'll see you at the warehouse tomorrow."

"Are you going now? Alone? At this hour?"

"No one would dare touch William Cormac's daughter."

"Just the same—" he hesitated. "I'll come with you."

To this day I cannot explain to myself my infatuation for James Bonny so I cannot explain it to my judges. Perhaps it would have remained an infatuation that would have passed when Hornigold returned if it had not been for Mr. Mackay and father.

Mr. Mackay was worried about father. "We must do something for the poor soul, Annie, or drink will be the death of him. I was thinking, if you could persuade him to go to the plantation to oversee the spring planting, it would keep him busy enough that he'd forget about drink."

"Do you think he should be out there alone? He has plenty to do here, but he won't do it. If it weren't for us the business would be ruined."

"Aye, his heart is no longer in this. It's lying in the grave with his Pegeen. But the land is curative, lass. Planting and watching things grow and come to life again, that mends a man. If he was in the air all day, working alongside the overseer, jollying the slaves, he'd have less time to tipple. He'd be early to bed and out at dawn. He'd sweat the liquor out of his flesh and have less craving for it."

"If he did crave it, there's a well-stocked cellar there. He could fill all the cups in Charles Town if he had a mind to do it."

"You could keep the key." Mr. Mackay laid his finger aside his nose and winked.

We laughed and I agreed to speak to father. I didn't think it would cure him but it was plain something must be done.

To our surprise, he agreed to the plan. He was so frail from drinking but never eating that he had to be carried down the stairs and lifted into the boat. Gillah was to go along and she had orders to feed him well. Mr. Mackay and I accompanied him, and a wild ride it was. Father was half-crazed and to keep him from overturning us or throwing himself overboard we had to ply him with liquor as if it were medicine.

He cried when we left. "You know well, beauty," he said, " 'tis happier I'd be and not sodden with booze if you and Colin had married and a wee lad were on the way. A laddie to inherit all this," he gave a sweep with his hand that sent him staggering, "a laddie I could watch grow and teach as I taught you. And later a little daughter called for Pegeen. But there, I know Colin's heart was set on helping folk in his own way. Mayhap if he'd already been learned in medicine he could have saved my darling."

With father out of the way I moved James Bonny into the town house. Its grandeur impressed him. He roamed from room to room, gazing about him, smiling ruefully.

"If you think this is grand you should see the plantation," I said.

"And it's all yours?"

"It will be."

"God!"

He was something new to me in the way of a lover. He had an air of being honored and grateful that I found appealing. His truculence vanished and he made an effort to be pleasant, even gay. He told me he had no desire to be either a pimp or a smuggler but an honest merchantman with a little sloop of his own. "But I've never had a chance to go honest. I've never had a chance to be anything but what I am. It's that or starving."

"You can begin by leaving off pimping for Tilda. I'll pay you whatever you make off her. That should keep you in rum and tobacco."

"I don't think a real gentleman would let you do that."

"You'd be surprised what some real gentlemen would do. How much does she pay you?"

He named a figure that astonished me. I questioned Tilda later and found she gave him less than half the sum. Rather than let him know I distrusted him, I paid.

I thought he would rather be busy than spending his days in idleness, and I tried to interest him in helping at the warehouse. After a couple of days he said he found it dull stuff and the figures I set him to add gave him a headache. It didn't occur to me he could neither read, write, nor tell a six from a seven.

So he spent his days wandering around the waterfront gazing wistfully at sloops, jawing with the seamen and pirates. We spent the evenings in the taverns drinking and dancing. He danced as well as he made love.

He looked better these days. Having regular meals had filled out the hollows that had made his eyes appear sunken. His skin had lost its pallor, his hair had been washed and shaped, and was as fair and soft as corn silk. I was as proud of him as if I had created him, and in a way, I had, so it was a shock when Mr. Mackay came to me one day and asked for a word in private.

"Lass, I wouldn't be speaking in this way except that I think of you as a daughter, as you would have been if Colin hadn't taken that daft notion to go off to be a leech. But speak I must. It's that pimp whose company you're keeping.

He's no good, Annie. He's a scoundrel and he'll exploit you and ruin you."

"You mean James?"

"Himself."

"But he isn't pimping anymore. All he wants is a chance to go honest. I'm thinking of asking father to buy him a sloop and set him up as a trader. It would make sense to have our own trader who'd cut out the middleman."

"I'm begging you not to do it. Listen, lass, I've a scheme and Mrs. Mackay is willing and your father is for it, too. Aye, I've been to the plantation and spoken to him."

I began to feel nervous.

"It's for your good as much as it is for your father's. We're sending you to Edinburgh. It'll do Colin no harm to have a wife while he's at his studies. You'd see to it he eats instead of keeping his nose at his books forever and aye. You'd cosset and encourage him, and there'd be an heir in the making for the warehouses and plantations, just as we had planned. I don't know why we didn't think of it before, but there was your mother's death and the trial over Clara, and all. But never too late to mend, Mrs. Mackay said when I told her, and your father is that pleased. He didn't take so much as a drop the whole time I was with him."

"You mean, it's all arranged?"

"And a letter posted to Colin!" He beamed at me. "In ten days there's a packet leaving for Glasgow and you'll be on it."

Any other time I would have broken into a stream of oaths that would have turned Mr. Mackay's red hair white. But I felt as if someone had punched me in the chest. I sat there, going hot and cold. The room whirled, and to prove I was my mother's own daughter, I fainted.

Mr. Mackay sent me home. The nice old fool was so pleased with himself he didn't notice my vexation.

No sooner was I in my own house than I picked up a china clock and flung it through a window. I broke a chair, kicked a footstool, and beat my fists on the wall while James Bonny stared at me in alarm.

"Don't stand there looking like a frightened dog. Get me some aqua vitae and be sharp about it," I snapped.

He almost ran to obey and I tossed down two tumblers of the fiery liquor before I was calm.

"There! James Bonny, will you marry me?"

"Marry you?" he echoed. Then he looked around the room. "Marry all this?"

"All this and me, too. If you don't, you'll lose it."

"I don't understand."

"You don't have to understand. All you have to do is say whether you'll marry me."

"Will your father let me have you or will he throw me out?"

"Lucifer's dog! Do you think I'm such a fool that I'd send you to ask for my hand? Of course he'd throw you out. We won't tell him until the deed's done."

"It sounds chancy."

"Everything's chancy. Be bold, man. Come, what's your answer? Aye or nay?"

I forgot how rapidly news travels on Charles Town's waterfront. The news reached the plantation before us. The house was barricaded like a fort. Mourning crepe still festooned the doors and windows. No one opened the door to my pounding. No voice answered my demands to be admitted.

"He's either dead or dead-drunk." I beat on the door with my fist.

A shot singed my hair. We threw ourselves down and crawled to the dubious safety of a moss-draped oak. A volley of fire followed us.

I made a trumpet of my hands. "Father, it's Anne!"

The ground beside me seemed to explode. I was shocked to hear James whimper.

"Father! Do you hear me? It's Anne."

"I hear you, you whore of Babylon, you spawn of Lucifer." His voice was like the God of the Old Testament, but I could tell from the way he slurred his words that he was the worse for drink. "I'll see you dead before I see you set foot in this house. You've brought it nothing but shame, and now you would be disgracing it further by bringing that panderer, that thief, that snotter, that firk to soil it!" A shot emphasized each epithet.

"He must have a damned arsenal in there," James said. "We'll be picked off like dogs."

"Nonsense. He'll calm down soon. We'll break down the door. Come, all we have to do is to shoot off the lock."

"You'd better go alone. It's plain the old devil wants no part of me. I'll wait here until you calm him."

"The hell you will. There's one name father forgot to call you, coward!" I jerked him to his feet and pushed him ahead of me. We ran, dodging the shots. Father was shooting wildly so we were in no real danger.

I had to take the gun from James's trembling hand. Even after I shattered the locks the door wouldn't open. It was barred within. I heard someone moving on the other side so I tried pleading again. "Father, please see me."

The wood splintered as another shot rammed through it. James dived off the piazza and ran back to the tree like a frightened rabbit. I followed and father's voice bellowed in the night.

"I'll have the militia on you. I'll see you in dock. You'll hang in chains at White Point."

"Jesu!" James rubbed his forehead with his sleeve. "What have I got myself into? All for money to buy a sloop and make a living that wouldn't land me in jail. It'll be the rope if that crazy old fool calls the militia."

"You've a damned hanging look, come to think of it. And you can leave off calling my father a crazy old fool. If you

((72))

end on a rope it'll be your own doing. Once you got that sloop you'd smuggle for the first rascal that offered your price."

"You're a hellkite and I wish to God I'd never got mixed up with you."

While we were upbraiding one another Dove came so silently that I cried out when he touched my arm. James, craven that he was, howled. It took me a moment in that dim light to recognize my runaway slave. He had fattened, living on the plantation, and his leg had mended so he didn't limp too badly. I all but threw my arms around him, slave though he was. He stepped back as if he saw my intent, and I regained my composure.

"Come!"

He led us to quarters and settled us in one of the deserted cabins. God knows it was primitive but the earthen floor was swept smooth. A fire glowed in the pit and a pot of red beans bubbled on the coals. There was even a pipkin of rum and a screw of tobacco.

Dove's kindness touched me, but James paced about, bumping his head on the rafters and cursing. He knew some lively expressions I'd never heard.

"Lucifer's balls, I never thought to be sleeping in stinking slave quarters. Jesu, Anne, what have you got me into?" He collapsed suddenly on the pile of skins that served as a bed and put his head in his hands and sobbed.

I had been doing some silent cursing myself for having got married to this spineless fool and alienated father. But his tears touched me. I reminded myself he had never had anything, he had lived off the garbage of Bristol, and his hold on life was so precarious that any untoward happening was a threat. I remembered all I had promised him, that it was not turning out as we had planned, and he had come near being shot.

I put my arms around him and explained how grief-

((73))

stricken father was, how he blamed me for mother's death, and was disappointed because I had not married Colin. "It will be all right," I promised. "I'll get father to give me my inheritance and we'll clear out."

James calmed down and kissed me. I brought him a bowl of beans and curled up at his feet to share it. For a few moments I even felt happy.

It was strange, considering we had been married only for a day, that there was no love-making that night. It wasn't my unwillingness. James pushed me away. "That would be a fine sight for the militia when they walk in. They'd drag me off you and there you'd be with your skirts up and they'd take it as an invitation to have a go themselves."

"God's teeth, will you forget the militia? Do you think they'll come all the way out here to fetch us? Nothing will happen until morning."

James was no countryman. Every bird call, every rustling tree, every breath of wind, awakened him and he would rouse me to tell me the soldiers had come. I began to wish they would come and carry him off to jail so I could sleep.

The roosters began crowing at false dawn and continued until sunup. James swore and pulled the covers over his head. Finally he gave up trying to sleep and began pacing the floor again. He wouldn't even go outside to piss until I had gone first and assured him it was safe.

Gillah brought us breakfast. She looked James up and down and sniffed. Seeing him with her eyes I knew he would never pass as a gentleman. I followed her outside and asked her to bring my clothes. "And Gillah, leave the door unlocked so I can slip into the house."

She shook her head. "No how! You got nothing to lose except what you already lost marrying with that in there. *I* get sold if I don't do what Master William say. He tell me, don't let that girl sugar-talk you into let her in the house. 'Cause I swear to the God if I lay eye on her, I shoot her dead."

"Father said that?" I couldn't believe it. "Is he sober?"

"There a smell of spirits."

"I had the key to the cellar."

"You think that stop him? He have Cuffee take off the door."

"All right. Tell him I want to talk to him. If he doesn't want me in the house I'll talk through a window."

I told James to stay where he was and followed Gillah.

She was gone a devil of a long time. I could hear her arguing with father but I couldn't make out what they were saying. Once he pounded the table and all the shutters rattled. Later there was a crash and sound of shattered glass.

It was one of those humid days when the scent of flowers is too sweet on the air and the sun has turned the sky molten. Mother's garden had gone wild. The breezeway between the house and kitchen had not been swept for days. I remembered the exact spot where Clara's body had lain, though there was nothing to mark it.

Silks and stomachers, petticoats and shawls, slippers and fans suddenly showered from an upper window, the skirts ballooning as they fell.

After what seemed an endless time Gillah came out the door and I heard the barricade being shoved into place behind her. Her mouth twisted as if she had drunk vinegar.

"Him! Bull 'gator's twice as friendly. Had to throw clothes out the window and put your jewel box under my skirt."

"Will he talk to me?"

"Just you. Not that one out there. Go to the side door."

The side door. The help's door. I advanced warily.

"Father?"

He growled like an old dog.

"Father, I'm sorry I angered you by marrying James, but you would like him if you would consent to meet him." I was beginning to doubt that he would, however.

"I'll meet him in Hell." His words were slurred.

"Father, won't you give me your blessing?"

"Damnation's what I'll give you."

For a moment I couldn't speak for my tears. "Father, as I have displeased you I'll—I'll go away. Give me my inheritance and I'll never trouble you again."

"You could have had everything, this land, this house, the slaves, the house in Charles Town, the warehouse, the gold I've hoarded for you, if you had married Colin. But you've scorned it as if 'twere dust, thrown yourself away on that fortune seeker. Inheritance be damned! You'll not have so much as a crooked copper. I've drawn up a new will disinheriting you. Cuffee is carrying it to Charles Town now, along with a warrant for your arrest and banishment, and the arrest of that pimp you've hired to pander for you. You're a pirate's trull and I want no part of you."

I was weeping, partially from sorrow, partially because I was so angry at his unreasonable behavior. "Father, you know we have always loved one another."

"Lucifer, get thee hence!" He wailed like a soul in Hell. "God, stay my hand from murder!"

I threw myself down the steps as a shot tore the jalousies. I cowered under the piazza, glad James couldn't see me, trying to think what to do. If he had really sworn out a warrant I'd better get out of Charles Town as soon as possible.

The wood for the fireplaces was stored under the rear piazza. A boy fetched a pot of hot coals there every morning so if the fires had died in the night they could be easily rekindled. As the coals winked at me a wicked thought entered my mind. I must have been possessed.

I spread the dried moss and twigs used as tinder under and over the logs, sprinkled them with the oil stored there, and emptied the pot of coals over all. The tinder flared. I blew on it and fanned the flames with my skirt. Soon the fire was lapping at the underflooring.

I ran back to quarters. The door was bolted. I had to scream at James to let me in.

"Come, if you don't want the militia after you. We've got to get out of Charles Town and damned fast."

He stared at me, white-faced, and I felt like kicking his shins.

"Good God, what have you done now?"

"Fired the house. He can roast in Hell for all I care."

"You fool woman. He might have forgiven you once he got used to the idea we're married."

"He wouldn't forgive me as long as I'm married to you. Come on, damn you."

Smoke enveloped the house and towered over the roof, turning the sunlight an ugly orange. The slaves were running toward the fire, shouting at one another, totally disorganized.

Dove was at the landing with my clothes tied in a lumpy bundle. He motioned us to a boat and got in himself.

"Are you coming, Dove?"

"I belong to you. I go where you go. Away from here." He smiled and heaved at the oars.

"Help him, James."

"I'm no slave."

"You'll be indentured if the militia catches us."

James swore and took an oar. We pulled out into the current.

Behind us flames touched the roof. The moss on the oak trees caught, flared, and fell to ash.

Leaving the men at the tavern where I had first had the ill luck to lay eyes on James Bonny, I went to the warehouse. I worked quickly but Mr. Mackay caught me before I got away. He pulled a long face, shaking his head as if he had a bug in his ear.

"You made a sore mistake, lass, when you let yourself be wed by that trash. Why did you do it?"

I was wondering that myself but I couldn't tell him it was

all to keep from being sent to his precious Colin like a bartered bride. I started to lie and say I was pregnant, but a lie sometimes brings the ill luck of becoming the truth. I shook my head, dumbly.

"You've broken our hearts, lass."

If he went on like that I knew I'd start crying again.

"For that I'm sorry for I wouldn't have broken your heart, Mr. Mackay, for anything. But if I stay here to mend them I'll be imprisoned or indentured and I've no desire to be either."

"Don't be hasty, lass. He'll come to his senses once he leaves off drink."

If he isn't burned to a crisp. "I can't chance it, Mr. Mackay. Do what you can for him. Perhaps one day he'll be willing to see me again."

"I'll pray for it, Annie."

I kissed him good-bye, hoping the sack of money I had taken from the warehouse chest and pinned to my underskirts wouldn't clink as he embraced me.

"You're a nice man, Mr. Mackay, and I'll always think fondly of you."

He stood in the door and watched me go. I blew him another kiss before I turned the corner.

The truth is, I was beginning to enjoy myself, but James was sweating with fear. "There's not a ship leaving for the next two days except for a smuggler's sloop. Jesu! In two days we'll be found and cast in jail."

"Won't the smuggler take us?"

"He's going to New Providence."

"Good! When does he sail?"

"We can't go there, you fool woman. It's a nest of pirates. Prison's one thing but hanging's another."

"Hornigold is there. He'll help us. When does he sail? Didn't you ask? Do you want to end up in dock?"

"On the evening tide."

"Then we should board now."

"I don't want to go to that hell-sump."

"Then stay here and greet the militia for me. Come, Dove."

James came panting after us. "You'd leave me here to be arrested, wouldn't you? And without a copper to my name."

"You didn't have a copper when I met you and I'm damned if I'll force you to go to New Providence."

"I'm coming, but I'd never have married you if I'd known you were going to be disinherited."

I stopped in the street and glared at him. "You damned miserable firk! Father and Mr. Mackay are right. You married me for my money. To think I was taken in! I've a damned good notion to make you work your passage."

He sulked the rest of the day, leaning on the bulwarks looking back at the harbor. Dove and I ignored him. I was glad to be on the sea again, excited by the prospect of new lands, at the thought of seeing Hornigold, facing an unknown future.

When the anchor came up, wet and encrusted, when the sails were hoisted, when the shudder of movement ran along the keel, I could have shouted with joy.

We tacked out of the harbor. Charles Town dwindled until it looked like a toy village against the pearl pink western sky.

A toy village, and I had put aside childish things.

CHAPTER

IV

STEDE BONNET

BY THE TIME we reached New Providence I was as sick of James Bonny as he was of me. Once I even considered pushing him overboard, but there was no need to make a habit of murder, and if New Providence was as rough as James said I would need a man. Besides, without him I would have had no protection against the captain, except Dove who didn't count, being black and a slave.

The captain was a knave if there ever was one. He saw at once how things were between James and me, and made freer than he should have. I pretended to think him quite a fellow. I didn't doubt that if we displeased him he would throw us overboard with nary a backward look, and help himself to our property. He would have been disappointed to find how skimpy it was. He was too stupid to think of looking under my skirts for money though he was anxious enough to get under them for another reason.

He taught me a bit about navigation. I learned to distinguish between a jib and a flying jib; how to judge the depth of water by the color; how to read the stars. He even let me take a turn at the wheel, though he stood by, closer than necessary, to see I did not bring us to harm.

James was jealous. After all, I held the moneybags. I had to make it up to him with lies and endearments I didn't mean. A tumble in our corner of the deck under the warm night sky did me no harm and to give the Devil his due, he used that tool of his with skill.

But often, after our love-making when James was sleeping, I watched the stars swinging back and forth overhead, and felt an awful sadness. I regretted having been a fool, all my wickedness, reproached myself for not having been a better daughter, and almost wept with loneliness for my father. I had adored him and I had tried to burn him alive.

I hoped the slaves had succeeded in putting out the fire. I doubted it from the way they had run about, squawking like frightened chickens, carrying pails of water that slopped over as they ran so they arrived at the house with scarcely a spit in them. I wondered what madness had possessed me.

But at two o'clock in the morning even a crack in a clay mug is a tragedy. When the sun came up turning the sea as gold as doubloons, the past was unimportant compared to what lay ahead. I made plans for the future. First I would find a way to get rid of James Bonny. Then I would take on Hornigold. He wouldn't have to worry about marrying me. Then— My plans went no further.

The smell of land was heavy on the air long before we sighted it. Every land has its own aroma. The Brethren who have sailed the Indian Ocean have told me that for miles out to sea you can smell the cloves of Madagascar. Charles Town smelled of oleander and boggy lowlands and pine. Jamaica of sugar, as my judges must know. Nassau smelled of tar and rotting garbage. By the time it appeared on the edge of the sea like a low-lying cloud bank the Turks-eye blue water had turned brown and turbid with a mixture of seaweed, broken jugs, smashed casks, feces, rotting fruit, coconut shells, dead fish, even bodies, the flesh torn by fish.

When the Brethren had taken it over New Providence had been deserted. The Spanish didn't want it because it yielded neither gold nor jewels. They abducted the aborigines and took them to work their mines in Spanish America. The English had tried to settle it next, but even the fort they had erected on the hilltop could not protect them from constant raids by the Cuba-based Spanish. During the War of Succession the Spanish carried off all the settlers, black and white, leaving the island a ruin.

It was an ideal base for the Brethren, the pirates. The climate was mild, the land fertile, there were fresh water springs, and it was between the east- and westbound shipping lanes, which made for an easy living. The harbor was guarded by an island so two ships were required to bottle it, and at low tide it was too shallow for the frigates of the Royal Navy.

We eased into the harbor where three or four hundred crafts rocked at anchor. There were vessels of every kind, some battered, half-sunken hulls, some taut, but most of them the worse for battle and lack of care.

"They're poor seamen," I said.

The captain laughed. "Why waste time swabbing paint? When a ship's wore out they capture a new one,"

A crowd gathered on the white coral beach, cheering and firing muskets into the air. The cannon on the old fort roared black smoke. Drums rattled, trumpets blared, and the captain fired a round from the ship's guns in answer.

Dove had collected our baggage and stood guard over it. James sweated in his velvet suit. I was dressed in my best. The captain leered at me. "You'll be setting them on their ears. They've never seen the likes of you there. Even swabs know a lady when they see one."

James glowered but the captain laughed and took my arm as he pointed out the sights. Not that there was much to be seen.

Beyond the dazzling white beach the jungle grew in a green and golden tangle. The fort topped the hill like a broken crown, and the sky was as deep a blue as the depths of the waters through which we had sailed. Birds flew singing among the foliage or soared into the air like loosened blossoms taking wing.

It looked like Paradise, but the outskirts of Hell lay at Eden's feet. The dwellings were made of tattered sails draped over broken spars. The grander ones were constructed of driftwood tied into a frame with threadbare lines. Those were roofed with thatch. The kitchens were open campfires. The bedrooms hammocks strung between two trees. Dogs, swine, and buzzards rooted in the offal, and the stink intermingled with the heavy scent of tropical flowers and spices was almost too much for my stomach. But I was damned if I was going to give James a chance to crow over my being sick.

The captain helped me over the side, squeezing my hand in parting, and it was Dove rather than James who helped me down the rope ladder. As we got closer to land I gave in and held my handkerchief to my nose. James sneered.

"You would come. I warned you."

"Yes, I would come. I think neither father nor the militia will find us here."

A collection of riffraff greeted us. Trulls and slatterns of every age and every degree of filth and ugliness with their naked brats tugging at their skirts stared at me. Drunks, scoundrels, men of every color and those born white so burned by sun and wind, so unwashed, to look as if they were wrought from bronze, leered. Many of them were scarred or disfigured in some way and looked like the Devil's brother. A few seemed to be fairly decent fellows. The older ones had the same disreputable dignity as Hornigold. And there wasn't one of that tag and bobtail rabble that wasn't gaping open-mouthed as fools at the sight of a decently dressed female.

A wispy old gentleman in frayed breeches and a raveling shirt, wearing shoes—or what was left of them—but no hose, hobbled up to me, swept off a battered hat, and bowed.

"Governor Sawney at your service, m'lady. May I welcome you to Nassau?" He gave me a sweet, toothless smile, but his eyes had the vacant look of one whose mind had strayed. I guessed this was the demented governor who, Hornigold had told me, had been the only man to escape the Spanish raid.

"Not that he's the real guv'nor. The real guv'nor is who-ever happens to be in port. We've a council of sorts and some loose regulations because even scoundrels like ourselves need laws to live by. We call Sawney guv'nor and see to it he's fed."

I curtsied. "Thank you, sir. This is my husband, James Bonny, and if you will be so kind as to give me your arm and lead us to Captain Benjamin Hornigold, I shall be grateful."

It was too much for his mind. Spittle threaded down his chin. "Hornigold?" His eyes searched the crowd. Hornigold certainly was not there, but a man who could be described as almost a gentleman came forward.

"You're friends of Benjamin? Then you're welcome. Jennings here, ma'am."

I gave him the smile that my father had said would charm the Devil into Confession. I haven't noticed it charming my judges into granting me a pardon.

"Captain Jennings who rescued the Spanish Plate? Hornigold has sung your praises. I'm delighted to meet you."

"I'm the one who's delighted, ma'am. I know Hornigold's a devil with women but you've a husband—" he gave James

((84))

a puzzled look and James nodded glumly. "Benjamin's not here, ma'am. He's taken his new lad, Teach, on a voyage to the Carolinas. I doubt he'll be back before hurricane season."

"Then we'll wait."

I was disappointed but there was nothing I could do about it. There was no place else we could go, and for the time being, James and I would have to make the best of one another.

For the first few weeks I behaved like a prudent wife. I selected the site for our house up wind from the settlement, far from the ceaseless cacophony of dogs, brats, and brawling females.

That climate doesn't require much shelter so the house was little more than a pavilion with another, smaller one, set apart for Dove. Almost anything we wanted in furnishings was available on the dock that served as a marketplace. It was all pilfer, of course, but there's no use being picayune in the company of thieves.

In those days I was still a lady and I wasn't going to lower myself to living the way the others did. We had a table and carved chairs of Spanish oak (the pirate who owned them as a part of his share of a prize was glad to get rid of them), a Turkey carpet, porcelain, pewter, even a French clock with golden nymphs casually supporting it as they simpered at one another.

Dove and I enjoyed our expeditions to the market and haggling over some treasure we fancied. James tolerated our foolishness since he didn't have to pay for it, and he enjoyed living in the grandest lean-to on the island.

With Captain Jennings's aid James had signed on a turtle boat. It was an easy living, which I suppose is why he chose it.

James was enthusiastic about his new profession and he wasn't bad company when he was cheerful. Of course he spoiled my lapse into fondness by saying, "When we have enough money we'll go back to Charles Town. When your father sees I've done all right by you, perhaps he'll relent. If you didn't burn him to death."

He was fool enough to think I didn't know he was still after my fortune.

The turtling sloop was gone sometimes for a week, and with James out of the way, I enjoyed myself.

The petitioners would have my judges believe that I was shocked by that crude and immoral society. The truth is, in those early days I found it exhilarating. There was no polite pretense about those hearty folk who gambled, fought, and fornicated without any pimp of a parson to reprimand them. When money ran out they went back "on account," which meant to go a-pirating.

Once the women got over their initial distrust they accepted me, though they teased me about my clothes and what they called my "airs." I took the banter good-naturedly and went out of my way to form friendships. Women can be vicious foes, smiling to your face and pointing a knife at your back.

Dove found a woman and asked permission to move her in. I told him to do as liked, that he was free now, and I wrote it on a paper and gave it to him. Slavery always seemed unfair to me. It's not as if the poor devils had walked on the slave ships voluntarily.

So with Dove as watchdog and his woman, Phibba, to cook and wash, we lived in style. We swam and fished in the mornings, dozed in our hammocks through the heat of midday, and gathered in the taverns to drink and gamble and gossip in the evenings.

At first I drank more than was good for me. The rum punch went down so easily I never knew I had had too much until I stood up to leave and found my legs unsteady. There was always some swab eager to help me home and more than once I woke up with someone I'd never seen before and wouldn't have chosen in a sober moment. After that happened a few times I was more cautious.

It's not immodesty but truth to say I was the toast of the taverns. There wasn't a man who wouldn't have abandoned his doxy if I had given him the nod. I'd have taken on Jennings in an instant but I liked his doxy. Besides, I was waiting for Hornigold.

One morning near hurricane season we were awakened by a cannonade that made me think the Spanish were attacking. That was something we lived in fear of, being so close to Cuba. James was away and for once I was sleeping alone. I leaped up, threw on some clothes, and ran to town with Dove and Phibba at my heels.

Two sloops were riding in on the tide, trumpets blasting, drums beating, guns smoking, black flags flying, and the crews hanging on the shrouds waving and shouting.

I pushed my way to Jennings's side. "What the devil's happening? I thought it was the Spanish."

"It's Hornigold. Don't you recognize his sloop? And us thinking he'd not be back until winter. He must have taken some rare prizes to return so soon."

Thank God. That meant my days with James were over. I could scarcely wait to boot him out, he was so dull.

I couldn't decide whether to stay and be among the first to greet Hornigold or make myself more presentable. The night before had been stormy in the tavern and my brains were still swimming in rum.

Vanity won. I had a rub with wet sand under Phibba's firm hands, a swim, another rub with coconut milk, and a drink of Phibba's concoction, which she called Kill Devil. It was eggs, fruit juice, fiery spices, and a dash of rum. It cleared the mind and settled the nerves.

I dressed slowly, put Hornigold's bracelet on my arm and a wreath of yellow flowers in my hair, and set out for the settlement.

I was so self-important I didn't heed the sly looks or nudges the women gave one another. I supposed it was because I looked grander than usual. If they assumed I was out to win Hornigold, they were right. I'd show them.

As I walked into Westminster, our principal tavern, pausing at the door the better to make an entrance, the talk and laughter died and everyone seemed to be waiting. Some folk behind me tried to peer over my shoulder and I had to snarl at them to get back.

Then someone said, "The Devil bless us, it's an angel. Judgment Day's at hand. Ladle out the rum, boys. Let's die drunk."

It was the most ferocious man I'd ever seen, but I had no time for him. At his side sat my Hornigold with a bare-breasted doxy on his knee. One hand was squeezing her breasts, the other was about to lift a mug to his lips.

He turned pale under his weathered skin, staring as if I were a ghost. Then he set down his mug so hastily it overturned and jumped to his feet. The doxy crashed to the floor.

"Anne! Anne Cormac!"

"Anne Bonny, it is now," Captain Jennings said. "She told me she's a friend of yours."

"Aye, aye, a friend. I heard in Charles Town you had married that pimp and fled after damned near sautéing your father."

"Well, he damned near shot me." Then the implication of "damned near" struck me. "He's alive then! Thank heavens."

"He's alive all right and read me a lecture for seducing his daughter and ruining her. I told him you were no virgin when I got to you and you'd taught me some tricks I hadn't known before."

"That was a filthy thing to do. However, I forgive you." I stepped past the doxy, Elena, who was getting to her feet, rubbing her backside. I lifted my face to be kissed but he

((88))

stepped back as if he'd like to run. "What's the matter with you?"

"I didn't expect you to be here."

"Where else would I come but here? I've brought the money from the goods James sold."

"I thought you'd foxed me."

So that was what was worrying him. "I wouldn't steal from you. Come, buy me a drink." I was about to sit down when Elena grabbed my arm and jerked me around.

Elena was some mixture of Spanish, Indian, black, English, and perhaps a little monkey thrown in. Her breasts, always bare, had dark garnet nipples. Her skin was the color of molasses and milk, and her eyes as black as bottomless pools. Right now they were boiling like lava.

"You blond bitch of the Devil's dog! Stay away from him! He's my man. He doesn't need any she-shark who thinks she's Queen Anne of Nassau. He's got me!" She pounded her chest so her breasts bounced. "I'm his woman."

I pushed her aside. "From the way you act when he's away I thought you were the woman of anyone who had the price."

She lunged at me. Hornigold caught her by the hair and held her while she writhed to be free.

"Is she your woman?"

Hornigold, big as he was, squirmed. "When I'm here—"

I interrupted. "I see. Just as I was your woman when you were in Charles Town."

"But that was another port."

So James wasn't the only man who had taken me in. I shrugged. "All right." I turned to Elena. "I don't want your man. You've probably given him every kind of pox there is. French pox, Spanish pox, English pox, black pox, Indian pox, monkey pox, dog pox—" I was going too far but I couldn't stop. I was so damned mad at having been gulled, so damned mad at Jennings for not having warned me, so disappointed because my plans were ruined, I was drunk with anger. "Cow pox, parrot pox—"

She jerked free leaving a handful of hair in Hornigold's hand and jumped me. We crashed to the floor, upsetting a bench as we went down. She was small and had the advantage. I was impeded by my skirts. But she didn't know how to fight. She went for my throat instead of my eyes.

I was ready to scratch out hers. I clawed her lids and she shrieked. I rolled her over and straddled her. She made a mistake with those bare breasts. I gave them a wringing that warmed my heart. When she tried to pull my hair I twisted my head around like a snake and bit her, tasting blood.

We rolled over and over, scratching, biting, beating, kicking, until we panted for breath. All those years of fighting bullies in the schoolyard had prepared me for this, which all her years of lying on her back while some seaman pumped away at her had not. I was more worried about my gown than about any hurt she might inflict on me. I got her by the shoulders and rapped her head against the floor until her teeth rattled.

Suddenly she went limp. I got to my feet feeling sick, hoping I hadn't killed her, remembering how suddenly Clara had died. She was a bloody mess but she wasn't dead. She lay there with her eyes closed, moaning. That damned Hornigold didn't make a move to comfort her.

I threw the wreath that was hanging over one eye across the room, smoothed my skirts, and called for rum all around. I took the sack of Hornigold's money I'd brought from Charles Town out of my skirts and threw it on the table. He started to reach for it. I shot it from under his hand. Doubloons flew everywhere.

He mopped his forehead with the tail of his neckerchief. "Damn my blood, Anne—"

"Damn it, indeed! The drinks are on you if you can pick up your gold. After that pick up your trull and carry her home and tend to her. She probably has some money for you, too. She worked hard while you were away."

I sat down beside Jennings and pounded the table. "Landlord! Rum! Fighting makes a lady thirsty."

When the drinks came, to show those knaves how a lady behaves, I knelt besides Elena and held my tankard to her lips. Then I dipped her skirt in the rum and bathed her face. "Come, you silly slut, you aren't dead. Next time you fight aim for the eyes. If you had blinded me first I'd never have got the better of you." Then I did something I have regretted ever since. I took off the bracelet and put it on her arm. "There. Alchemists say gold is a cure-all. Let's be friends."

She blubbered like a child and Jennings's doxy—Nell, her name was—had to take her out.

Hornigold looked at me with wonder. "By Jupiter, Jezebel, was there ever such a woman as you?" He reached for my hand.

I jerked away. "You have your woman. Don't touch me."

"Cow pox, monkey pox, dog pox," the ugly fellow beside him bellowed with laughter. His voice made the rafters shake.

He had the fullest black beard I had ever seen, braided in ten plaits and tied with colored ribbons and hooked back over his ears. He wore a brace of three pistols, matches in his hatband, a cutlass, two dirks, and had a musket leaning against his knee. The man was a walking arsenal. He was as large and brawny as Hornigold, but if he had bathed since the day of his birth he had rolled in the gutter immediately afterward.

"Who the devil are you?"

"Ned Teach of Bristol, ma'am, better known by the merchants I've taught to fear me as Blackbeard. At your service, ma'am, for by Neptune, you're the kind of wench I admire. If it's a husband you're wanting, I'm your man."

"I have a husband, Ned Teach, and he doesn't stink the way you do. Any wife you had would have to lie upwind to avoid asphyxiation."

"I had ten at last count, ma'am, and so far none of 'em has complained."

"They must be after your fortune."

"When I make my fortune no one but the Devil and I will know where it's hid, and the one who lives the longer shall have it."

"I doubt the Devil will allow you near enough to whisper in his ear. Do you never wash, man?"

"It might put out my fire. Where most folk have guts I have a bed of coals. Lookee!" He took out his powder horn, sprinkled gunpowder on his rum, set it afire, and drank it down. It was a frightening and impressive sight, lighting his ugly features as he held it to his lips.

I said to Hornigold, "You've got one of Lucifer's own for an apprentice." But I thought to myself, What a braggart.

Hornigold nodded. "He'll be the best of us all."

"Best be damned," Teach roared. "I'll be the worst of us all. I'll frighten my victims so they'll beg me to take their gold. I'll be the terror of the seas and it'll take the Devil himself to stop me."

"We all think 'twill when we're young and new to the profession," Jennings said. "I'm getting old and come too close to Execution Dock too many times. Luck runs out, you know."

"When luck runs out, blow up the ship. It's better to swim with the fish than feed the crows."

"That's easy to say, Teach."

I was bored with his blustering. "If I ever go on account I'll come to you for lessons," I said mockingly.

"It'll be a black day for the profession when women take to it," Teach said. "They'll sail us right into Execution Dock."

"If you think that you've known some frail females, probably your stink smothered them. Don't tell me women aren't equal to men. I've seen women, white and black, work alongside their men planting, building, plowing, doing whatever needed to be done, keeping the family fed and clothed, the house clean, the children cared for, slaving long hours after the men were dozing by the fire with their feet up, cosseting themselves for having worked so hard all day."

Hornigold backed me. "It mightn't be so bad as you think, Ned. If the women were like Anne I'd trust 'em with a sloop and look to see them take every ship they sight. You should have seen Anne in Charles Town in her buckskins clambering up a ship's rope, swaggering around a deck and beating down the price of an honest pirate 'til he damn near makes her a present of the goods."

"Stow the soft-sawder, Hornigold. You'll have Elena starting another fight with me."

For Nell and Elena had come back. Elena's eyes were blackened, her lips split and swollen, her breasts bruised. She knelt at Hornigold's knees like a faithful bitch. He patted her head absentmindedly. I half-expected him to say, "Good dog."

It was time for me to leave. Jealousy was twisting my guts. I still had a hankering for that man. We'd had some good times, and despite the fact he hadn't wanted to be anchored and wasn't faithful, he was more of a man than any I had known. I drained off my drink and made my excuses, pretending I expected James the next day and would need a good sleep and a clear head. Hornigold didn't know I was lying but Jennings did. He said he and Nell would see me home. As we said our good-byes Hornigold stood up and touched my arm.

"Why did you do it, Anne? Why did you marry Bonny?"

"Every woman's bound to make a fool of herself over a man at some time in her life." I left him to guess which man I meant.

It was one of those nights when the scent of night-blooming flowers is so heavy on the air you can't smell the offal and open privies. The sound of the sea was soothing and the phosphorescent algae set the beach aglow. We walked in silence a little way, then I said to Jennings, "Why didn't you tell me?"

"I didn't know that's the way it was between Hornigold and you. You had a man."

"But when I said I was his friend—"

"I didn't guess, though I own, I kept pondering where I'd seen that bracelet."

"For a wicked old man you're mighty innocent."

"I am."

"Never mind. Hornigold's getting old and men are as plentiful as fish in the sea. I'll go fishing one of these days."

Ned Teach sailed a few days later in order to get north before hurricane season. Hornigold had taken a French Guinea ship and turned it over to Ned's command. To the amusement of everyone but Elena, Ned christened it *Queen Anne's Revenge.*

Hornigold stayed behind. He was rather shamefaced in my presence, which made me sad. No one likes to see a good man humbled. Elena and I became friends. Not good friends, but friends enough that we could drink together without embarrassment. I used to wish we could put James and Elena in the same sack and drop them in the harbor, leaving Hornigold and me a clear field. But when it came right down to it, I didn't want any part of him after he had acted like a dog over Elena.

My plans had hinged on him, and now that there was no luck there I didn't know what to do. My money had run out, thanks to my extravagance, and I was dependent on James, which didn't please either of us.

I had been in the settlement long enough for the novelty to have worn off and monotony to set in. I don't know how those other women stood it. There were days when I thought the idleness would drive me mad. It was different for the men. They could work on the ships—which they didn't do half enough to keep them in any kind of condition—and leave whenever they took a mind.

I spent a good part of my days brooding about the past, remembering the good things about life in Charles Town: the smell of the warehouse, hunting in the forest, the gusty winter days when waves crashed over the seawall and challenged me to be abroad, the parties at the plantation when there were merchants and planters from Jamaica, Barbados, the Bermudas, Virginia, and the northern regions of Carolina; pirates, officers, and ladies; music, dancing, and rich food. I hoped father wasn't busily drinking himself to death and said a crude prayer that we would meet again and he would forgive me. I even thought of Colin and wondered if he was happy in Edinburgh.

Mostly I thought about myself. I was not exactly unhappy but I didn't want to stay here forever, drifting from day to day until I was so old no man would want me unless he was blind drunk. Moreover, I didn't want just any man. No woman does. She wants the ideal man. I knew I stood little chance of finding him on New Providence.

There were several days of breathless weather when the trade winds died. Not a leaf moved, no birds called in the jungle, no lizards scuttled in the thatch and the reek of human waste was sickening on the air. The sea was lifeless and oily, and the sky looked as if a thin, watery veil wavered across it. Every morning the sun rose, blurred behind the vapor. The sunsets were so gaudily red that the sea and the island looked as if they were afire. Tempers were frayed and a man was knifed in Westminster over the price of a drink.

Jennings said we were in for a blow. The Brethren busied themselves making their lines fast and cursing themselves for not having gone up Boston way before the winds struck. Day after day the blow held off, the white sands glistened and to walk on them was like walking on coals.

I went swimming because it was too hot to do anything else, but the water was tepid as a bath. I had closed my eyes to the glare and was floating, half asleep, when the water that had been smooth and still began to tremble. I felt the first stirring of wind I had felt in days.

Opening my eyes I saw a bank of dark clouds had edged up the horizon and encircled the island. They moved in fast like a steep towering wall. As I waded ashore there was a moan of wind. All the trees seemed to twist and shiver.

A sloop was entering the harbor, running before the storm with every sail hoisted. It looked as if it were going to run right up on the beach. The captain was no seaman and he and the crew were obviously frightened.

So was I. The thatch on our pavilions was being torn apart and carried away like straws. Dove and Phibba were burying everything we owned. I thought they had gone crazy but just then the wind sent me staggering. At the same time it caught our iron caldron, tossed it over and over down to the sea. I chased it and brought it to Dove who put it in the pit he had dug. The wind shrieked so we couldn't hear one another speak. I gestured I was going to the settlement. I don't know why I thought I'd be safe there.

It seemed an endless journey through Hell. Often I had to embrace a tree trunk to keep from being blown away. Half my clothes were torn off and carried away like the vines that were torn from the trees and snaked across the sky. The wind lifted the sea and flung it at the island in blinding mists of spray.

The clouds burst and rain pelted down so hard it bounced into the air again. It bruised like grapeshot. Overhead clothes, branches, birds, roofs, sails, and garbage soared away.

I was soaked to the skin by the time I reached Westminster. Everyone with his woman and squalling brats was there. The windows had been nailed shut but they bulged with the wind and the oil lamps flickered and the roof rattled like a drum as the rain beat upon it. In a corner some hen-hearted numskulls were praying and singing hymns. It seemed a little late to repent.

I wrung out my skirts as best as I could and pushed my hair out of my eyes. Elena spotted me and waved me over. The wind had all but torn off my waist so I had no right to criticize Elena for her exposure except that my hair was long enough to cover me like a shawl. I sat down and drained off the corker Jennings thrust at me.

"Lucifer's dog! If this is a hurricane I've had enough."

"It's only begun. It'll be a long night, Jezebel." I didn't know why Hornigold looked so pleased.

"Jezebel? I thought it was Botticelli's Venus risen from the waves."

For the first time I noticed the newcomer. It didn't take more than one glance to see he was a gentleman. I didn't know who Botticelli was but I knew Venus. I blushed because I looked so terrible.

"This is the lady we told you about," Jennings said. "We were laying wagers as to your safety, Anne, but only the Devil would have gone to see if you were safe. This is Major Stede Bonnet, late of Barbados. He made it to port just in time."

"So that was your sloop. I thought you were going to beach her."

Hornigold kicked me under the table.

Major Bonnet had risen to his feet when he referred to me as Venus. Now he kissed my hand and seated me beside him. "I am no seaman, my lady, but I am learning. The wind had the better of me."

"No one could handle a sloop in that gale," I said. It had been a long time since I had felt so flustered in the company

of a man and even longer since I'd been with a gentleman.
I looked from Bonnet to Jennings and Hornigold and saw
how crude they were. I was glad James was away turtling
for I would have been chagrined to have Major Bonnet see
the pitiful example I had married.

"The Major's gone on account," Jennings explained.
"He's taken four ships and came here to hire more crew."
His eyes twinkled.

Nobody *hired* a crew. All you had to do was promise a
fair share of the booty and you'd have men fighting to sign
on. But it was what a gentleman would do. "You shouldn't
have any trouble. If I were a man I'd offer my services."

Hornigold kicked me under the table again. "She may
offer anyway, but not as a crew member."

"Shut your saucy mouth. You'll have the Major thinking
I'm a trull."

"I would never be so mistaken as to think that, my lady.
What are you doing in the company of these rogues?"

James Bonny had asked me that when we met, which shows
how much alike males are, gentlemen or not.

"I could ask the same of you."

He wasn't as handsome as Hornigold. Hornigold still had
a fine head of hair and the Major was already balding. He
was, I learned later, nearly twice my age, and his face was
lined, not with age but with melancholy, which tinged his
smile. But he had the fine features, grace, and dignity of
a gentleman, and in a way reminded me of my father.

"I prefer this company to that of plantation owners who
talk of nothing but yields and prices, or that of scolding
wives and whining widows. Besides," he added in a lighter
tone, "I've always yearned to go to sea."

"There are ways of going to sea without turning pirate
and risking your neck."

"I risked it in the army. Why not risk it living a life more
to my liking?"

"A short life and a merry one," Hornigold said.

"Merry until you swing for it." Jennings tapped his forehead and tipped me a wink to indicate he thought the Major was crazy.

"I'll take my chances. I've been happier in the past month than in all my life before, so whatever comes is worth it."

"You can't argue with that," I said. "It's you fellows have the fun. If I had been born Andrew instead of Anne I'd risk swinging and go on account myself." I called for another round of drinks and insisted on paying for them though I knew I'd have to account to James for every groat I spent. "If I can't sign on as crew I can pay for my own drinks."

"A new way of thinking," the Major said after considering.

For nineteen hours the wind shrieked, bits of roof blew off, and rain drenched us. There had been one lull when I thought the worst was over and rose to go outside. Hornigold wouldn't allow it. "It's the eye, Anne. In any moment it will start again, worse than ever." Of course he was right.

Gradually Westminster grew quieter as people fell asleep from exhaustion or passed out from drink. Elena laid her head on the table and snored. Hornigold promptly began pressing against my knee. I moved closer to the Major. Jennings's Nell went off to gossip with some friends and Hornigold, after a puzzled look, gave me up and fell into a long discussion with Jennings about former shipmates, long since drying in Execution Dock. Which left the Major and me to our own company.

He told me about his life in Barbados. "The plantation was inland but the island is small enough that I was always conscious of the sea. There was a tree I used to climb and watch the ships through my spyglass. My father warned me if I didn't forget about the sea I'd never make a planter."

His father had died young leaving him a fortune, the plantation, and his mother to care for. His mother had engineered a marriage for him with a lady who was a shrew and a nag. "But perhaps she realizes I don't love her."

His younger brother had died of fever leaving a widow and four daughters to Bonnet's care. Then his sister's husband had been killed in a duel. "Again, I was the one turned to for help. I was surrounded by women and orphans and could stand it no longer. They are well cared for but I'm free of them, thank God."

I was a little drunk by then and I cried over the sad story. The Major wiped away my tears. Any other time it would have amused me to see Hornigold twinging with jealousy.

The air was stinking by now. The keg the landlord had supplied for our needs was overflowing. One of the trulls was doing a lively business in the corner where the hymn singers had given up hope.

The Major laughed. "If my lady folk could see me now they'd go down in a faint one by one like tipped dominoes. Yet here you sit aloof as if you were in your own drawing room."

"Perhaps I am no lady."

"You are Venus come to earth to teach us heavenly love."

That sounds flowery and foolish on paper but it sounded neither coming from him. Once more it was brought home to me that I had been a fool to throw myself away on James.

An eerie silence startled us. Then a bird called and a shaft of sunlight pierced the room.

Noah must have felt as we did when the waters receded. The nightmare was over. Devastation remained. The trees that were still standing had been stripped of foliage. Vultures lay dead, battered by the wind. Mongrels were already at work tearing apart their dead brothers. Crafts had crashed ashore and were like broken toys. Dead fish glistened on the sands. Everywhere was an already stinking green pulp of rot and vegetation.

I scarcely recognized the place that had been my home. The wind had moved the earth and the torrents of rain furrowed it. I found scraps of kindling that had been the carved chairs, and under a fallen tree the oak table cracked through and flattened. All the treasures I had gathered so proudly were lost except what Dove had buried, and it took a day of hard digging to find those.

Dove and Phibba came creeping out of the grotto where they had hidden and we set to work to restore our lives.

I kept thinking James could not have survived this storm and I was probably a widow. I fluctuated between joy at the thought of being free and worry because without money I didn't know what I would do. But there was no time to brood.

The Major found me toward evening. He brought fresh red snapper, rice, papaws, and French wine. Dove was no fool. He recognized the Major as a gentleman and gave me an unspoken blessing. While Phibba cooked our feast Dove finished throwing together a shelter and slung my hammock.

Major Stede Bonnet is no part of my defense. He was with me for a week while his battered ships were being repaired. I have never known such contentment or so tender and gentle a man. To him I was no quick gallop, a convenient wench in a certain port, but a lady, "a lively lady," he called me laughingly, as much in love as he was.

If I had been his wife he would never have left Barbados. If he had been my husband I would never have left Charles Town. If we could have belonged to one another we would have been happy forever. Perhaps.

The day came when the repairs to his ships were complete. Still he lingered. One evening he seemed more melancholy than usual. I asked what troubled him.

"My crew is fretting to put to sea. A fortune isn't made by sitting in port waiting for your victim to come to you, my dear."

"I have been thinking about that." I took his hands across the table. "I'm coming with you."

"My dear—"

"Listen to me, Stede. I'll put on seaman's dress. I'll cut my hair. I'll take my turn at the work. I can handle the ropes. I'm a better seaman than you when it comes to that. I'll fight beside the men. I'll *be* a man. No one need know. And if we appear to be more than friends—well, Stede, you cannot be such a gentleman that you don't know seamen often practice a different kind of love. There's not a member of the Brethren who hasn't at one time or another—" The expression on his face silenced me. Then I said stubbornly, "It's true. Ask Jennings if you don't believe me."

"I believe you. I am not as you say such a gentleman, so innocent a gentleman." He stared at our hands.

"I see," I said after a moment. "I forgot. You went on account to get away from women." I tried to withdraw my hands but his grip tightened.

"My dear, I would take you if I could see a way of doing it. But already the crew is drolling me about our affair. They call it by a cruder name. Even if you were to put on men's clothing they would see through the disguise. It would be disaster."

"I can't see—"

"Disaster, Anne. Trust me, my darling. I'll voyage until I make fortune enough to support us without care. Not here. Not in this den of carrion, though I call many of them friend. Somewhere that we can live decently, as we should."

"It will never happen."

"I promise you, it shall."

I wanted to believe it. I stood on the dock and waved farewell until his fleet was out of sight. Deep in my heart I knew I'd never see him again.

A day or so later James came limping home. I was not the widow I had hoped to be. The turtling sloop had put in at one of the minuscule islands, more reef than land, when they had seen the hurricane coming. The boat had been tossed on the beach and a part of the hull bashed. It had taken more than a week to mend. The men had suffered exposure and hunger, and all the turtles had escaped making the voyage profitless.

"But you weren't lost," I pointed out in answer to his complaints and added under my breath, more's the pity. "Turtling isn't the only way of making a living. If you're so set on getting rich why don't you go on account? If I know you, you wouldn't throw your share of the booty away on rum and women. You'd bury it and die rich."

"I did my bit of pirating and didn't swing for it. I'm glad to be going honest."

"So don't complain about a lost turtle! If it hadn't been for me you'd have come back to a heap of straw."

"If it hadn't been for you trying to burn your father alive we'd be living in Charles Town. He'd have forgiven you by now. He doted on you, Hornigold said."

"Stop going on about my father. If it was his money you wanted you should have bilked him instead of me."

"I didn't bilk you. It was you wanted to be married."

I couldn't deny that. He looked so pathetic I forgave him for being such a suck-up. He couldn't help it if he was as common as a barber's chair and I didn't love him. Besides, he now held the moneybags.

CHAPTER

CALICO JACK

As MY JUDGES know, 1718 was a good year for the Brethren. The shipping lanes were so busy it required little effort to take a prize. The ships coming from Europe yielded the better haul as they carried merchandise for the colonial markets, but no one scorned the gold and jewels from New Spain.

Often there were three thousand pirates in port at once, set on having a good time, spending their loot freely.

The turtling trade flourished. James was never home more than two or three nights between expeditions so we didn't have much opportunity to quarrel. He was hard put to find fault with me because, except for my wifely duties, I remained celibate and sober. James didn't know it, but I was being faithful to Stede. James was pleased with me and being pleased made him generous. I had a wardrobe a princess would have envied. He bought a slave to fan us while we ate, which made him feel a grand gentleman instead of a sow's ear.

All in all he was well satisfied with himself and had even ceased to upbraid me for having been disinherited. I think at the back of his mind was the idea that we would return to Charles Town someday. Perhaps he had convinced himself that my father would accept him.

As for myself, I was marking time, waiting for the day when Stede would come back even though I didn't believe he ever would.

We heard news of him from time to time from Brethren who had seen him. Stede's lack of seamanship hadn't prevented him from taking ships and sailing as far north as Long Island, but it had created a great deal of disorder and a lack of respect among his crew. So much so that when they met up with Ned Teach, Teach as good as took Stede prisoner and put one of his own men in charge of Stede's sloop.

This worried me. Teach's reputation as a terror had grown. He had married four more times, his most recent bride being a girl of fourteen on whom he showered jewels and money, then forced her to prostitute herself for his crew. His own men were rumored to be afraid of him. I spent some sleepless nights worrying about Stede until another ship came to port with the news that he had regained command of his sloop and was in Honduras. Ned Teach was somewhere on the Virginia coast being entertained by the planters who were apparently as dazzled by his gifts of rum and sugar as his bride had been by his gold.

If Stede could go to Honduras he could have put in at New Providence on the way. I couldn't believe he had forgotten me, but I could believe he was avoiding me. The thought came close to breaking my heart.

During that year I learned a great deal about the profession of piracy. If ever there was a School for Scoundrels it was in Nassau. All I had to do was sit and listen, and I could have gone on account with the best of them had the profession been open to females.

I learned, for instance, that the old legend so often told in Charles Town about forcing captured victims to walk the plank was laughable.

"Why go to that trouble?" Jennings asked. "If they resist throw 'em overboard and be done with it. Or tie 'em to a cannon and blow off their heads. But that's a waste of good powder when all the sea's there. A man's a poor swimmer with his arms bound."

"God's blood!"

"It's not done often, Jezebel," said Hornigold. "Oftener'n not the swabs give you no trouble. They know if they don't fuss they'll be set free. If we don't want their ships we set 'em adrift after we've taken the spoil. If we do want the ship, we put 'em in a longboat with bread and rum. They make it to port somehow. Men have a fierce hankering to stay alive. The officers now, they're a different matter, especially if they've been brutal to their crews."

Jennings agreed. "Aye, a different matter. Them we generally flog before we let 'em go. Give 'em a taste of their own whip. Most times we talk those crews into joining us. Always make use of a good man, see? A carpenter, a metalsmith, a cook—a crew fights on its belly timber—a surgeon. A skilled man is worth half the loot. And if the captain's been a bastard, the men'll not hesitate to come."

Hornigold gave a bellow of laughter. "Fight to sign on, they do, but if we're captured, they're always the first to whine they were pressed and were lily-white afore we tarred 'em."

"Can you blame them, Benjamin? It's a dirty way to die. Not fit for dogs or hogs. Remember Symon Harley? He danced on air an hour before he finally choked and me sweating in the crowd knowing I should be there as well if I'd been caught."

"Marooning now, that's another thing. If you've mutiny on your hands, if some swab starts objecting to the rules, there's naught to do but maroon him. Once a troublemaker, always a troublemaker. Not that I like it. It's hell to see the poor devil looking after you knowing he'll either drown at high tide or have put a ball through his head afore the water gets him. Swabs you've been comrades with and drunk with."

"But there's no help for it," Jennings put in.

"No help at all. Not when they don't abide by Articles."

The Articles were the codes of pirate law that every crew member swore to and signed. I read Hornigold's copy and no government could ask for fairer rules, save one. It was I who objected to that. No women were allowed on board and if any man induced a woman to go to sea in disguise he was to suffer death. It made me understand Stede's position a little better, but I still resented it.

"I can shoot as well as any man," I argued. I had a bad case of island fever and was feeling more depressed than usual. "I can fence better than most."

"It wouldn't do, Jezebel. A woman aboard a ship is trouble. You couldn't keep from giving yourself away—showing off your breastplate or prettying yourself. And fencing with a foil isn't like handling a cutlass. A cutlass is a man's weapon."

That was all he needed to say. I began to have a nagging fear that all this dissolute and idle living had dulled my skill. I still carried my gold-chased sixty-caliber pistol but I hadn't had to use it since the day I had shot the doubloons from under Hornigold's hand.

Now every morning I took myself off to a favorite cove. It was a place I called my own because no one else ever came there. I spent hours practicing. It was true my eye had grown less sharp but a few days' shooting soon put that right. If Colin had been there I could have shot off his hat without stirring a hair, just as I had done in the past.

The cutlass was a different matter. Long, wide-bladed, and brutally heavy, it required strong muscles and fearless technique. Instead of flicking the opponent's weapon out of the way and making a lightning thrust when you saw an opening, the cutlass was all cut and thrust and hack. Fortunately I was tall enough that the length didn't bother me, but it was some time before I had the strength or skill to handle it easily.

Dove and I constructed a straw man for my opponent and I spent every day opposing its wooden staff and often getting the wind knocked out of me. Dove didn't approve. He had his ideas about what a lady should be and do.

My judges will assume as Dove did that I was already planning to go on account. Perhaps, unconsciously, I was.

Another hurricane season passed, this one leaving New Providence more or less intact. I was so restless that had my pride permitted, I would have gone crawling back to Charles Town to ask my father's forgiveness.

One afternoon when even the company of the Brethren, of whom I was heartily sick, seemed preferable to my own, I walked over to the settlement. The place was babbling with excitement.

A sloop had come in on the morning tide with strange loot. It was a bale of notices en route to the Indies, a proclamation by the King. Copies had been tacked on every post and wall, and before each a crowd had gathered while some literate member of the island earned himself a rum by reading it aloud to the unschooled. I didn't need anyone to read it to me. I shoved my way through the listeners and had taken in the whole thing while the literate one was still struggling with the first few lines.

It was impressive, right enough, all flowing tails and curlicues as befitted such a document.

BY THE KING,

A proclamation of Suppressing of Pyrates
Whereas we have received Information, that several per-

sons, Subjects of GREAT BRITAIN, have, since the 24th
Day of June, in the Year of Our Lord, 1715, committed
divers Pyracies and Roberies upon the High Sea, in the
West Indies or adjoining Plantations, which hath and may
Occasion great Damage to the Merchants of GREAT
BRITAIN and tho' we have appointed such Force as we
judge sufficient for the suppressing of said Pyrates, yet
the more effectually to make an End to the Same, we have
thought fit, by and with the Advice of our Privy Council
to Issue this our Royal Proclamation . . .

It went on and on and the crowd began to get rude and
ordered their readers to stow the fancy talk and give them
the gaff.

The jist of it was that any pirate who by the fifth of Sep-
tember of that year, 1718, would surrender to any governor
or deputy governor, would be pardoned for past piracies.
If they did not accept the pardon or surrender themselves
they would be hunted down, seized, and hanged.

But the real shocker was saved for the end. A governor was
being sent to Nassau to "rout out the Sea Wolves, this
Viperish Nest of Pyrates." The governor's duty would be to
grant pardons and establish a colony of "Decent Men."

Shocked silence met that statement, then one man pushed
to the front and demanded, "Where does it say that? Show
me." He ran his fingers over the written words as if they
could read what his mind could not.

In Westminster rum was flowing. You would have thought
from the discussions being carried on that there were more
than two choices: to take the pardon or defy the King. Everyone had a different opinion and wanted to express it.

Jennings who was, as much as anyone, our acknowledged
governor was looking worn and serious as he tried to speak
over the uproar.

"It could be worse, mates. Woodes Rogers, him as has
been appointed governor, is a decent man, a seaman like

((109))

ourselves. He's sailed around the globe and how many of you swabs have done that? Remember, he sacked Guayaquil and took the Spanish Plate ship on its way from Manila to Mexico. Eight hundred thousand pounds, lads. None of us has ever seen the likes of that. He's half-pirate himself, so perhaps there'll be reasoning with him. He won't be like those governors who've spent their days mincing around at court. I've known men who crewed for Rogers and they said he was right as rain and fair as the weather. Not one spoke a word against him. He'd sense enough to know sailors need good liquor more than they need good clothes or a good berth.

"We've had our way and our day. Mayhap times are changing. Let's not be hasty and swing for it after. Let's belay action until all the Brethren have had their say. What we do now is, we go after those out on cruise and call them in for a palaver. That's fair and square and according to Articles, and as I'm governor as much as any appointed by Hampton Court, I'm saying, that's the way it is."

By nightfall everyone had agreed that a general council was the only way to handle the crisis, but there were some mumbled threats about what they would do to Rogers once he set foot ashore.

Naturally, James was on the side of authority. He began to make plans to get himself appointed to a government post so he wouldn't have to turtle anymore.

"I don't know what makes you think the governor will give a second look to a man with no learning," I said. "Or why you think I want to be the wife of some low-class clerk, curtseying and smirking every time some official snaps his fingers at us. Better you should go back to pimping. It's all the same thing."

"And make you my whore? Damn it, woman, can't I ever please you?"

"No."

The day of the palaver there were so many of the Brethren ashore the meet had to be held outside. Naturally the females had to crowd in there, too, to hear what was going on. Not that many of them gave a damn. They had nothing to fear from the edict unless the King had decided to suppress fornication. In true female fashion they spent more time gabbling with each other and slapping their brats than they did listening. I'd like to have sewn their mouths shut.

Because, of course, I was there, too, as near the front as I could get. I had dressed for the occasion in a pale-green lawn dress with a skirt so full I didn't need petticoats. God knows, no one needs petticoats in that climate. My hair was piled on my head to keep my neck cool and I wore Spanish emeralds in my ears and was shielded from the sun by a parasol. James's slave fanned me with a palm leaf, and all the other females were giving their usual look of mingled resentment, envy, and wry amusement.

Charles Vane's crew was late in arriving. I didn't know Vane well as he spent most of his time sailing from Virginia down to Jamaica, Honduras, and on down to Brazil. He had a reputation of being ill-tempered, high-handed, and contemptuous of his crew. "If ever an argument's started when Vane's around, you can wager he was the one who started it," Hornigold had told me.

But as he was one of the Brethren he had been called in, and late or not, he was determined to have his say. He was pushing his way toward the front, none too gently, and causing a lot of snarling, which he disregarded. He was self-important until the day they hanged him.

Behind him was the first man I'd given more than a second look since Stede had left. It was his clothes made me notice. He wore bell-bottom trousers of red and yellow flowered calico, a yellow striped shirt of such gossamer stuff that the dark hair on his chest showed through. The red bandanna on his head was topped with a wide-brimmed hat woven of palm leaf. The traditional gold earring swung from his ear and a chunk of green serpentine, which seamen wear to protect them from drowning, was suspended from a thin gold chain around his neck. Black hair curled from under the bandanna, his black goatee was carefully trimmed, and his moustache was waxed and twisted into two half circles. His skin was burned dark but he looked clean, which was more than I could say for most of the Brethren.

I stared admiringly, thinking Raleigh must have looked like this. He felt my gaze and turned back and accosted me with eyes as dark as mahogany. Then he laughed.

"Yo, Vane, see this! The governor's lady has already arrived."

Everyone laughed, those jealous bitches the most loudly. I turned red and nearly knocked over the slave as I leaped up. It's impossible to ram someone with an open parasol and what with it in one hand and James dragging at my other I couldn't get at my pistol or I'd have maimed him.

Hornigold called, "Devil help you, Jack, that's not the guv'nor's lady. It's Anne Bonny, Hell's own kite. She'll shoot you as soon as look at you."

The man laughed again. His teeth were even and white, not stained with tobacco or pocked with decay. He swept off his hat and bowed. "Forgive me, m'lady. I didn't notice your horns but now I see them I recognize you as Lucifer's wife. Tell me, do you have a forked tail, too?"

Without waiting for an answer—as if there were one—he and Vane pressed on to the front row.

"Who is that dog?" I asked James.

"John Rackham. They call him Calico Jack. He always dresses in that gaudy manner the better to attract attention. The same as you."

"Is he one of us?"

"He's none of me. He's a damned pirate. Why else would he be here? He's Vane's quartermaster. They say Vane had better look to his guns or Rackham'll end up captain and Vane will find himself on a spit of land with nothing but biscuit and a pistol with a single shot."

"If it was the other way around I'd supply the pistol."

But I couldn't keep my eyes off the man. I kept craning my neck to watch him sitting cross-legged on the ground, and thinking what I would say to him the next time we met. My thoughts were so busy with him that I only half heard the discussion.

What it amounted to was that Jennings and Hornigold along with some of the other older leaders had decided to accept the pardon and advised the others to do the same.

Vane bounded up and shook his fist under Jennings's nose. "You're old men. You'd rather laze around on shore than go to sea. You've escaped Execution Dock so long that now you're afraid to die. But you've no right to deny the young bloods their fun and fortune. If you want to live safe go to Boston, go to Philadelphia, go to Virginia. The governors'll welcome you. They'll wink at your sins. But leave New Providence to us." He turned to the crowd. "What do you say, mates? Shall we fortify the island and defy this fellow Rogers? Do you want to be pardoned so you can work like dogs to make the world safe for planters and merchants? Or do you want to be free, make the sea your home and what's on it yours for the taking?"

There were some enthusiastic ayes and grumbling nays, and a fight started near the front that had to be stopped before the discussion could continue.

"You're moonstruck if you think this island can be fortified, Vane," Jennings said. "We've no harbor defenses. The fort's in ruins and the only cannon up there that'll fire is an old nine-pounder with a crack in it. It'll blow up any day."

"We'll block the harbor with ships. We've cannon on every vessel and powder a-plenty. We'll blow Rogers out of the sea before he knows what's hit him."

"And bring the Royal Navy against us. It's New Providence that'll be blown out of the sea if that happens."

"You're a bunch of hen-hearted numskulls."

"Name-calling won't settle the problem." Hornigold and Jennings were purple with anger.

The fight started again, this time with dirks instead of fists. It wasn't stopped until blood was drawn.

The day wore on. Nothing was settled except that the colony broke into three factions: those siding with Jennings and Hornigold, those with Vane, and a wait-and-see-what-Rogers-has-to-offer group who could jump either way.

If the government wanted to destroy the Brethren they couldn't have made a better start.

From a practical point of view my sympathies lay with Vane. What kind of work could government find for rogues who had never done an honest stroke in their lives? There weren't enough merchantmen on the sea to take care of them all and they'd mutiny the first week out if things weren't run the way they were accustomed. If government thought to press them into the navy—well, that was another fool idea. Nor would they be of any use as planters because that involved hard work.

But Jennings and Hornigold were my friends so I joined them at Westminster after the meeting, and kept my opinions to myself. It was a dull evening. Everyone was chewing over the afternoon's arguments and nobody was changing his stand. I was yawning and wishing the musicians would strike up a tune so we could dance. But they were busy arguing, too, for as my judges know, all pirate ships carry musicians and they stood as much chance to hang as anybody.

I had just said to James that we might as well go home because I was sick of Governor Rogers and pardons and everything to do with them, when Calico Jack Rackham walked in the door. A hush fell over the room. Everyone knew he was Vane's man and no one knew whether he'd come to start a fight or join Jennings's side, which would be the first break in Vane's contingent and probably lead to his capitulation.

"Halloo, mate," Jennings waved across the room. "Have you come to join us?"

Rackham smiled so all his white teeth showed and came to our table and bowed to the company in general. "I've come to join the hellkite." His eyes twinkled as he appraised me. There was such open lust in his look that no one could doubt his intent.

James, of course, was instantly on the defensive. "You weren't invited, Rackham, and you're not welcome. I'm the lady's husband."

Rackham looked James up and down, then shrugged. "You have my sympathy, m'lady. I'd prefer to hear from you if I'm welcome."

"Of course you're welcome." I moved over to make room for him beside me.

"I thought you wanted to go home," James said.

"I don't know why you thought that."

Glaring, James squeezed down on the other side of me. Hornigold grinned, enjoying what he foresaw would happen. I kicked him under the table.

"Have you decided to take the pardon?" Jennings asked.

"The pardon can wait. I've come to do some pirating. I saw this fine-rigged vessel and decided to board and loot her."

James leaned around me. "What do you mean by that, Rackham?"

"Unless you're a fool you bloody well know what I mean."

"This lady is my wife."

"You repeat yourself, sirrah. The prize belongs to the man bold enough to take it."

James stood up. "Come on, Anne. I don't like the company here."

I could have refused but Rackham was looking so pleased with himself that I wasn't going to give him the satisfaction of thinking I wanted to stay. I took James's arm and we left. I knew I would never be satisfied until I had Rackham begging for my favors.

Vane's sloop left on the morning tide. James watched it until the topsails disappeared. Then he glared at me and said, "Good riddance."

"Pooh. I don't know what makes you think I'd bother with him."

"You must think I'm a fool."

I didn't bother to answer because I wouldn't have been able to deny it.

James was busy making plans to go with Jennings and the others to accept the King's pardon with the excuse that while he hadn't been pirating, it was best to be on the safe side. I was glad to be shut of him for a while.

It was quiet with the men gone. The women settled down as happy as hens in a dust bath and just as amiable. It was only when the men were present that they argued with one another. The harbor was empty except for the sunken hulls, and Westminster was like a haunted house. Governor Sawney had to be reassured a dozen times a day that the island was not being deserted again and that he wouldn't be left stranded.

One day I was swimming in a quiet cove well away from the settlement. I had removed all my clothes as I often did when it was unlikely that anyone would come around and was floating, letting the waves lift and lap over me. Suddenly someone hailed me. I submerged hurriedly, doubling my knees so I was underwater up to my chin. Not that much of me was hidden in that clear water where you can almost count the grains of sand on the floor of the sea.

Who should be coming toward me in a coracle and showing how inept he was at paddling it—though they are the devil to handle—but Jack Rackham. His shirt was open and the serpentine was lying in the black hair of his chest. He'd need that serpentine if he couldn't handle a sloop any better than he handled the coracle.

"They told me I'd find you here," he said, and the way he looked at me I knew it wasn't grains of sand on the floor of the sea he was counting.

"Who told you?" I'd wring their necks if I ever got out of there and into my clothes.

"Your blacks. I had to bribe them. That man's as jealous as your husband." He was so close I could have reached up and tipped him over, but I didn't want him in the water with me. Not with that look in his eyes.

"Damn their skins! I'll teach them to take bribes." I caught hold of the coracle and hid myself against its side. "I thought you had gone with Vane."

"I did, but we're back. We were only waiting for Jennings and his henchmen to leave. Vane's taking over as governor of the island."

"He'll serve a short term."

"That's as may be. I hear your man went with the others."

I wondered how much he had given Dove to make his tongue so loose. "James is so cowardly he's afraid he'll get hanged for association." I hadn't meant to say any such thing, but treading water, hanging on to the coracle that swung

((117))

around in every wave that caught it, and trying to keep decently hidden, made me lose my head.

"How did you manage to get married to a whelp like that?" Rackham was enjoying the situation even though he didn't have the coracle under control.

"Lucifer's dog! Every man I meet either asks me what I'm doing in their company or why I am married to James. Don't a one of you have an original thought? There's nothing wrong with a man who makes an honest living."

"Don't lie to me, wench. It's easy to see you despise him. But perhaps he's got more ammunition in his cannon than I think by looking at him."

In spite of myself I laughed.

"I gather he didn't always make an honest living or your father wouldn't have thrown you out. But fathers are a bad lot. Mine threw me out, too. He's a merchant like your own —a London merchant. Wealthy as sin and straitlaced as a Puritan, though he's Anglican on the Sabbath for business' sake. I'm the family blackguard. Father paid me to get out of London and stop disgracing him."

"I'll be glad to listen to the story of your life some other time," I said, treading water. "That is, if there is any more. You didn't have to tell me you're a blackguard. A gentleman would go away and let me cover myself."

"I like you better uncovered. There's too much modesty in the world, Anne Bonny. You can blame the damned Puritans for that. You're a well-rigged female. It's a pity you aren't as well manned. But you will be."

He stood up, the coracle tipping dangerously, and shook off his shirt and stripped off his trousers before I recovered my wits sufficiently to swim away. He was well rigged himself with his mainsail up.

As he dived in I dived under the coracle and let a wave carry me out of his reach. Once he almost caught me but I was the better swimmer and slippery as a mermaid. We sported in the water, playful as fishes. Then, unexpectedly, he rammed me head on and speared me.

Being locked together in the water, lifted and dropped by the waves, required less effort than coupling on land. No wonder there are so many fish in the sea.

Gillah had not mentioned seawater in her list of preventatives but I hoped it would work. I'd never be able to convince James that a black-haired child was any of his.

Eventually we tired, and went ashore and dressed. I wondered if Jack's bribe to Dove had been generous enough to allow me to take him home, but suddenly he struck his head and cursed.

"If I don't get back, Vane'll have blood. We're supposed to be taking over the island, not one member of it."

"It's a fool notion. Who does Vane think he is? Henry Morgan?"

"All we have to do is bottle the harbor with the sunken hulls and man the fort. We've a crew of ninety-five and every man jack of us is ashore."

"If they are spending their time the way you've spent yours it's not the fort they're manning."

He put his hands on my shoulders and looked at me, his eyes sparkling with laughter and passion. If James had ever looked at me like that I would never have cuckolded him— except perhaps with Stede.

"It's called subduing the population, Anne. Now, lookee, m'lady, I've taken you fair and square, boarded you, manned you, claimed you. From now on you're mine even if that ill-looked husband comes back. Which he'll have the Devil's own time doing if Vane's plan succeeds."

"Ninety-five men can't succeed against the number the Brethren have. If you block the harbor with sunken hulls you won't be able to get out yourselves. There's something called island fever that'll soon produce mutiny in your ranks."

"Save your breath for coupling, woman. Come along, I've work to do."

We needn't have hurried. The women had been without their men for a few days and Vane's crew had been at sea even longer. There was scarcely a hammock that wasn't swinging, Elena's among them, and not with the trade wind.

"So much for Vane's take-over," I laughed.

"All the damned swabs can think of is their tails. It'll be their necks they'll be thinking of if Rogers lands."

"That's one crow calling the other black. Let's have a corker while the population is being subdued."

"You're a disrespectful woman, Anne."

Vane was in Westminster sulking drunk. The fort was manned right enough and a couple of light cannon had been brought from his brigantine to back up the cannon rusting up there. So far he hadn't been able to call a council to organize the defense of the island.

"We should round up all the trulls and drive 'em into the sea and drown 'em. You, too, m'lady." He was so bleary-eyed he could scarcely focus on my face. " 'S only way to get order."

"It might be easier to cut off the men's parts. That would save lives and keep the men from getting itchy."

He glowered at me. "You're all alike, woman." He turned to Jack. "Got to bottle the harbor. Bottle one end. That'll do it. Guard the other with cannon. Hold it against God and man. And the Devil. Him, too."

"Blocking the harbor may keep out God, man, and the Devil, but it will keep you in as well," I said. "The Brethren can fence you in, and who knows how many warships the new governor will have? You'll need the other end open to give them the slip."

Jack looked at me admiringly but Vane banged the table with his tankard and shouted, "I'll hang before I'll take the pardon." He sat down suddenly and passed out.

Jack and I went home. Dove, instead of acting like an anxious old mother, had Phibba fix our meal, then retired discreetly. I was puzzled.

"How much did you give him?"

"I filled the soup caldron with gold doubloons."

My mouth fell open. That meant Dove could buy and sell me, which was just what he had done.

"I wanted you, m'lady, even though you're too damned wise to be a woman." He took my hand and drew me to him.

My loyalties were shallow shoals. I completely forgot Stede.

Vane held the island for two weeks. Held it because there was no one trying to wrest it from him.

Jack and I lived well during that time. Vane's most recent prize had been a French ship laden with brandy and wines. I hadn't had such wine since I had left my father's house and it was a welcome change from rum.

There had also been brocades, watered silks, fans, slippers, lace, and other pretties aboard, and Jack lavished his share of the booty on me and Phibba. I lavished him with passion. I was as besotted as I had ever been with Hornigold or James or Stede.

Those days were full of love and laughter and fun. When Jack was away I waited for him as impatiently as any bride. When he was with me I wanted no one and nothing else. He talked over his and Vane's affairs with me and listened to my opinions, even took my advice, passing it on to Vane as if it were his own.

The Brethren returned, radiant and pious as converts. Vane's defenses crumbled after a short exchange of shot. The old nine-pounder on the fort exploded killing two men and maiming another. Jack had managed to persuade Vane not to bottle the harbor with sunken hulls and the ships holding the harbor's mouth mutinied, the men having decided it was better to take the pardon than to be blown up. Vane sailed off in his brig with only three quarters of his crew.

Rachkam stayed behind.

CHAPTER

VI

THE GOVERNOR

WOODES ROGERS ARRIVED on an evening in June. His fleet
consisted of two tall frigates and two sloops. Richard Turnley
went out to meet him and act as pilot.

I haven't mentioned Turnley because I never liked the
man with his shifty eyes and buttonhole of a mouth. He was
a turtling companion of James's. Hornigold and Jennings
said he was the best pilot in the waters. He was also an informer who would sell a secret for a groat.

The tide was low and before he left Turnley said he
would advise the new governor to lay by until dawn.

"That way he can swagger around aboard the governor's
ship and talk big and ingratiate himself," I told James.

Turnley wasn't the only one who would be throwing his
weight around. As luck would have it, Vane had come in the
day before with his own sloop and a brig he had taken.
He was boasting and spending his gold, jeering at the men

who had taken the pardon and proclaiming he'd hang before he'd accept it. He had said it so many times I thought it a pity someone didn't accommodate him. Nor could he keep from taunting Jack.

"Worse luck you weren't with me, mate. I'd have given you command of the brig and your own pick of a company to man it. But, no, you deserted me for a petticoat. You'll never get rich chasing skirts, mate."

Jack was looking down his nose. It was obvious he wished he had gone with Vane in order to share some of that loot. I didn't know it then, but he was low on money.

Hornigold and Jennings were furious. They didn't want the celebration to welcome Rogers ruined. "Mark me, blood'll be drawn if that cock is still ashore tomorrow," Jennings said to Hornigold. "I'm ordering him back to his ships and I'm looking for you to stand by me."

"You know I'm square, Henry."

"Aye, I know."

We were in Westminster, as always. Jennings got up deliberately, slowly, and walked to the table where Vane was laying on the rum for all who would drink with him. Vane ignored Jennings at first, but finally he sneered, "Well, old man, do you want a free drink, too? Now you're done with pirating do you have to beg for your corkers?"

Jennings turned purple and Hornigold leaped up, dirk in hand. Elena and I held him back and he sat down reluctantly, but he didn't sheath his dirk.

Westminster had fallen silent so Jennings's next words rang out. "Vane, you're a soft-headed fool and you'll never change until you're drying like buccan. We drove you off the island once. This time we want you to go quietlike. There's no room here for swabs who haven't taken the pardon. Not anymore."

"I'll shove off when I'm ready, old man."

"You'll shove off now. I'm an old man, aye, and an easy one, but I've men rough and ready who think as I think. I'm advising you to cast off and if so much as a skiff belonging to your fleet is in harbor at dawn I'll ask Rogers to put the frigates' guns on it."

If looks had been daggers there would have been blood, then Vane laughed and shrugged. "Drink up, lads. This place stinks like bilge. All right, old man, all right. We're shoving off. Go back to your easy chair before I swat you like a fly."

Jennings stood his ground until Vane and his crew were away. They went shouting profanities and singing ribald songs directed at Rogers. They didn't stop even when they reached their ships. Their voices carried well over the water. Every threat, every word of ridicule, could be plainly heard.

We knew Rogers had heard because the frigates changed position and moved up to the east mouth of the harbor. They had scarcely got into position when Vane's captured brig fired a four-gun salute, damaging the rigging on one of the men-of-war.

The Brethren were furious. Hornigold paced up and down shaking his fist in Vane's direction and letting fly some obscenities Vane had forgotten.

Jennings sweated with rage. "The guv'nor'll think we're revolting against him. That dog! We should've given him broadside before he left Westminster. Lucifer knows what he'll do next."

"We've got to stop him, that's certain," Hornigold said. "And we should send a man out to Rogers to tell him we've no part in what's happening."

"Better send a man to halt Vane."

No one volunteered. There wasn't a man there wanted any part of Vane. Hornigold's eye lighted on Rackham. He jerked his thumb at him. "You. You were quartermaster along of Vane. You should have some influence. You go."

((125))

"I'm not sailing along of him now."

"Nor've you taken the pardon," Jennings said. "How is that?"

"I wasn't here when you went off. I'll take it off Rogers when he comes ashore."

"He'll have a hard time coming ashore if that swab out there keeps on like this. You're going, Rackham."

Jack was sweating but he finally agreed to go. Not that he had any choice. Like a fool he gave me a good-bye kiss right in front of James.

"For luck," he said.

He got away before James could start a fight.

Before Jack reached Vane's vessels the man-of-war fired the eight-o'clock gun. Vane knew damned well what it was, but he answered with another round, putting a hole in the frigate's hull.

Across the water we heard Jack shout to Vane for a line. Then everything was quiet.

"Maybe he's talking some sense into that stinking tar-barrel's bloody head," Hornigold said. Hornigold was so nervous he couldn't stand in one spot. He kept pacing up and down, chewing at his moustache and hitching at his breeks.

"And maybe he isn't," Jennings said. "It's gone too quiet." He squinted out to where the sloop and brig lay at anchor. "There's something going on aboard the brig. I wonder what that shark's doing? There're torches—" He interrupted himself with a howl. "They've fired the brig. The damned dog's fired the brig and turned it loose. It'll ram the frigates sure as Lucifer's his name."

A stiff breeze blew down the harbor and the brig rode before it, full speed. Flames lapped at the canvas and ran in a fiery line following the powder trails Vane had trickled round the deck. As the fire reached the guns they exploded sending balls and round shot in every direction, but mostly at the frigates at which they had been aimed.

The frigates cut cable and headed out to sea, crippled through they were, and just in time. Suddenly the sea, the harbor, the island were alight as an earsplitting explosion threw us to the ground. The fire had reached the magazine and Vane's brig leaped out of the water and disintegrated in a shower of glowing brands that soared like shooting stars and hissed as they fell into the sea.

During the few moments the explosion lighted the sky we saw Vane's light sloop speed out of the other end of the harbor, the crew shouting with victory as they went.

Jennings mopped his brow. "God almighty! There's a bold bastard for you. Even in the old days I'd never have dared a trick like that."

"Rackham doesn't seem to have stopped him," Hornigold said. "It wouldn't surprise me but what he was in on it all along."

"The devil he was," I said. But I wasn't certain. The only thing I did know for sure was that I was furious with Jack.

When James put a tentative hand on my breast that night I knocked him out of the hammock.

Rogers's fleet entered the harbor at daybreak. Everyone on the island was there to greet him. It was laughable to see those regenerate rascals clutching their Certificates of Pardon.

The captains lined up their men in double file. As Rogers came ashore with his escort a volley of musket fire greeted him. Cutlasses flashed in the air and the Brethren cheered as their trulls pelted the path with flowers.

After last night's experience Rogers might have thought they were there to murder him, but he never flinched when the muskets blasted. He walked with steady tread, nodding right and left as if greeting old friends, saluting the captains as if they were the King's Own. He even patted the head of a brat who escaped its mother and darted into his path. I had my troubles with Rogers later but that day I admired him.

It was reassuring to see he was as battle-scarred as any of the Brethren. Part of his lower jaw had been shot away by a Spanish musket. Powder burns had blackened his lips. In healing the scar had pulled back his mouth so his teeth were bared in a wry smile. He looked tough and fearless, and I said to myself, the Brethren were in for a bad time.

They soon found out what they were in for, and some of them whispered among themselves that Vane wasn't such a fool after all.

Rogers established himself and his staff in the ruins of the fort and soon had it repaired and made impregnable. He put the island under martial law—that caused some grumbling—and recruited an army from the pardoned captains and their crews.

He appointed justices of the peace, magistrates, constables, and public work officers. James got a commission as some sort of subordinate officer. I never understood exactly what it was, but then I never bothered to ask.

Turnley was made chief pilot. A factor was appointed to examine all the shipping in the harbor to decide which belonged to the pirates, which to the Crown, and which could be legitimately claimed by merchantmen and tradesmen. This caused an uproar because the pirates had accepted the pardon with the understanding that they could keep all the plunder they had taken up to that time. Fortunately, it took so long to form a Court of Admiralty, and those who sat on the bench were all former pirates, that in the end, there were few complaints.

The next order of business was to clean up the island.

The ramshackle shelters were condemned and torn down, and replaced by new, sturdier ones. Any man willing to construct a permanent dwelling for himself, timber provided by government, was given title to 120 square feet of land. Men who had never owned anything but what they had plundered and the clothes they stood in became proud as squires.

Four days a week every man had to donate his labor to public works, rebuilding, fortifying, scavenger work, planting, and clearing the sunken hulls out of the harbor.

I watched and wondered how long it would last.

One night in Westminster—for Rogers had the wisdom to keep the grog shops operating—James, all officious and self-important, had gone off to quiet a couple of rowdies in a corner. I said to Hornigold, "The man I'd like to see walk through that door right now is Stede Bonnet."

"Not Rackham?" Hornigold cocked an eye at me. "I heard you and Rackham were keeping hot company and sharing the same berth while we were in Bermuda."

Elena couldn't keep her mouth shut any more than she could keep her legs together.

"Not Rackham." Although I wouldn't have minded him either. "Stede."

"Devil knows where that gentleman is now," Hornigold said. "Didn't anyone tell you he was in Bermuda taking the pardon?"

"It didn't take him long to tire of pirating," I said. But an awful depression settled on me. By now he was probably back in Barbados with his nagging wife.

So much for that dream.

Somehow the weeks passed. I was not the only one finding life dull and disappointing. Some of the Brethren had stolen small craft and slipped off in the black of night, back to their old ways. If they wanted to go, full-knowing they would hang, it was their affair. A man should be free to choose his own fate. But James was not of the same opinion, as I soon learned.

Often when we turned up at Westminster, more to avoid one another's company than to enjoy ourselves, men shied away from us, some actually turned their backs, refused the offer of a drink, and made us feel as welcome as a plague. Even Jennings and Hornigold seemed uncomfortable when we joined them.

I thought little about it. I didn't care that much for James myself, but finally I asked Jennings's Nell what it was all about. We had gone outside to relieve ourselves and as we squatted side by side I asked what the devil ailed everyone.

"You don't know? You don't know what that lousy dog is doing?"

"I suppose you mean James."

"You may call him James. I call him a lousy dog."

"I know more than one lousy dog. I wanted to make sure we're talking about the same lousy dog."

"You're droll, you are, Anne. Aye, it's James Bonny I mean." She stood up and shook out her skirts. "The devil! I got my petticoats."

"What has James done?"

"Turned spy and informer, that's what he's done. You know there's a bit of sleight of hand going on with some of the Brethren. Nothing dishonest, just to make a bit on the side with the guv'nor so strict and all."

"And James found out and turned them in?"

"Not only that. You know some've found the work too hard. They aren't used to it, Anne. Quiet days at sea, a bit of slosh down the deck, mend a sail, tar the ropes, a tipple in the evening, and a fight when there's a prize to take, but all in all, an easy life. Guv'nor, well, he's set on blistering their hands and keeping 'em jumping like Billy Black."

I had heard the complaints.

((130))

"You know some's gone back to their old ways and were so unwise as to say their plans in your James's hearing—"

"Don't call him *my* James."

"Well, seeing you're married to him. Not that it's held you back. Anyway, the lousy dog goes running to the guv'nor every time he hears of a backslider. And the guv'nor, well, he's planning to send out a sloop to round 'em up and he's swore he'll hang everyone as is caught. Hang, Anne. We've never had a hanging here. It'll be Execution Dock. What's it coming to?"

"The miserable firk. I'll soon tend to him."

"What'll you do?"

"I'll think of something."

But it was going to take some thinking because, as I said earlier, my money had long been exhausted and I was dependent on James for everything.

I supposed Dove still had the money Rackham had lavished on him but I couldn't go begging off my former slave any more than I could go crawling back to my father. Nor could I come up with any kind of plan.

I told James what I thought about him and his informing, but what I thought didn't matter to him, and there was no reason why it should have. We continued to share our pavilion but ours was no longer much of a marriage.

Those were depressing days. I had a bad case of island fever, which as my judges know doesn't put you to bed with boils and delirium, but makes you sick in your soul.

Sometimes I drank myself into oblivion. The pity was when the drink wore off the world was the same as when I had left it and I had a raging head.

Sometimes I thought I would swim out so far I couldn't come back. Then the sea would take me. I had reached the depths where there was no cure, then Fate intervened. It's strange Fate saved me from drowning myself so that I could be hanged.

James and I didn't talk to one another much so it is surprising he told me the news. Likely it was to see how I would react.

"By the by," he said one evening after a silent meal, "a friend of yours is back."

My first thought was Stede Bonnet and my heart began to thump. I got hold of myself and said, "I haven't any friends who've been away."

"Don't tell me that tale. I hear more than you think I do and I heard John Rackham was your friend in more ways than one."

"That traitor? He's back?" I tried to sound cool. "I suppose Vane's come to burn the settlement the way he keeps boasting he'll do. Those notes he sends to the governor are laughable."

"Vane's not with Rackham. Seems they captured a sloop and Rackham got command of it, set himself up as captain and told Vane to shove off. Rackham's come to take the pardon." James watched me narrowly but I kept my eyes on the papaw I was eating. "He claims he didn't have any part in that attack on the frigates. He no sooner got on board than Vane took him prisoner and all the pleading in the world didn't set him free."

"The governor believed that?"

"More fool he."

"Maybe it's so."

"So or not, he's back and I'm warning you, stay away from him."

"I will, James, I will. I'll do whatever you say."

"I don't know how I came to be saddled with such a bitch." He got up. "I'm for Westminster."

"See to it you don't get dirked coming home."

He hadn't been gone more than a quarter of an hour and I was wondering whether I should go along to my cove on the chance that Jack would be there, when he came strolling into the pavilion as if he were master of it.

I ran into his arms and between kisses he told me he had come back because he couldn't stay away from me. I begged him never to leave me again and threatened to dirk him if he tried.

"But what are we to do?" I asked, remembering James.

"Do?" His voice was muffled because he was kissing the hollow between my breasts. "We're going to get into that hammock of yours first. Then I'm going to the governor and take the pardon and live the life of a decent man so I can have you."

"But James—"

He stopped my words with kisses. Then he picked me up. I'm a big woman, as my judges know. He staggered under my weight. Just as he threw me into my hammock and climbed in on top of me, James came back, livid with rage.

"I knew I'd find you here, you sneaking cur. I knew it, so I doubled back and I've been standing there all this time and I saw it all and heard it all."

Jack fell out of the hammock as fast as he had fallen in. He began calling James every name that came to his tongue while he was trying to button his trousers again. Then he broke off.

"The truth is, Bonny, the only reason I despise you is because you're married to Anne. I want her myself and I'll buy her off you."

"Buy her? Like a slave, you mean?"

"I've no use for slaves. I'm talking about Divorce by Sale. How much do you want?"

"Is Divorce by Sale still legal? I've seen it at public auction but that was back in England."

"If it's done at public aution it must be legal and what's good for England is good for Nassau now we've got a good

((133))

English governor. But I won't have Anne put up at public auction. I might lose her. We'll hold our auction here and now. How much? Five shillings?"

I had got out of the hammock and pulled my blouse back together and shaken my skirts around my ankles where they belonged. But things were moving too fast. "Five shillings? I hope I'm worth more than that."

"Shillings aren't any good here. I want doubloons and reals."

"You'll have them. I want papers and witnesses."

"All right, all right."

"Good-o, then. You stay here, Anne. Bonny and I'll go to town and get someone to draw up the divorce and witness the handing over of the money. Then I'll be back for you. We'll sleep beneath the stars tonight and tomorrow I'll marry you."

Dove and Phibba were pleased because they didn't care for James any more than I did. They began packing my things and their own. I had to convince them they had better wait until I had a place to go before they decided to come with me.

I was ready when the men came back. James was still saying he wasn't sure Divorce by Sale was legal and maybe they should have consulted Governor Rogers. But he seemed pleased with the price he had been paid to be rid of me. Jack hoisted my belongings on his shoulder and as we walked off into the darkness James called, "I warn you, Rackham, she's a faithless bitch."

For just a second I remembered Stede and realized that James spoke the truth.

I thought my troubles were over. Jack told me that Governor Rogers had allowed him to keep a part of his plunder and that there was plenty more buried on a certain islet, safe from confiscation.

We fished for our breakfast and cooked our catch over an open fire. We had just finished our meal when four members of Governor Rogers's militia came marching along as smartly as they could, slogging through sand. They weren't members of the Brethren but men who had come with Rogers from London.

"We have callers," I said to Jack and went down to the sea to wash the fish off my hands.

"Halt!" The sergeant pointed his musket at me.

I thought he had gone off his head, London men not being accustomed to our sun.

"You want me to halt?" I asked.

"You're under arrest."

Jack got to his feet. "What the devil for?"

"You, for consorting with a woman who's not your wife. Her, for consorting with a man who's not her husband."

"Are you arresting everyone on the island?" I asked.

He gave me a spiteful look. "Never you mind. You come with us." He turned to his men. "Bind them."

If we hadn't been so astounded we would have put up a fight, but it's as well we didn't for the way the sergeant swung his musket around someone might have been hurt.

They bound our hands behind our backs and hobbled us just loosely enough that we could shuffle. They marched us through the settlement, prodding us with the butts of their muskets. We got some surprised stares but no one stayed around to catcall. A good many people remembered important business, which took them inside their houses, and it shows how the settlement had changed that they didn't even peek out their windows.

We stumbled up the hill to the fort and were butted into the miserable room that served as the governor's office. There were James, and to my surprise, Turnley.

"I had a feeling you were in on this," I said to James and was rewarded with a thud from the musket.

Governor Rogers was busy with some papers. He gave us a glance and went back to them. We stood there the better part of half an hour while he read and wrote and sharpened his quill, scratched a few more lines, and passed the papers to his clerk.

The room, being in the fort, had mere slits for windows and they were as high as windows in a jail. The walls had been limed but it was still necessary to have an oil lamp burning on his desk. The desk was big and old and had got well-battered on its journey from England. The inkwell was turtle-shaped pale-green glass and there was such a profusion of quills I swear you could have constructed an eagle from them. A map of the Caribbean was on the wall, and after I got tired of glaring at James I studied it. I was surprised to see how many little islands there were and how large Cuba was and how close, and how small Barbados and how far away it and Stede were.

Rogers put down his quill, sanded the paper, and handed it to the clerk. He folded his hands on his desk and studied us with his calm, stern eyes. With his disfigured face and perpetual smile he looked grotesque and foreboding in the flickering light, which threw his gigantic shadow up the white wall. I thought of all my sins and was ready to repent then and there.

The clerk, a young Londoner, had the pallor of the city on his face. I suppose Rogers never gave him time to get out into the sun. I gathered he hadn't yet found himself a woman either for whenever he looked at me he wetted his lips with his tongue and gulped the way Colin used to do.

"You are Anne B-Bonny?" Colin used to stutter a little, too.

"Yes."

"The wife of J-James Bonny?"

"I was until last night."

A flush tinted his pallor. He turned to the others and

asked their names in turn. Then he looked at Rogers who nodded at him.

"J-James B-Bonny, did you agree to a D-Divorce by S-S-Sale of this w-woman to John Rackham?"

"Yes."

"Is that t-true, John Rackham?"

"Yes."

"Did you, Richard Turnley, w-witness the s-signing of the papers and the exchange of money?"

"I did."

"Were you aware, James Bonny, that D-Divorce by S-Sale is ill-illegal?"

"I told them." James jerked his head at us savagely. "I told them but they talked me down."

"Were you aware, Richard Turnley, that it was illegal?"

"I suspected as much but Rackham said it was done at public auction in old England so how could it be illegal? James was willing and it was his wife, and damned lucky to be rid of her, he is, in my opinion—"

Rogers silenced him with a gesture.

"Were you aware it was ill-illegal, A-Anne B-Bonny?"

"No. If everyone who does something illegal on this island is to be arrested you'll have to build a jail as large as Cuba to hold them all."

The clerk looked at Rogers who frowned at me. He wrote something, spraying ink as he did so, and handed the paper to the clerk who read it silently and gulped again before he read it aloud.

"Do you deny your l-l-loose and ob-obscene behavior, Anne B-Bonny?"

"Of course I deny it."

"You have been cohabiting with John Rackham during your husband's absences and again last night after the p-papers were signed?"

"Why not?"

((137))

The clerk took a deep breath. "Anne Bonny, you w-will return to the house and b-b-bed and board of your husband, James Bonny. Should any further lewdness come to our attention you will be committed to prison after first being s-s-s-stripped and publicly flogged, and John Rackham will, perforce, handle the whip." His face was scarlet as he passed the papers back to Rogers. Rogers gave him a hard look and wrote some more. It dawned on me that the musket ball that had blown away his jaw had blown away his voice as well. It was true I had never heard him speak but I had heard, "Guv'nor says this and guv'nor says that . . ."

"You are all dismissed. Anne Bonny, g-go with your husband."

We went out together about as friendly as a passel of curs ready for a fight.

"All right," I said, rubbing my wrists where the ropes had burned them, "which of you went blabbering to the governor and got us into this?"

"It was him," James jerked his thumb at Turnley. "And after witnessing the papers, too."

"I knew it wasn't legal," Turnley said.

Jack was fuming. "Then why the devil did you witness for us? You've been aching to get at me ever since Vane gave you the slip the night the governor arrived, haven't you? You told Rogers it wasn't safe to cross the bar at low tide so it was you kept him sitting out there and gave Vane the chance to get away."

"I don't give a damn about Vane or you, Rackham. It's lawful behavior I care about and keeping sluts like her from turning this island into a bawd house."

I jerked out my pistol, which those fool soldiers hadn't the sense to take off me and I would have killed Turnley if Jack hadn't deflected my aim.

"Lucifer, Anne! You just escaped prison and a flogging. It'd be the rope if you killed him."

Turnley paled like the coward he was. "She'd be locked up now if I was guv'nor." He made a sneering mouth at James. "You've got your hands full. No wonder you were willing to risk the law to be done with her."

James wasn't looking too happy to have me back. He grabbed my arm and marched me off as briskly as the soldiers had done, leaving Jack gazing after us.

CHAPTER

VII

THE *KINGSTON*

NOR WAS IT CALICO JACK who led me into piracy. It was I
who led him back to his evil ways.

Jack and I continued to meet at my cove. I doubt James
would have cared. He hadn't returned the divorce money—
Governor Rogers had overlooked that—so I figured the
divorce was legal no matter what the governor thought.

I made it clear to Jack that all he had bought was my
freedom. I was more than willing to enjoy him but I didn't
want to belong to anyone. We couldn't be married without
creating further trouble and I had had enough of marriage
anyway.

"You'd be glad enough to marry me if I could claim my
title," Jack said one day when we were lying on the beach.
"You'd like being a duchess. It would suit you, too," he
added admiringly.

I was watching a sloop so swift it seemed to dance across

the water. It belonged to a trader named Haman, and it was so beautiful it made my heart contract every time I saw it.

"What do you mean, duchess?" I asked without taking my eyes off the sloop.

"I'm the illegitimate son of the second son of William the Third.'"

"And I'm Queen Anne. I didn't die. I got tired of all that royal bilge and abdicated. Georgie always wanted to be King so I gave him the Crown."

"You don't believe me." Jack turned away petulantly and sifted sand through his fingers.

"You told me you are the son of a London merchant who threw you out."

"That was the story my father, the duke and I, settled on. I thought it would please you if you thought my father was a merchant like yours so I didn't tell you about being a duke."

"You're lying, but lie away if it makes you happy. I don't care who you are or what you are. And I don't want to be a duchess. I want—" Suddenly I knew what I wanted. "I want John Haman's sloop."

He had been prepared to be angry but my statement was so unexpected he gaped at me.

"Will you buy it for me?" I shaded my eyes watching until it disappeared. "He might sell. He's made such havoc of shipping off Cuba the Spaniards are laying for him. They can't catch him. The *Kingston*'s the fastest sloop in the Caribbean. But if the Spanish ever discover where he lives they may revenge themselves. I heard he's thinking of moving to the settlement for safety now the governor's here."

"What would you do with a sloop?"

It was as if I had always known what I would do. The door had always been there waiting for me to open it.

"I'd go on account. There must be ships for the boarding

out there now that so many of the Brethren have taken the pardon. Rocking along at sea, unsuspecting, smug, thinking they're safe as porridge because Georgie's made honest men of all the pirates by giving them his Grace. Lucifer's dog, doesn't it whet your appetite?"

He didn't answer for a moment. "Aye, it does. But it's no use. I took the pardon."

"So did many another fellow who's gone back on account."

"I'm a man of my word."

"Like your father, the duke?"

He ignored that. He was looking out at sea. "Where does Haman live?"

"On one of the little islands off Eleuthera. Haman's Cay, they call it. He and his family are the only ones who live there. He's a wife and four children. All legitimate." I knew all about the Hamans because a legal family was so uncommon in these parts. "They come to Nassau once or twice a week. Next time he comes let's ask if he'll sell. The sloop's a forty ton. How much do you think she's worth?"

"Whatever she's worth it's more than I can pay. I haven't a cob."

"What do you mean you haven't a cob? You said the government let you keep your plunder."

"There was damned little of it, and of course, I bought that worthless divorce."

"I suppose there isn't any buried on a little islet known only to yourself either?"

He shook his head.

"If lies were gold doubloons you'd be a rich man, Jack."

"I was afraid of losing you."

The judges must know by now that I was a fool when it came to men. Furthermore, I preferred Jack's company to that of James's. So instead of being angry I laughed.

"Since we're high and dry without a cob to spin between us we'll have to steal the sloop."

"God's blood, Anne, you wouldn't dare!"

"We'll need a crew."

"A crew's no problem. I could pick up twenty brisk fellows hungry enough to go back on account in less time than it takes to drink a corker."

"Then do it. You get the crew. I'll get the sloop."

"By God, I believe you will."

At first I didn't know how I was going to do it, but the more I thought about the *Kingston* the more determined I was to have her.

My judges will begin to understand that my father and I are cursed with an Irish madness that seizes us unexpectedly and with disastrous results. The terrible thing is, Fate plays into our hands, the better to trap us.

As soon as Jack realized I was determined he fell in with my plans. We agreed I must don my breeches again and keep the fact that I was a woman hidden from the crew. My sharing Jack's cabin wouldn't cause so much as a wink, as I have explained before. It's a pity seamen must turn to their own kind for their relief but until they rid themselves of the superstition that women aboard ship are ill luck, there's nothing else for them.

There was small chance of my sex being discovered. At no time would I need to be uncovered in front of the crew. The Brethren sleep in their clothes. As for the ship's arrangements, the privy—the head, as it is called aboard ship —is at the head, the bow end. Being below the breast-high bulwarks it is secluded and out of sight. Frigates usually rig a crude seat, one starboard for the officers, one port side for the common seamen. But that's the Royal Navy for you. The Brethren are not so choosy. All hands share alike. Often there's no seat at all. That's a refinement they scorn, and perch on the fore-chains swinging like a monkey on a bough in a high wind. The ship cutting through the water and the splash of spray keep the area washed clean.

But this is all by the way.

Fate, as I have said, played into my hands. A few days after our talk John Haman and his family came to Nassau. Haman was meeting with the governor seeking protection for Haman's Cay. That failing, he would look for a suitable place in the settlement to establish his family.

Mistress Haman had her doubts about bringing her children to such an immoral place, but decided it was better than having them raped and murdered by the Spanish.

The *Kingston* was anchored in the harbor, and it didn't take long to find out that a good part of her crew was ashore enjoying the immorality that Mistress Haman feared.

James was away at one of the other islands rounding up fugitives from the pardon.

I sent Dove shopping for shag breeches and checkered shirts and one of those hats with the sides tacked to the crown so they look like a triangular apple pasty. He got me a red-lined kersey jacket and gray woolen stockings as well. But it was too hot for those. I hid them and the hat and tied my hair in a red neckcloth. I even put a gold ring in my ear.

Dove was very sniffy about the whole affair. I hadn't told him what I was up to but he knew it was to no good.

Jack had left the coracle ashore at my cove and I shoved it into the water and paddled off. The weather had been unsettled for days, alternating gusty showers of rain with steamy stillnesses.

A coracle is a light craft and I bobbed across the choppy water like a cork and with about as much direction. I can handle a skiff or a jolly boat as well as any man, but anyone seeing me in that coracle would never have thought so.

The man standing watch on the *Kingston* must have been daydreaming or watching the particularly lurid sunset, for he didn't see me approach until I had tied alongside and called for a hand up.

There were two men aboard, innocent as lambs and glad for company.

I put on a crude accent and asked if the cap'n was aboard.

"Naw, mate, he's ashore for the night with his missus and young ones. He's a great one for family, is Cap'n Haman."

"Blast. I was hoping for a word with him. I hear he's honest and an honest cap'n's what I'm looking for. Is he signing on hands?"

"Not as I know of." Watch scratched his head. "But honest he is and honest men is what he wants. Pillaging Jack Spaniard's one thing but pillaging from old England's another, and that he won't hold with. Are you honest, lad?"

"Honest as mother's milk. But even with the new guv'nor setting things right, an honest cap'n and honest crew are rare as a dog without fleas."

"Aye," they nodded.

"It's a fine vessel, this," I said and by damn, it was, taut and sleek and clean as paint. "Could I have a look around? It's not often you see a vessel as well cared for in these ill parts."

"Aye, we treat her fine, we do. Haman'll have it no other way."

"Then he's a rare one and one'd be a pleasure to serve under."

We jawed awhile, me praising the *Kingston* and the way she was kept and them accepting the praise as if she belonged to themselves. They showed me around and we had a drink of rum and they promised to put in a good word with the captain for me.

I told them my name was Andrew Bonn and I was camping out up the beach, not like some of the company in the settlement.

"Guv'nor may have cleaned it up, but it's still rough company and not to my liking. I was raised proper and though I was forced when our ship was captured, I stayed clean. But

I'm itching to have the sea under my feet again." They nodded understandingly. "But it's a right ship I want." I lowered my voice and said, "Isn't it chancy having only the two of you on watch? I've heard some of the gentlemen of fortune have been stealing back to sea."

They laughed and said no one would dare to attempt to take the *Kingston*. "Guv'nor'd have every sloop in the harbor after the swabs that dare that."

"They'd have the Devil's own time catching her," I said.

They laughed the harder at that. I think the rum had gone to their heads. "Aye, catch her if you can! But there's not a soul would dare, see?"

I smiled to myself and said I must be shoving off or I'd lose my way back to the cove in the dark. "I'll see you tomorrow when I come back to see Cap'n," I said.

"We're off dooty tomorrow and 'll be ashore. You want to come afore noon because Cap'n 'll be ashore again the rest of the day and night."

I promised I'd do that and added I'd meet them in Westminster the next evening to return their hospitality.

"I don't go around the grog shops much but when the company's good, that's different."

I left, wondering if I had overdone the pious act.

Jack had lit a signal fire on the beach and was pacing up and down before it.

"You damn well took your time," he said helping me drag the coracle ashore.

"It had to be done right or they'd have been suspicious. If you could have done better you should have gone yourself." I pulled off my bandanna and shook out my hair. "But you couldn't have done better. I played the innocent lad—"

"Damn few of those around. They should've been suspicious right off."

"I found out all we need to know. They leave only two

men aboard at night and they help themselves to the rum when things get dull. They think no one would dare to seize the *Kingston*, Governor Rogers being a benign God holding his hand on its anchor."

"We'll soon see to that."

"There's just one thing I'll regret."

"What's that? Leaving James?" He laughed and slapped my backside.

"Leaving before I've made Turnley crawl."

It amazes me now, though I don't suppose it amazes my judges, that I went about the plan so coolly. I never gave a thought to the fact that it was wrong or to the consequences if I was caught. I had made up my mind to go on account and nothing could have changed it.

When it came time to leave I was half sorry. I wished I could say good-bye to Hornigold and Jennings and my friends. But I was afraid Hornigold would turn me in if he knew what I was about to do.

I packed a few possessions I couldn't bear to leave behind, even some gowns though I didn't know when I would have a chance to wear them again. I cut my hair and donned my sailor dress, took my pistol and cutlass, and at the last moment my parasol because it reminded me of the first time I had seen Jack.

Dove and Phibba and I cried when we said good-bye. They clearly thought I had gone mad but it didn't keep them from weeping over me.

Jack and I met at the cove and made a supper of bread and cheese and beer. The weather was thickening. A cold wind harried clouds across the sky and hacked the water into whitecaps. It was too cold to sit still. We paced up and down the beach, buffeted by the wind, waiting for midnight when the crew Jack had recruited would join us. Jack would have made love but I was too nervous and excited to roll around in the damp sand and that annoyed him. Sometimes I think all the wits he had were in his cock.

In the harbor the *Kingston* hung out her lights. She rocked with a steady, even roll unlike the lighter, less well-crafted vessels, which jerked at their lines.

"It was a good choice," I said. "The *Kingston,* I mean. Look at the way she rides even in this weather."

"Do you think you can pull it off?"

"If I didn't would I be here? I can do it if the men you give me are sound and will take my orders."

"They're sound. Sound and tough and don't give a wink at drawing blood if it comes to that."

"It won't come to that," I said sharply. I'm not queasy but it didn't seem necessary to baptize our venture so soon.

"Dead men don't bite."

"The live ones won't have to. The settlement'll know who's taken the *Kingston* as soon as we turn up missing."

Jack grunted. For a man about to return to his chosen career he didn't seem happy. "I could do with a rum."

I could have done with one myself but I wanted a clear head. There'd be time for rum when we were well away.

The foul weather brought early darkness and soon we heard the sound of oars and a boat grating on the beach. We doused the fire so anyone offshore wouldn't see our gathering.

Jack's boast of getting twenty men had been just that. He had got ten but he swore they were trustworthy, good fighters, and knew the trade. I had drunk with two of them, John Fenwick and Richard Corner. They had sailed with Jennings and I knew they would be well trained. I chose them to go with me in the coracle. I hoped they wouldn't recognize me, but even Jack had blinked in disbelief when he first saw me in man's dress.

Jack loaded my possessions into the skiff and pushed the coracle into the water. I took an oar and as we pulled round to the harbor I explained the plan to my companions. I'd go aboard first and give them a whistle if all was clear. Meanwhile Jack and the rest of the crew would be waiting to loosen the cables as soon as we hailed them.

As we drew alongside the *Kingston* it began to rain. It was one of those heavy tropical cloudbursts that give no warning but suddenly pour down, drenching everything.

"God's with us," I said, for the sound of the rain and wind would cover our moves.

"With the likes of us?" Richard Corner asked.

Fenwick chuckled. "I allays figured He hadn't the wits to discriminate between knaves, fools, and parsons. Sometimes it seems like He favors us the most."

Except for the port and starboard lanterns, the only light aboard was in the cabin. No one hailed us and there was no movement on deck. John Haman's crew was mighty trusting, such was the power of Governor Rogers.

I climbed up the line and waited. Rain thudded around me, the lines creaked in the wind, and the lanterns swung shining red and green glades across the wet deck. I was alone.

I whistled up the men. The coracle bobbed away into the darkness. I was glad to see the last of it.

We moved stealthily but any sound we might have made would have been covered by the storm. I held my pistol in my left hand and my cutlass in my right. Corner had a pistol in each hand, Fenwick a dirk and cutlass. A line of light showed under the door of the cabin. Someone was moving around inside. The only other sound was snoring.

I kicked open the door and burst in with Corner and Fenwick so close behind me we jostled one another and had to regain our footing. We interrupted Watch as he was raising a cup of rum to his lips. He gave a strangled sound and dropped it. His companion who was asleep in his hammock stopped snoring for as long as it takes to catch a breath, then resumed.

I put my cutlass to Watch's throat. "Don't make a sound unless you want your brains blown out." He shook so much it was a wonder he didn't pinion himself. "Bind him," I told Fenwick. "If he makes a move, shoot him."

The snores stopped again and the sleeping man opened his eyes and stared at us as if we were a part of a nightmare. But he didn't move. We bound him easily.

Leaving Corner with his pistols to guard them, we went on deck and signaled the longboat. The men clambered up the side. Fenwick and I hoisted the jib, the men heaved the anchor, and Jack took the wheel. We drove down the harbor passing so close to the fort my heart nearly stopped. The guard ship hailed us as we rode past.

"Cables've parted," Jack bellowed at him. "All we've got is a grappling. Won't hold in this weather."

"Do you need help?"

"We'll put to sea 'til the weather clears."

The fool waved us on our way.

The jib gave us steerage until we cleared the harbor, then we put on every sail we had and stood to sea.

Corner brought up the prisoners and removed their gags and we offered them a cup of Haman's rum. They refused although they'd been making free with it earlier. Corner took the helm while Jack explained to the men that we were going on account and they were welcome to join us.

"Join a gang of bloody rascals?" Watch exclaimed. "I'd take my chances with sharks first."

"You're a pious one, aren't you? How about your mate?"

His mate shook his head. He seemed still to be half asleep, and from the reek of him I guessed he had been sleeping off his share of the rum. "Same as him," he said. "It's not the company. It's the hanging. You'll all hang in the end. Haman says so and he's a friend of Guv'nor."

"We'll be a long time free before we hang," Jack said. "All right, mates. We'll put you over the side in a boat and you can row ashore. It's not a fit night to be bucking the waves but it'll not be so far to go as if we waited 'til morning. Good luck to you, and tell Haman we'll return his sloop when we've done with it."

"Huh! I reckon he's seen the last of it. And him a good man, too."

They must have made it to shore because their murder was not mentioned at our trials.

As soon as we were rid of them we broke out the rum. The celebration lasted until dawn came, pale blue and silver. Sometime in the night the rain had eased off and finally ceased, and the winds had abated.

We went south, gliding among the Exuma Cays looking for an islet with a secluded cove where we could lay by without detection until we had organized.

Weary as Jack was, and the worse for rum, he took the *Kingston* into an inlet so shallow I expected every moment we would go aground. Corner had the lead, taking soundings all the way, and the men stood by with sweeps in case they were needed. If we hadn't been so busy the men would have seen what a greenhorn I was. Jack kept me near him, supposedly reading the charts, and by staying quiet, listening, observing, I learned a good deal of seamanship that day.

After we dropped anchor Dobbin, who had volunteered as cook, and I went to see to our supplies. They weren't as extensive as we had hoped. Being anchored in Nassau most of the crew was eating ashore. There were the usual barrel of salt meat, biscuit, eggs, hard cheese, limes, spices, and of course, sack, rum, and beer.

We soon had a fire going in the box of sand at the foot of

the mast, and Dobbin made us a concoction of eggs mixed with sherry and spices and plenty of cheese. Eaten with biscuit and washed down with beer it was a fine feast.

After that we all had a sleep on deck in the warmth of the sun, and except for the lapping of water and the birds calling onshore, there was a silence such as I had never experienced. I decided this was the life!

The next few days were spent drawing up Articles, which all hands signed or put their mark to. Article six worried me.

"No women allowed. If any man be found carrying one of the sex to sea, disguised, he is to suffer death."

Jack gave me a wink as we signed and I hoped if we were found out, he would be the one to die, not me.

Then we set to work cutting down the deckhouses and raising the gunwales, filling the casks with fresh water, turtling, taking stock of supplies and powder, and making hand grenades from empty bottles by filling them with gunpowder and nails salvaged when we tore down the deckhouses.

Fenwick dived and found the bottom clean, well daubed with sulfur and tallow to deter worms, and well caulked.

"It's the best vessel I've ever stood on," Jack said. "By damn, it was a lucky day when I decided to take the *Kingston*."

"You? You'd still be sitting in the settlement doing your four days a week volunteer work and cursing your bad end, if it weren't for me."

Jack laughed, started to caress me, and turned it into a hearty thump on the shoulders. We were having a difficult time remembering my new role and new name. The crew chuckled over our bumbling and drolled with Jack saying they had always thought he'd been a one with the ladies, but that Andy was a fair lad for sure.

Every evening we had a bit of music and dancing before lights were extinguished at eight o'clock. Fenwick had served with the navy and knew some doleful songs, which he sang in a doleful voice. We all joined in on the refrains for, as Corner said, "A song where all hands can't join in at the coal box isn't worth the singing."

One fair morning we hoisted anchor. I took my place on the cable alongside the men and as they shouted, *"I, Boys, Oh, Boys,"* I had one of those vivid flashes of memory. Instantly I was back on the Thames, holding the hands of my father and mother, while the capstan creaked and gulls circled the tall masts under the misty English sky. Where was Clym now and where my doll, Jack? I knew where the child was, the child who had said solemnly to Clym, "I mean to have a ship of my own one day." She was on a stolen sloop with a band of rogues, a ruined woman, the rope burning her hands, and tears blinding her eyes.

The memory passed in less time than it takes to tell. I had no regrets. I had set my course and would sail it.

We were clear of the inlet. The sails began to draw and a fine spray rainbowed in the sun.

We took our first ship that same day. It was just past midday and hot as Hell when the lookout called, "Sail, ho, dead ahead."

The crew had been sprawling about, listless in the heat. Now they sprang to life. Harwood, our gunner, began laying out muskets, grenades, axes, boarding pikes and hooks, and that done, prepared to load and prime the cannon.

I felt as if I had swallowed a bird and it was fluttering in my stomach. Since that day I've always imagined fear as being a blackbird beating its wings inside me. Sweat trickled down my temples and into the corners of my eyes, formed on my upper lip and between my breasts. Harwood kept me busy, giving me running orders in his calm voice, and a cuff on the shoulder when I didn't perform quickly enough. I wanted to see the approaching sail but there was no time to hang over the bulwarks and gaze at the sea.

"Leave that to Lookout, lad," Harwood said when he caught my eyes straying. "Him'll keep us informed. Stand the grenades up for easy grasping, see. You got the pikes too close together. We'll get in each other's way when we take 'em up. That's better."

"A sloop," the lookout called. "Low in the water. Must be well laden. Twenty to thirty ton, I'd guess."

"Smaller'n us," Corner said and licked his lips.

"Two guns. Swivel."

"Thundering pieces," Harwood said. "That's what we call swivel guns, lad. They're nasty. I've never handled one. Always been on the receiving end." He must have smelled my fear for he gave me a sharp look. "First take, lad?"

I nodded.

"Where the devil did Jack ever get you, eh? Well, lookee, the first is always hardest. Soon as the fight starts things move so fast and get so hot you forget to be scared. All you think about is killing before they kill you. But take an old hand's advice. Go to the head while there's plenty of time or you'll be soiling your breeches later."

I found out what he meant for when I was swinging on the chain I found my guts had turned to water. All the while the lookout was calling.

"Merchant ship. Slow. Riding deep. Must be from London. Timbers on her deck to act as ramparts. She's sighted us."

I came back on deck looking pale and feeling limp. Jack frowned and asked if I was all right. I nodded.

"Then look to your guns. Get your weapons ready. Watch me and stick close. Don't let me down or they'll heave us overboard."

It was his saying not to let him down that cured me. He had been willing enough to take me to sea but when it came down to it, he doubted I could fight. I swore to myself I'd be the first to board the prize.

We crowded on sail but it was two hours before we were

in hailing distance. There was plenty to do during that time. Pass out the rum to prime the crew with courage, clear the deck of gear so our movements would be unhampered, draw the water for swabbing the cannon, use the head again. I was calmer now and my guts had ceased to churn, perhaps because there was nothing left inside me to be emptied.

Jack motioned me to his side. "Do you know what we've forgot? The Roger."

I confess I laughed, but he wasn't amused. "Damn my blood, the men'll think I've gone off."

"Does it have to be black?"

"Or red. It was always red in the old days."

"I can take the lining out of my kersey jacket."

It would have saddened Dove to see me rip out the lining with my knife. Once again it took me back to the day I had ripped a flowered lining from a cape to make sailor pants for my wooden doll. I was getting altogether too sentimental. I cut up a pair of drawers for the skull and stitched it with sail thread. It was crude but its very crudity made it more ferocious. It pleased the crew. Fenwick wanted to add a black heart and Corner suggested a dripping dagger, but there was no time for refinements. Later I added two crossed cutlasses for mine and Jack's. I got it finished just in time. The merchantman was close on, and we took our places beneath the gunwales, out of sight.

My hand sweated on the butt of my pistol. I rubbed it against my trouser so the gold shone in the sun. Father would be shocked if he knew the use to which his gift was about to be put. Or was he beyond being shocked by me now? Perhaps it was just such an end that he would have predicted. I wished to God I'd stop thinking of the past. I wished I could see what was happening. I envied Harwood's calm. He squatted by his cannon and puffed at his pipe as if he had the rest of the day to smoke it. If I had lighted mine I would have bit through the stem.

A voice called across the water, *"Queen of Indies,* Bristol. Arthur Gillmore, Master."

"Aye," Corner told us. "There's the Jack. She's square."

"What ship? Who are ye and whence do ye come?"

"Gentlemen of fortune, from the sea," Jack bellowed and hoisted the Roger.

At the same time Harwood fired an eight-pounder and yelled in delight as he scored a hit. Dobbin beat his drum and Carty gave several shrill blasts on his trumpet.

Their swivel guns ripped our shrouds scattering nails and glass. Blood spurted from Harwood's arm. It didn't prevent him from firing again and knocking out the *Queen*'s gunner.

Stinkpots showered on our deck, the sulfurous fumes choking us. We returned the favor with hand grenades, but I threw wild because my eyes were running with tears from the smoke and I was coughing my lungs out from the sulfur fumes.

Corner brought the *Kingston* round downwind and a moment later I was nearly knocked off my feet as the ships ground together, timbers groaning and squealing.

After that I don't remember anything clearly except throwing my grapple into their rigging and leaping onto the shrouds. I clung to them a moment to catch my breath. I heard Jack yell something at me, then I jumped the timbers the *Queen*'s crew had set up as ramparts. I was face to face with a frightened lad whose pistol had jammed. His blue eyes were wide with fear and his mouth open in surprise. Without thinking, I hacked him down.

"That Andy," Corner said of me later, "he fair flew on to the *Queen*. It was as if he'd sprouted wings."

It was a fast, bloody fight, and the wonder is they put up so little resistance. We had only two more men so we were fairly evenly matched. Maybe it was the sight of that lad's blood staining the deck, making it slippery. It seemed to me only a few minutes had passed when the captain bawled, "Quarter! Quarter, damn ye!"

I was about to hack off the mate's head. Jack grabbed my arm. "Quarter it is, Andy."

I felt deflated, almost disappointed, and very tired.

The cargo was gin, bales of jute sacking, bolts of linen, muslin and calico, shoes, stockings and periwigs—one of which Corner promptly put on—needles, thread, pewter mugs, and glass cups.

"Christ," Jack said. "You've got a grab bag here, Captain."

"I have that. The owners won't let an inch of space go empty. It's why we ride so low and heavy. But the seas are supposed to be safe now, so there's no need to go light. I tried to tell 'em different in London, but they know everything. It's their loss, not mine."

"When you get back to Bristol you tell them the seas won't be safe as long as Calico Jack is sailing them. Bring the punch bowl, Dobbin, and we'll refresh ourselves. Then we'll lighten the cap'n's ship for him."

Dobbin made a huge punch of rum, lemon, sugar, and beer, and we all sat down together, friend and foe, and passed the bowl and 'baccy, jawing away as if we were old friends. It seemed strange to me that less than an hour ago we'd been out to kill one another and now we were drinking together, but that was the way it had always been, if the captain was wise. Those who resisted too often ended up swimming.

After a time the captain looked over at the poor dead lad. "Who killed him?"

There was an embarrassed silence, which was no wonder since we were so chummy. Then I said, "I did."

"He was only a lad. My sister's son." He drained his cup and held it out to be refilled.

It was dark before we finished transferring the cargo to

our gunwales and my legs were stiff from going up and down the ladder as we stowed the plunder below. I had had nothing to eat since breakfast. I was half drunk and the rum was sour on my stomach. I regretted having killed the lad, and rued the day I had decided to go on account.

Back in the settlement Phibba would have served one of her spicy stews, my friends would be gathering in Westminster, and I would be in a silk dress instead of rough trousers black with powder stains and flapping at my knee where I had torn one leg when I leaped over the timbers.

I didn't even care to take part in the conference as to whether we should take the *Queen* as well as its cargo. They haggled so long I finally put in, "Oh, hell-fire, let her go. We'd have to tow her, wouldn't we? We haven't crew to man two sloops and they've already said they won't join us."

"Three of us could man her," Corner argued.

"It's got swivel guns," Harwood said.

"It'll fetch a good price."

It was finally put to vote and came out half for, half against. We reached a compromise by deciding to remove the swivel guns. But that would have to wait until morning.

We remained lashed together all night, sails furled, rocking at anchor. The boats grinding together moaned. I dreamed it was the lad screaming as I killed him.

We waved the *Queen* off the next day and headed north. We had to mend the shrouds, which was weary work. Sitting cross-legged on the deck, I was soon burned by the sun glaring off the water. I peeled for a week.

There was another palaver over whether we should sell our cargo in Cuba to the Spanish half-breed settlers or take it to colonies where it had been intended to go.

"Trouble with those half-breeds in Cuba is, they buy below market value," Fenwick argued. "And what the devil would they be wanting with periwigs?"

"Same as Corner wants with his."

"It don't match his hair and looks bloody silly. I say, take it to the Carolinas. It's fancy stuff, this lot. The Carolinas will pay up. They're hurting since the guv'nor's trying to clean up the sweet trade."

Jack and I exchanged a look. When the vote was taken I voted for Cuba. Carolina won.

We came within hailing distance of another ship on our way north, a heavily laden merchantman, but her crew outnumbered us and her guns, while they weren't murdering pieces, were heavy. We laid on sail and retreated. The merchantman wasn't interested in pursuit.

Two days out of Carolina we sighted a brig and two sloops in close formation. They sighted us, too, and made straight for us. Jack swore as he searched the ship for Haman's ensign, hoping if we hoisted it, we could pass as a respectable trader. He ran his hand around the neck of his shirt as if he could feel the rope. Finally, he jerked off his neckerchief and threw it overboard. The wind brought it back and wrapped it around the topmast where it fluttered like a netted bird.

"I don't see why you're so worried," I said to Jack.

"That's because you're new at the trade. Damn my blood, look at those guns! They must be government sloops sent to hunt us down."

Already the fleet had spread out with the obvious intent of flanking us. The sun glinted off the round brass mouths of their cannon, and the lookout reported all three ships were swarming with crew.

"They're readying for battle," he called down. "Say your prayers, mates."

As before my guts turned to water and that damned blackbird flapped in my stomach. Still, I couldn't resist saying to Jack, "That's what greed gets you. We should damned well have gone to Cuba."

((159   ))

"It won't be Cuba we're going to if they take us."

The sloop on our starboard hailed us. "What ship?"

"What the devil does he mean, what ship? He's supposed to give his registry first."

"What ship?"

"The *Kingston* out of New Providence!" Then, "Where the devil's the ensign? I suppose some fool flung it overboard or used it to swab down the cannon. Who are you and whence do you come?"

"*Queen Anne's Revenge.* Gentlemen of fortune, from the sea!" The black flags went up on the three ships. Our crew began to yell and wave before their cannon could blast us. Harwood fired a round into the air, Dobbin hoisted our Roger, and the rest of us grabbed our muskets and fired at the sky. Their guns answered. The water was pocked with shot falling harmlessly and great spouts where the cannon balls landed. It was beautiful with the sun sparkling through the splashing spray and the vessels gliding around one another as if in movement of an intricate dance.

"You know who it is, don't you?" I asked Jack.

"One of the Brethren and me sweating!"

"It's Ned Teach. That's his ship."

"Is it, by damn? I've never met up with him. Vane was so afraid of Teach he'd have risked hanging rather than meeting him."

"Vane must be a coward. Ned's harmless. He's nothing but a show-off and a braggart."

"Harmless as poison from what I hear. Will he recognize you?"

"Lucifer's dog! I hadn't thought of that. What shall I do?"

"Keep your mouth shut, if it's possible." Jack grinned at me. "Your own father wouldn't recognize you. Your face is the color of the Roger and flaking like a boiled fish. I don't know why I let you into my bed at night."

"Go to the devil!" I tied my bandanna low on my forehead and put on my apple-pasty hat, cocking one corner low on my forehead like a beak. I helped lash the ships together, then brought the bowl and rum for Dobbin to mix the punch.

It was easy to stay in the background. Teach had a crew of forty and everyone swarmed over all four ships, tippling, bragging, exchanging tales. The musicians brought out their viols and drums so there was dancing and singing. I joined in the dancing for I love the hornpipe.

Once Ned Teach interrupted his conversation with Jack to point a pistol at me. "That lad trips a fine step. Do you know a jig, lad?"

I nodded, and the musicians changed their tune. I kept my back to Ned as much as possible. But even I can dance only so long. Soon I dripped with sweat for the October day was muggy and the sun glaring on the brine-encrusted decks burned my feet. Ned didn't choose for us to stop. He shouted us on, cursing at the musicians, "Faster, damn ye, faster! I don't want a funeral dirge. I want a fandango." He primed his pistols and shot among our feet, laughing to see us jump.

"You fool man, what're you doing?" Jack tried to deflect his aim.

"Keeping 'em hot, damned hot." Ned fired again.

One dancer limped away with a bleeding foot and another crumpled, holding his leg and moaning. I decided it was time to sit in a quiet corner with a rum.

"I have to keep 'em frightened or they forget who I am." Ned shook with laughter. "Had to maroon some swabs awhile back. They'd got brazen. Didn't leave 'em so much as a spit to drink or a moldy crust to chew."

Jack looked as if he wished the party were over. "I thought that was against Articles."

"Articles be damned. I make my own Articles and change 'em when it pleases me. As longs as there's plenty of rum the company's no right to complain. And there was plenty. It's when they get sober you run into confusion. But there was rum to pour in the sea and they still talked separation. I separated them all right. All seventeen of 'em. Wouldn't wonder by now they're living like cannibals."

"Where did you do this?"

"Off Virginia. I didn't stay. Spottiswoode ain't too friendly to the Brethren. Not like Eden in Carolina North. He's a man for all he's a governor. Gives a good price, has his Customs Collector well reined, and don't wink at sitting down to drink with you and providing the rum himself."

"We weren't figuring on going that far, but maybe we should if the price is good. We were figuring on selling in Charles Town."

"Charles Town! You must want that lad to dance on air. Haven't you heard what's happening in Charles Town? Governor Johnson's taken courage from Woodes Rogers and sworn to clean up the seas. He's got some colonel—Rhett or Brett, however he's called—outfitted with two sloops and crews of seventy to eighty men. Four of the Brethren got hanged there awhile back and they've another lot sitting in the Guard House awaiting trial. They'll hang, too. Not but what they got there by their own fool ways. Stede Bonnet's no seaman or he'd never have been caught."

"Stede Bonnet!" I forgot Jack's warning to keep quiet.

"Aye, Major Bonnet. You've heard of him, lad? Stupid as bilge, Bonnet is. He was careening his ship in Cape Fear when they nabbed him."

"I thought he took the pardon."

"Oh, he took it all right. Took it and changed his name to Captain Thomas and has been working north of the Virginia coast as far up as Delaware. He was aiming to amass a fortune as big as the one he'd left in Barbados and go back to some hen in Nassau. Any fool'd do that deserves to hang," said Teach.

So he hadn't forgotten me, though I'd damn well near forgotten him and been unfaithful and gone on account myself. He wouldn't want me now but I didn't want him to die.

"Why don't we rescue him and his crew?"

Ned Teach wasn't the only one who stared at me. The whole company stared, then Teach began to laugh. "Rescue, says the lad. Rescue! Lookee, lad, when you go on account you take your chances. You go free or you get caught. You get your head blown off or you feed the crows. You may even live to be an old man like Jennings and Hornigold who are two swabs as could give you a few lessons, if they hadn't gone nancy on us. Your end is your own doing, see. You knew it when you signed the Articles. There's none but yourself to hold in account and none but yourself to save you. Don't fret about Bonnet. He's a God-Almighty gentleman, the Major is, and he'll die like one." He broke off and stared hard at me. "Do I know you from someplace, lad? You got a mighty familiar look about you."

I shook my head. "I've never seen you before, sir."

"I'd swear I've seen you. No matter. Stick by Rackham here and do as he tells you and look sharp to your guns. But don't try to interfere with the law when it takes a hand and don't expect any swab to come a-rescuing you if you're caught."

I gave a lot of thought to his words that night before I fell asleep, half drunk as I was. I have thought about them these past months when I've been hoping for a pardon. I do not expect my petitioners' efforts to save me to succeed, but there is one person I wish I could have saved. Mary.

But I have not yet come to Mary.

We took Ned Teach's advice and sold our plunder in North Carolina, giving Charles Town a wide sweep. Even so, I could smell it as we sailed up the coast: oleander, roses, acacia, swampland, each odor blended with the other and yet distinct.

I kept thinking about Stede sitting in the Guard House. I got it into my head that his present plight was my fault. If I had remained faithful, he would never have been caught.

Jack noticed my melancholy and asked what ailed me. I answered with a shrug. But Jack was no fool. One night, lying in my arms he asked out of the clear blue, "What was between you and Stede Bonnet?"

"He was my friend."

"When?"

"Before I met you."

"What if he should escape and we met him the way we met with Ned Teach?"

I hesitated too long to answer, but the truth was I didn't know what would happen if I was to see Stede again. Jack twisted away from me. "Bonny was right. You're a faithless bitch."

"Don't be a fool. Do you think I'd go off with another man?"

"Aren't you the woman he was going back to Nassau to give his fortune to?"

"How do I know?"

"You know, Anne, and I know. By God, the Brethren are right. Women are good for only one thing. I was a fool to bring you along."

"*I* stole the sloop."

"Stop throwing that at me. I know you stole the sloop. Any silly fool can steal a sloop. I could have done it myself."

"But you didn't because you're a firking coward, just like Bonny. All you were thinking about was your tail. You couldn't see any further than under my skirts."

"You were willing enough to lift them."

"Because when I met you I forgot all about Stede Bonnet."

The anger went out of him. "Is that true, Anne? Is it

true? Even though I'm not a gentleman like Bonnet?"

"I thought you were the son of a duke?"

"I was lying, Anne. My parents were strolling players. I was born behind a May hedge between acts."

I began to laugh. "Whatever you are, you're entertaining, Jack. Yes, it's true, from the time you took me in the water, I forgot Stede and every other man. I've been happy here on the *Kingston*. It's strange, isn't it? Happier than I've ever been."

Reveling in evil.

The weather turned wintry. Day after day high gray clouds hid the sun. The wind was north by east and chilly. The seas were strong and leaden-color. Sometimes it was too rough to cook on deck and we supped on biscuit and cold salt pork and cheese without so much as a hot rumfustian to warm our guts.

The crew complained about the cold, their blood having been thinned through the years in warmer waters. I got a new jacket and some breeches to replace my torn ones and some warm drawers, but I, too, felt the cold. My hands were so raw and chapped from the icy cold ropes that they bled. Jack ignored our grumblings.

Pickings were good in those coastal waters. Governor Eden paid well, and the whores were plentiful and willing for a crew that had been a long time at sea. It was good for all of us to go ashore and stretch our legs at a tavern fire and have a meal that wasn't salt meat.

Then Ned Teach got too high-handed with Governor Eden. A whore told Corner there were two war vessels hunting Ned. Jack decided to sail south.

"It'll make the company happy," he said.

"And keep us from being mistaken for Teach."

"That, too."

We didn't feel safe until we were well off the coast of Florida. We were sixteen now and fairly formidable. Four new men had joined us, recruited from two of the ships we had taken, a carpenter, a surgeon's apprentice, and two common seamen fed up with conditions of their own ship and glad to leave the captain who fed them on maggoty beef and weevilly biscuit. Later, when we were captured, two of them claimed to have been pressed and went free, which is gratitude for you. I saw them fight alongside us every bit as bloodthirsty and anxious to share the loot.

One day as dawn broke we saw sails silhouetted against the sky. The ship had come up in the night and might have passed us had morning not come when it did. She was a merchantman, lumbering along, low in the water. When we challenged her she answered by turning her guns on us. They had made a shambles of our deck before we were close enough to board. Then it was six or seven of their crew that boarded us. We had boarding axes in hand and cut two of them down, but half the time the fight was going on on our own deck as well as theirs. I've never been in such a battle. It lasted until past midday, though it seemed much longer. I kept thinking the sun would set soon and when dark came we'd have to stop. Once I found myself fighting beside Jack, though he was scarcely recognizable under the powder burns. He grinned, showing his white teeth, and said, "Christ, their hold must be full of gold the way they're fighting. We'll be rich enough to retire."

There was no time to load muskets. I thrust my pistol into my belt where I felt it cool and hard against my stomach and fought with ax and cutlass. I was blood-spattered and a cut in my side trickled like a worm crawling down my thigh. It was damned distracting. There wasn't a one of us who hadn't some injury. The surgeon's apprentice would have plenty of practice that evening.

It's strange in a battle, how one part of you fights and thinks of nothing but cut and thrust, while another part is detached, thinking of other things in a slow, dreamlike way. I kept thinking of my cove in New Providence and how clear the water was and the white sand beneath the water.

The decks were slippery with blood. A couple of times I damned near had my head chopped off when I stumbled over a body. My arms ached and I was so hungry my stomach rumbled.

"Why the devil doesn't your captain call for quarter?" I asked the man I was fencing.

"Why don't yours?"

I didn't answer because I knocked him broadside with my cutlass and he fell on his own ax. It wasn't a nice sight.

The moment came when we stood panting, begrimed, bleeding, staring at one another, with no one left to fight. Two of their crew were still alive. One had lost an arm and a leg and lay there bleeding and moaning, begging someone to kill him. Corner obliged and also dispatched a man who was staggering around, falling over his dead shipmates, because someone had piked out his eyes.

The surgeon's apprentice vomited and didn't have the decency to go to the side of the ship.

Jack leaned on his ax and gasped for breath. "Christ! I've never seen such a mess. I wonder what's under the hatches that made 'em put up such a fight?"

"Sooner we find out, the better. In this heat the blood's going to begin to stink," Fenwick said. "You, Bones, if you're finished spewing like a whale, come tie up my arm so we can get at the hatches. This is one ship I wouldn't have if you gave it to me for Boxing Day."

The stench on the deck was nothing to the stench from below. It rose like a fog, thick and foul, the stink of bodies and excrement, spoiled food, fever, dysentery, and rotting dead.

Timothy Davis was sent below and Corner volunteered to go with him, "to keep him in line and see he don't help himself to anything of value."

"There's nothing of value down there," Fenwick said. "Not stinking like that. Seems to me we've made a whopping mistake and bled for nothing, mates."

He was right. Davis and Corner were back almost at once looking as sick as Bones who was vomiting again.

"It's convicts," Corner said. "The whole god-bedamned hold is full of convicts from Newgate. They're being shipped to the penal colonies. From what I've seen they'd 've been better off hanged."

Fenwick's rage and disappointment were so great he went to the captain's body and gave it a dozen angry jabs with his cutlass.

We were all sick at the effort wasted but we were too weary to say much. I felt rotten, shaking with hunger and weariness. I wanted to lie down in a shady part of the deck and sleep, away from the stench and the dead. And I didn't want Jack bothering me. Every battle excited him so he couldn't rest until he'd had me three or four times. I suppose that's one of the differences between men and women. After a battle all I wanted was to bathe, as if the water would purify my having done murder.

In the end it was Jack who decided what should be done. He found the key to the shackles in the captain's cabin, along with some fine tobacco and Spanish sack, which revived us all. Poor Timothy Davis—though why I should pity him when he's walking around Jamaica free as if he owned it, I don't know—had to go below to set the devils loose.

They were a wild-eyed lot, slavishly grateful at their release. Jack made them clean the deck and throw the bodies overboard. They performed some obscenities on the mate and captain, which turned my stomach, before they threw them over the side.

Jack selected a crew for the ship with Corner in command and we set off for the north shore of Jamaica where Corner ran the ship aground and set the criminals free. With them

to bedevil him, it would take Governor Lawes's mind off
bedeviling the Brethren.

Not quite all of them chose to go free. Six joined us.

It was now close on to Christmas. We planned to spend
it ashore careening the ship and making repairs, taking inventory of our stores, and generally refreshing ourselves.

We took one more ship before we beached. This time,
thank God, there was almost no resistance. The lading was
Spanish sack, gin—both English and Holland, Madeira, and
beer. That captain must have taken on potables at every port
between Holland and the Indies. We lifted it all.

It was good to be ashore. I wasn't the only one who
thought so. Half the company was sick with flux and some
fever we'd got from the convict ship. Fenwick's arm had
festered and turned black. Jack told me privately he would
not be surprised if it had to be sawed off. Fortunately, it
burst open on Christmas Day. For a week pus poured out,
so foul-smelling no one wanted to be near him.

I felt wretched myself, though I made an effort to appear
as merry as any of us. Christmas dinner was a salmagundi
and two kinds of punch. Dobbin made some sweet hot
cakes filled with raisins and nuts, which he baked in the
coals. We mixed the English gin with the lime juice, which
had also been aboard our Christmas ship, as Bones called it.
We gorged ourselves on the fresh fruit we found on the
island. It made our flux worsen. Corner did a hornpipe on
top of a keg of Hollands without falling off. We finished off
the celebration with theatricals.

My judges may not know there is a favorite play performed by the Brethren. It's a mock trial. Every performer
gives his own interpretation but the general outline is always
the same.

Jack played the part of the judge with a jib sail for a robe
and moss and vines draping his head like a wig. Fenwick

was chief justice and the company the jury. Corner was the condemned.

He was led in making doleful faces and the jury hissed at him and pelted him with sand. Dobbin pounded his crowbar on the barrel of Hollands and announced court was in session.

Fenwick presented the prisoner. "He's a lousy dog and ill-whelped rascal, your Worship, and I beg you to order him hanged immediately."

Corner made a long speech telling how he had fallen into an evil life and pleaded not guilty. Jack silenced him.

"Lookee, you ill-living whelp, I'd be no kind of judge if I didn't order you hanged. And hanged you must be as it's time for my dinner. You know the law. If the trial ain't over by dinnertime there's nothing to it but hang the prisoner."

Corner fell to his knees wailing. "Please your Worship, I'm as honest as your own blessed father. I was forced to piracy by the notorious Captain John Rackham."

"Forced you may have been and forced am I. Forced to hang you."

The jury howled with laughter. Only Timothy Davis pulled a sour face. "You laugh and play the fool now, but one of these days it will be for real. Jack won't be sitting on the judge's bench then. He'll be in dock with the rest of you."

"They'll have to catch us first, Davis."

"They will."

"Damn it, man, it's bad luck to talk like that. You'll put a spell on us."

"Put it on yourselves and me along with you."

"We can always leave you here when we sail, Davis. Maybe you'd enjoy your own company instead of ours."

"Oh, I'll go along with you. And if I'm punished, I'm punished and it's no more than I deserve. Let's have some more rum."

I felt like throwing it in his face. He'd given me a grue.

I shivered, thinking he was right. It was all too real, ridiculous as it was.

Jack saw me shivering and asked what was wrong.

"I must be getting the fever."

"Well, don't get it yet. We're careening the ship tomorrow and need all hands."

That was my gallant lover.

I don't know how I got through the next few days. We unloaded the ship, took down the topmast and scraped it, hitched ropes from the ship to the trees on shore and heaved it over until she lay almost flat on her side. We sanded and scraped and daubed and tallowed and caulked and sweated. The carpenter repaired the planks that had been splintered in our last engagement. Fenwick and I went over supplies and I made lists of what we had and what was needed as he couldn't write. My head ached before I finished the lists, but that didn't spare my going over gunnery supplies with Harwood and medicines with Bones.

Jack was supposed to have been keeping the ship's log and wanted it brought up to date. I soon learned how sketchy his education had been from his spelling and his scribble. But all of this work was by the way of helping with the careening, and I began to think I was the one who should be captain.

We were ashore another ten days and I didn't feel myself a day of it. I blamed it on the drink, which was too plentiful since we had captured the Christmas ship, and on the heat. I longed to be back at sea with the wind and spray cooling my face. Fenwick said it was land sickness, but two other hands were so ill they couldn't take part in the work, and it wasn't pretense. One night they were both delirious and no one could sleep for their raving and screaming.

It was Corner suggested they be left behind. We were to sail two days hence. "They'll spread their fever and the lot of us'll be sick," he argued. "We'll be a ghost ship and there'll be no one to bury the last man dead."

Fenwick said, "I reckon getting back to sea'd be the curing of 'em. It's this island. I smelled fever the minute we came ashore."

"You smelled it 'cause we brought it."

"It's the bugs. I can't sleep at night nor can you, Corner, I've heard you say so, for their whining around our heads and in our ears. Wherever those flying bugs are, there's fever."

"We got it off the convict ship."

"We got the runs and foul stomachs there. This is different."

"You're saying that because one of 'em's Howell. You were always cozy with Howell, whispering together in the dark of the deck at night."

"I'll cut out your filthy tongue, Corner."

"Articles, Articles!" Dobbin shouted.

"Stow that, Dobbin. I'm not going to duel Fenwick. Those corpses aren't worth a duel. I leave it to Calico Jack. He's captain and he doesn't want a sick ship, do you, Jack?"

"We had a sick ship when we came here, Dick. Howell and Cary have been with us from the start. But I've never seen men sick as they are."

"That's how we'll all be if we take 'em with us." Dick Corner pointed at me. "Look at Andy Bonn. He's been helping Bones with 'em and getting sicker by the day himself. He could hardly haul at the ropes and was sweating and turning dizzy. You thought I didn't notice, eh, Andy? I noticed all right. Who helped you heave those casks aboard and who took the greater weight?"

Jack gave me a hard look. I said, "It's the drink. I'm not used to so much."

"Stow that," Corner said. "Many's the time you're still

on your feet when the rum was all out and every other hand like a chicken with the staggers."

"Who'll take care of 'em if we leave 'em?" Fenwick asked. "When'll we come back to pick 'em up?"

"No need to. They'll be dead and can rot. Not that there'll be much left to rot. Cary's skin and bones already and looks half green." Corner grabbed his nose. "And the stink! That's rot set in."

"Maybe Corner's right," Jack said.

We were all staring across the camp at the sick tent. Cary was out of his head again and crying for his father.

"That proves it," Corner said. "Any proper sick man calls for his mother even if she was a drunken slut that beat him every day."

"Not so," Fenwick said. "I knew a man cried for George. George, George, day and night until we were ready to George him. When he was well we said, 'Who's George?' 'George?' says he. 'I never heard tell of any George.'"

Harwood took his pipe out of his mouth and scratched his ear with it. "I knew a man who cried for his brother who was lost off Boston."

"I'd cry for my father," I said. "Not because I didn't love my mother. But it was my father who—" Who tried to kill me. "Who always helped me. Anyway, if we leave them, it's like marooning, isn't it? It's like hanging a man without a trial. Like burying him alive."

"Andy's right," Jack said. "We'll decide tomorrow."

As soon as I got Jack in our tent that night I said, "If you leave those men behind you leave me, too. I'm sick. Half the crew's sick. Nobody talked about heaving anybody overboard because he had the flux. Corner's turning into a troublemaker. You give in to him this time and next time it'll be something else."

"If it's a contagion they've got—"

I interrupted him. "I'm warning you. If you leave them I'll stay behind. I'll jump ship. And I'll shoot that damned Corner in the back as he climbs aboard."

"Anne, I'm captain and I'll decide what to do without you threatening me with your fool nonsense."

"You should at least put it to a vote."

"Are you sweet on one of those men? Have *you* been whispering in a corner with Howell or Cary? No, not Cary, he's ugly as bilge."

"I'm sweet on nobody."

He reached under my shirt and began to caress me. "Because if you are, I'll cut off his parts." He fumbled at the lacings on my trousers. I caught his hand. "You won't leave them, will you?"

He roared like a wounded bull. "No! No! No! Damn you, no!"

I released his hand and put my lips on his.

Cary's fever broke in the night and he was sane, if still weak. This gave Jack the authority he seemed to need to insist the men be brought along.

Corner sneered at me. "This is your doing, Bonn. Lucky for them you've Calico Jack as your lover. A woman couldn't have done better than you've done."

Both men had to be carried aboard. It was a week before they were able to be up and about.

I felt better, too, as soon as we were at sea. My nausea and dizziness passed, my appetite came back, and I put on weight. Jack said if my breasts didn't stop growing the men would get suspicious.

"Not that I don't like it, but Corner himself'll be wanting a feel." He laughed, then suddenly he reached out and touched my belly, his eyes suspicious. "When did you last have your woman's time?"

"I don't remember. The days at sea are all alike. It was—um—just before we met Ned Teach."

"That was October, Anne."

We looked at each other. "Lucifer's dog! I'm pregnant." I burst into tears.

That fool man picked me up and laid me in the hammock and kissed my forehead like a father kissing a child. "If I had known—you might have lost it, Anne. Oh, God, I'm as big a fool as you are. I should have noticed. I should be taking care of you. Don't move. Stay here. I'll tell the crew you've got the fever."

"And what will you tell them when the damned brat's born? That you found it floating on the sea in a basket like Moses?"

"Lie down, Anne. I'll tell them—I don't know what I'll tell them. But I know what I'm going to do. I'm taking you to Cuba and putting you ashore."

"Cuba! And let the Spanish rip open my belly? There are easier ways than that of getting rid of it if I could remember them."

"Not Cuba proper. Coxen's Hole. A place we sometimes sell our plunder. It's shut off from the mainland by a range of mountains. I've a house there I bought when I was sailing with Vane."

"What the devil were you doing buying a house?"

"I had in mind I'd retire there if I didn't hang."

"Well, I'm not retiring there. I'm going to find a way to rid myself of this bastard."

"Oh, no, you don't. I want this bastard. I've always wanted a son. We'll raise him to be a rare gentleman, Anne. Educated like you. *He* won't have to hire out as livery boy the way I did and get kicked and bullied and catch his death standing in the rain. From now on every bit of loot we take, we put aside a portion for him."

I let him rave. I thought as soon as I was ashore I'd find some wise woman like Gillah or Tilda Redhose and rid myself of the brat. Meanwhile, I pleased Jack by lying in the cabin all day, pretending to have the fever. The wonder is I didn't get ill, shut away from the sea and air. But I survived it, and one morning I looked out the port to see we were tacking into a bottle-shaped inlet through an opening so narrow I could almost reach out and touch the trees. It was Coxen's Hole.

CHAPTER

VIII

MARK READ

I STAYED THERE for seven months. The house sat on a knoll overlooking the lagoon. The windows opened onto a gallery that ran around all four sides of the house, so there was always wind blowing through it. The jungle growing close about us filled the rooms with wavering green shadows so it was like living in the depths of the sea. All day birds sang and I saw the bright green flash of parrots. The wind was sweet with the scent of foreign flowers. And I longed to be back on the *Kingston.*

The half-breeds were beautiful, gentle, and lazy. They seldom hurried, but their settlement, unlike Nassau, was clean. Every morning the offal was collected and the beach swept with palm fronds so the sand started the day smoothly patterned with long, sweeping ripples.

My maid kept the house, did the marketing and cooking. Her conversation consisted of giggles, shrugs, and droll faces because she knew so little English. Mine consisted of smiles and nods because I knew so little Spanish, but there was understanding between us.

As soon as Jack sailed I consulted the local bawd house where they did understand English, having served so many of the Brethren. They all told me the same thing. It was too late to abort.

"Too dangerous. You die, maybe. Maybe get sick and no get well for man again. See, lady?"

I saw. I was fated to have the brat.

At first I enjoyed my solitude because I was too gloomy to talk to anyone. Again I found my thoughts dwelling on the past, yet I knew if I had it to do over I would live none of it differently. My biggest regret was that Gillah wasn't here to take care of me and the brat when it was born.

There was little entertainment in Coxen's Hole. I would have spent more time with the bawds but I could see I made them uneasy. They were accustomed to being ostracized. When one of the Brethren's ships put in, it seemed best to avoid the crew for fear someone would recognize me. All in all, it was a lonely time.

Eight weeks passed before Jack returned. One morning I had set out to accompany Raquella to market and saw the *Kingston* gliding into port. I started to run down the hill before I recollected myself. The men must not see Andrew Bonn with his hair grown long, with a woman's swollen breasts, and a belly big with Jack's child. I gestured for Raquella to go on without me and turned back to the house where I waited at the window.

I thought the sloop would never drop anchor and make the cables fast. I thought the boats would never go over and the men slide down into them. They took forever to row ashore, and once there, to scatter. When Jack, his flowered trousers belling about his ankles, started up the path to our house, two people came with him. A man—a black man—and a woman.

Dove and Phibba.

I embraced them as tenderly as if they were my own color and kind. I cried as I thanked Jack for bringing them.

He had persuaded the men to allow Phibba aboard by pretending he had a market for her and Dove as slaves and was getting a good price, which the crew would share. Corner, as usual, had objected, then tried to force Phibba once she was aboard.

"Where are you going to get this good price?" I asked.

"We're selling your Spanish emeralds."

Although, as Andrew Bonn, I hadn't been able to wear them, I didn't want to part with them. But I did. Dove and Phibba were worth it.

Afterward I wondered why the plunder Jack had taken in his eight weeks' absence wouldn't cover their price, but he shrugged off the question. The *Kingston* had been doing well, raiding coastal shipping as far north as the Cape. But the colonial governors were wearying of the pirates' high-handed ways, and they weren't as welcome as they had once been.

"Mostly it's Ned Teach," Jack said. "He got so insolent that all his gifts of rum and sugar could no longer excuse him. They got him at Cape Fear."

"Captured him?"

"Killed him. He was shot five times and had twenty-five cutlass wounds. They said he looked as if he'd been flayed."

"I always thought he'd be a hard man to kill."

"They gave his head to the governor and threw his body into the sea." Jack shuddered. "I didn't stay long off the Virginia coast."

"He would rather have fed the fish than the crows. He always said so."

Jack was haunted by the whole affair. "Eight of his crew were killed in the fight and thirteen of the others stood trial and were hanged. One proved he'd been forced and Hands —d'you remember Israel Hands?—he was pardoned. God knows why. Teach had lamed him with a pistol shot in one of those mad frolics of his. Sometimes I think we should have stayed safe in Nassau."

"That would have been a dull life."

"Your other friend—"

"What makes you think Ned Teach was any friend of mine?" I interrupted.

"You knew him before I did. Your other friend, Major Bonnet, he had ill luck, too. They hanged him at White Point in Charles Town just before Christmas."

"Oh." Jack watched me but I could think of nothing to say. I wondered if my father had attended the execution and what he would have done if he had known the gentleman pirate had been his daughter's lover. I imagined Stede's body hanging at White Point. If I were still in Charles Town I would see, from my bedroom window, the winter sun rise behind the gallows.

"Do you have nothing to say to that?"

I shook my head.

The *Kingston* stayed at Coxen's Hole only long enough to dispose of their plunder, and there wasn't one of them, Jack included, didn't complain at the prices they received.

"These folk pay poor and sell rich. The whores charge more than any place this side of the Atlantic. Half-breed bitches is what they are, but Corner said they know every way of turning a trick that there is."

Jack spent the afternoons and evenings with me, but I began to look forward to the day when he'd be gone. Perhaps I had been alone too long. He paced around and around the gallery, pausing only when he was on the side that over-looked the harbor.

"Damn it, there's nothing to do ashore," he complained when I commented on his restlessness.

"I thought you had planned to retire here."

"Aye, when I'm old. It will be different then."

"It will be worse. You'll have been at sea so long you won't know how to live any other way."

He couldn't keep his mind off Ned Teach's fate or the ill times. "We've got to hurry, Anne. Those pious pimps of government are closing in on us. There are all those ships out there waiting for me to take them and the market getting worse all the time. We've got to hurry. It's getting so you never know when it's a real merchantman or a government trap." He started to pace again.

"Go, then. I wish I could go with you. I don't like being ashore any more than you do, particularly in this condition. As soon as I'm delivered of this brat I won't let you near me with your trouser laces undone."

"The day I see you celibate will be the day the world ends. Then you'll be seducing the Lord's angels if they have any parts." He swung me to my feet and kissed me. "I never knew I'd be so hungry for a woman and so miserable without one. You think I'm restless here! Ask Corner, ask Fenwick or Dobbin. Ask any of the company. I'm pacing the deck half the night because I can't sleep without you at my side."

"Just as you're pacing now, when I am at your side." I took his arm. "Come, we'll pace together. There are only a few more months. Lucifer's dog, how time drags! I wish you could make a raid that would yield some books or a spinet or some paints. I've no way to pass the time."

"The crew'd wonder what I wanted with them. They know Andy Bonn is lying fevered with a lung disease brought on by the pox, but I don't think they know he can read."

"The devil they don't. Andy Bonn used to keep the accounts, don't you remember?"

"That's so. I do remember. We all remember. Corner keeps them now. He's got damned matey with those convicts who joined us." Jack stretched and shook himself as if shaking off his boredom. "Let's have a tipple. Being ashore gives me a whale's thirst."

"I've noticed. You haven't gone to bed sober one night since you've been here."

"No more have you, and if you're going to complain about it, the sooner I'm back at sea, the better."

"I'm not complaining about anything except your company. You're damned dull when you're sodden with drink and fall asleep in your chair. Duller than when you're pacing the gallery until it's a wonder you haven't worn it through."

"You're damned dull yourself with that great belly. If it weren't that you carried the son I've always wanted I'd not be wasting time with you."

"You were anxious enough to waste it when you filled Dove's caldron with gold and spent a fortune buying a bill of divorce."

He made a rueful mouth. "You're right. I'm the same man, too, for all the ill you think of me, Anne. And I'd rather have you, great belly or no, nag or no, than any other wench."

But it was dawning on me that I was no longer the same woman. Something had happened to the passion we had once had for one another. I knew it was just that: lustful passion and little else. Jack was a liar, a braggart, a drunk, a good pirate, and a poor companion. It had been different in Nassau where there was plenty of entertainment and all my friends. It had been different at sea where there was always work to be done, and when there was not I could spend hours watching the sea and sky. It was apt to say that ashore we were like fish out of water.

* * *

Jack came back to Coxen's Hole to be with me when the child was born. The son he had wanted was a lusty-voiced girl with a full head of black curls like Jack's own and hazel eyes. We named her Joanna and I'll say this much in Jack's favor, he was a better mother than I was. I'd had my fill of motherhood before she was born. Jack carried her about all day, rocked her in his arms until she slept, got up a dozen times a night to gaze into her cradle.

If he had had his way he would have kept me ashore to take care of her. I soon convinced him he would sail with Andy Bonn or not at all. He gave in with bad grace, and we hired a wet nurse. I bound my breasts to dry them, and made it clear to Dove and Phibba that they were in charge.

One morning a day or so before we planned to sail, Jack was circumnavigating the gallery with Joanna in his arms when Fenwick appeared at the garden gate. I ran through the house thinking to step out a window and take the child from Jack before he came face to face with Fenwick. It was too late. As Jack rounded a corner, Fenwick bounded up the steps.

"Here's the devil to pay," I whispered to Phibba and tiptoed to the door to listen.

At first both men were speechless, then Fenwick took out his pipe and said, "Is that a babe?"

"What the hell does it look like?"

"It looks like a babe."

"You've sharp eyes, Fenwick. So sharp maybe we should make you lookout."

From the silence that followed I gathered Fenwick was thinking. "Rum thing," he said finally. "I had a feeling you had a woman ashore. I didn't think it was being without Andy Bonn was giving you that itch." He must have stepped closer and looked into the baby's face, for his next sentence was, "Looks a proper mate. How's he called, Jack?"

((183))

"He's called Joanna because he's a she."

"Good thing. Too pretty for a lad. Well, well, a babe. I wonder if I might hold her, Jack?"

"If you're careful."

"Careful as if she were her weight in doubloons. She's a robust one, isn't she, Jack? Would you say she's smiling at me?"

Phibba and I raised our eyebrows at each other and shook our heads. That bloody old fool who'd as soon hack off a man's head as look at him was cooing away over Joanna as if he were its granny.

"What I came to tell you, Jack, was I think we'd better heave anchor. A boat came ashore at dawn. Crew—or what's left of the crew—from an English sloop. A Spanish man-of-war had taken her and set 'em adrift. The captain said he heard the Spanish say they were heading for Coxen's Hole to take the *Kingston.* Spanish merchantmen are one thing. Spanish frigates are another."

"The devil. How can we be ready?"

"We'd better be ready or Joanna here'll run the risk of being orphaned."

As if she understood, Joanna set up a howl and Fenwick returned her to Jack.

"All right. Start laying in supplies and I'll be down the hill as soon as Joanna's asleep."

Fenwick paused on the steps. "Hasn't she a mother?"

"Of course she has a mother. I didn't find her by opening an oyster shell. By the way, Fenwick, Andy Bonn'll be sailing with us."

There was another thoughtful silence. "You're versatile, Jack. Versatile a man as I know." He was silent for so long that I thought he had gone. I stepped to the door and stopped. He stood on the bottom step sucking at his pipe. He looked at me, removed his pipe, and smiled. "Unless Andy Bonn happens to be yon woman."

Jack whirled around. "What the devil are you doing out here?"

"I thought he'd gone."

"Here's foul weather for sure! Fenwick, come back!"

Fenwick mounted the steps without taking his eyes off me. "Aye, you're Andy Bonn right enough." He laughed and slapped his thigh. "You fooled us all, ma'am. If it weren't for this pretty little figurehead you'd be fooling us still."

"The question is, what's to be done." Jack bounced Joanna up and down. "I suppose you won't rest until you've spread the news, then there'll be mutiny."

Fenwick's voice was dry. "Seems to me you ought to know by now I'm a man what knows when to hold his tongue, Jack, which is more than I can say for some. Corner, for one. I know a female aboard's supposed to bring foul luck, but look at it this way. All the time Andy was aboard we had nothing but good. He—she—he—Andy here, manned the ropes, stood watch, mended sail, caulked, tarred alongside the rest of us and never shirked. In my opinion he was the best fighter of us all. Who was always first to board the prize, eh? Andy here. But then I always held women were fiercer than men and more fearless. So if you want to know what I think, Andy here is welcome. And no one'll know from me that Andy's missing his mainmast. That's my say."

I took his hand and he wrung mine. "Thank you, John Fenwick. You're a loyal friend."

He pursed his lips together and tapped them with his pipe, laying his other hand to his heart, thus indicating his lips were sealed.

The lagoon at Coxen's Hole is, as I have said, bottle-shaped, and just inside the neck of the bottle is a cork that has been pushed in. The cork is an islet, little more than a rock jutting up like a huge tooth and topped with towering ferns. From the sea, due to the position of the island, Coxen's

Hole is hidden, but the Spanish know it is there just as do the Brethren. A frigate lying at the neck of the bottle, or just inside the neck, could fence in a sloop as neatly as if the bottle were corked. This was what Fenwick feared.

The *Kingston* was anchored close under the "cork" so it would be sheltered from the heat of the afternoon sun. I was glad to be back aboard her. I had come home again.

We worked at a frenzied pace all that day and I felt myself coming alive again. The lassitude that had held me the past months dropped away. I was so happy I sang as I worked and soon had the company singing with me.

But it disturbed me to see Jack bolstering himself with hourly tipples. It wasn't until late evening that the rum robbed him of his cunning. By then he was swaying, repeating orders, and cursing if they weren't carried out as quickly as he thought they should be. Dick Corner was openly sneering. By then, too, the Spanish had bottled us in.

They came, with the English sloop they had taken, at half-sail, as quietly as clouds. One moment they weren't there. The next time we looked up, they were. I blinked to make sure they were real. It was evening and the shadows from the mountains that shut Coxen's Hole off from Cuba proper made all the landscape, sea and shore alike, blue and unreal.

The frigate dropped anchor in the channel directly opposite us. She drew too much water to come close. The English sloop, manned by a small Spanish crew, anchored in the channel at the other side of the islet, boxing us in as neatly as two cats at a mouse hole.

The air was not only blue with evening light but also with the swearing Jack did. The rest of the crew pulled long faces and looked at Jack for orders.

"Christ's Nails, get those hanging looks off your faces. We'd have caught the afternoon tide if I hadn't had to drag half of you out of the bawd house. It's no fault of mine you

had to have one more go before we heaved anchor." This
wasn't true but Jack was in no mood for truths. "We all
knew the damned Spaniards've been hunting the Brethren
ever since Jennings took the Plate. And they've been laying
for the *Kingston* since before we took her. So now they've
found us, and if they sink us, they sink us, but we'll give 'em
a good dose of powder before we go down."

"Damn little chance we've got, not with them firing at
us from two sides," Corner said.

"We could sit here and toss 'em kisses. Or maybe you'd
rather go ashore and leave 'em to take the *Kingston* at their
leisure, Dick."

"Whatever happens, it won't be 'til dawn," Fenwick said.
"If they tried firing at us now they'd hit the English sloop.
Foolish of 'em to lay it in so close."

"Oh, it'll damn well back out of range at dawn and leave
plenty of room for error. So long as we've got 'til dawn we
may as well break out the punch bowl. Dobbin, brew us a
blackstrap with plenty of courage in it."

Perhaps I'd been ashore too long but it seemed to me the
punch bowl didn't solve all problems. "Wait. Hold off,
Dobbin. We don't need blackstrap now. We need our wits."

"You bloody well don't know what we need, Anne-dy.
I'm captain and I say we need rum."

"You won't be captain after dawn tomorrow if you don't
listen to me."

More than one of the men drew a quick breath and someone, I think it was Corner, choked back a chuckle.

"By God, I've a notion to put you ashore and leave you
there. I don't know why I agreed to let you come back."

"Because I'm going to save your skin for you. That's why."

"How do you think to do that?"

"We're going to steal the English sloop the same way we
stole the *Kingston*. What do you think her weight is, Fenwick?"

He peered at her in the darkening light. Night was closing down fast. "Thirty ton, maybe."

"Lighter than the *Kingston*. So we lose ten ton but we save our skins. All right, Jack?"

Jack in his rummy state had been thinking and it had kept him quiet. He started to speak now but Corner interrupted.

"Whether it's all right with Jack or not all right with Jack, we're with you, Andy. Jack'd let us stay here and get blown out of the water."

"He doesn't fancy being fish food any more than you do, Dick. He'd have come up with the same idea given time. Harwood, you speak Spanish, don't you?"

"Aye."

"Good. What we do is, we wait for the eight-o'clock gun and lights doused. Then we load all hands into the boats and attack the sloop from both sides. If there's a man on watch, Harwood tells him he's got a message from his captain, that plans have been changed, and to throw him a line. Up we go, overpower them, and hoist anchor. Remember, we've got the numbers and they're a skeleton crew. Once we're aboard Harwood tells them if they shout or make the least noise they're dead men. We lock them up below and stand a guard."

"What about our supplies?"

"Supplies. Yes. If there's time and things go right, we can come back and unload supplies. We'll have to work fast and we'll have to work silently. If the frigate should hail us as we're leaving we say the same thing we said at Nassau, that the cable's slipped. But I don't think they'll see us. They're going to be too busy watching the *Kingston*. We'll leave a light in the cabin and a port ajar so they'll think the captain is keeping late hours."

"It may work," Jack said. "It worked before. It may work."

"It will work," I said. "And now, let's have some belly timber."

It was a merry supper with the men chuckling over how we'd surprise the Spaniards. Even Jack recovered his good temper as the food sobered him.

The lights from the settlement shone on the water and I spotted the one on the hillside that was our house. I should have felt sad but all I felt was thankful that I was on the *Kingston* and not up there.

On the frigate guitars were playing and someone sang a song of bitter sorrow. Even without understanding the words it was enough to break your heart.

Supper done we put out all lamps except one in the hold. We brought everything we felt we could not leave behind onto the deck. We stumbled in the dark and cursed one another, but all in a friendly way.

The frigate fired the eight-o'clock gun. One by one their lights went out. The musicians played on.

"Damn their blood, why don't they go to sleep?" Jack said. "I don't want to stay up all night."

As if the musicians had heard the music ceased on a sobbing note that made me think of all the evil I had done in my life, but there was too much to be done to brood over it.

Sounds carry over the water so we bound the oars. A light wind came up driving waves against the islet and rocking the sloop. The blocks banged and the crossbars creaked. One by one we dropped into the boats. I took a place beside Jack and he squeezed my hand as we pulled away. I felt a pang of sorrow, leaving that sloop, but I had left many things I loved since I had gone off with James Bonny, and oftener than not, it had worked out for the best.

The dark hull loomed over us. Fenwick laid hold of the hawser. We listened. All I heard were the hundreds of little lapping tongues of water.

Harwood was the first up with Fenwick close behind him and Jack following Fenwick. Corner was in the other boat and was on deck as soon as Harwood was.

Those Spaniards never had a chance. We didn't kill them, though they expected to be killed when they had their heads tipped back and dirks held at their throats while Harwood rattled away in Spanish. We bound and gagged them and threw them on the ballast. Dobbin and I took a quick inventory of their stores. They were poor stuff and we decided to bring everything we could from the *Kingston.* Jack was the kind of captain who believed a crew fought best on good rum and good belly timber.

It was almost midnight before the transfer was complete. Some of the cargo I would have left but the Brethren are a stingy lot about some things, just as they are openhanded with their money. They picked the *Kingston* clean.

The tide was running and it was time for change of watch. I was nervous. I had hoped to be well away before dawn in case the Spanish discovered they had been fooled and came after us. We hadn't yet tested this sloop and had no way of knowing whether she was as fast as the *Kingston.* I seemed to be the only one concerned.

As we hoisted anchor a light showed on the frigate. The wind and tide were carrying us dangerously close to the islet but we didn't dare put on sail to show white against the night sky.

The light flashed twice as if signaling us.

"Signal back," I said.

"How? If we give the wrong signal they'll know something's foul. They'll see we've changed position, too."

"They'll think the tide has moved us. They've shifted a degree or two themselves. Do as they did. Flash twice. It may work."

We lay low while Corner lighted a lamp and passed his hand across it twice. Immediately the light on the frigate went out.

We used the sweeps to keep us from grounding. We drifted

out of the frigate's sight, behind the island, hoisted canvas, and glided out the neck of the bottle.

As we reached the open sea the moon came up silvering a glade for us to sail.

Jack slept late the next morning, snoring out fumes of rum so I could almost get drunk just by stepping inside the cabin. He was often drunk these days. He started drinking as soon as morning came to ease the pain of the drink from the night before. He'd lie in his berth, tippling and sweating, too weak to move.

"You take over, Anne. Tell 'em what I want done. You're as good a captain as I am anyway."

"Quartermaster's supposed to take over when you can't."

"I don't want Corner taking over. I want you, damn it." He rolled to his feet and staggered to the deck, all rumple-haired and red-eyed, and bellowed, "Andy here'll take over when I can't, see? I'll give him orders and he'll pass 'em on to you. You swabs understand? You understand, Corner?"

"It's not according to Articles."

"That's too bloody bad about Articles. If I say Andy's word is the same as my word, it is the same."

"If you'd lay off the rum there'd be no need for Andy to speak your words."

"You keep your tongue where it belongs, Corner, or you'll find it missing one day."

"That's enough, Jack," I said. "You keep your own tongue where it belongs and go back to your bed. We'll sort out things with no help from you." I propelled him back to his berth.

"I couldn't manage without you, Anne. You're a rare woman. Better'n I deserve. You aren't taking the bottle with you, are you?" He was reaching out for the rum the way a babe reaches for a teat.

"I damned well am."

"You damned well aren't. You're a coldhearted bitch!"

Later I had a private word with Fenwick.

"We've got to do something to keep Jack off the rum. When did he start drinking like this?"

"Jack was always one for the bottle, Andy, but he started drinking heavy after you were put ashore. Not one of us but was ailing for a while. Some complaint we'd got from the prison ship or off that island from the bugs. But his craving for drink got worse and many's the time one of us has had to take over." Fenwick squinted in the direction of one of the former convicts who was going over the ropes. "I rue the day we let them swabs sign on."

"Are they troublemakers?"

"Not that exactly. They take their share and don't complain. Do their share of work right and proper. I don't like them. They still smell of Newgate to me."

"The crew seems smaller. Who's missing?"

"The carpenter and two of the seamen who joined us way back. They decided to stay ashore Boston way. Michelson and Webson took the pardon. Davis, he's still with us, and Bones says this is as good an apprenticeship as any. That tall lad's Mark Read. He came off a Dutch ship. Funny thing, an Englishman serving with the Dutch. He seemed glad to join us. Guess he was tired of foreign tongues. All spit and gargle, the Dutch tongue is."

"I like the looks of him."

"He's a right one, though he's friendly with none but himself."

"There's no harm in that. You told me once it's when the men group together and talk in low tones it's time to watch out."

Fenwick gave me a long look. "Fancy you remembering!

Aye, it's true. And it's what makes me uneasy about those felons. They're too close."

"Jack said Corner is matey with them."

"Sometimes I think Corner hasn't the brains of a gull."

At midday we put the Spaniards into a boat with some biscuit and sack and pointed them toward Cuba. They shook their fists and shouted Spanish invective that had Harwood laughing until tears ran down his cheeks. He had a curious Puritanical streak in him and refused to translate because he didn't want to sully his tongue. The gist of it was they wished us all to be reborn as bulls who could find no cows to receive us.

Much later we learned the fate of the *Kingston*. At dawn the frigate opened a furious cannonade that turned the sloop into a worthless hull before they discovered that we had fled. So Haman never got back his sloop.

The *Mary Belle* didn't have the speed of the *Kingston* but she was a fit little vessel. I was glad to be back at sea. My muscles that had ached for action during the long months ashore now ached because of it. My hands bled until they became calloused again, and my face burned and peeled and burned until I regained my old bronzed look.

I tried to make friends with Mark Read but was rebuffed. Despite that I couldn't stay away from him. He looked to be little older than myself, fair-skinned, with eyes that changed from blue to gray depending on the color of the seas. His eyes fascinated me and I made excuses to talk to him just to see what color they were on that particular day. They had a hard, fearless expression, yet several times when I surprised him leaning over the bow gazing into the wake, I would see they were blurred with daydreams.

I wondered what he dreamed of and why he had joined us, he was so unlike any of the other Brethren I had known. He deliberately shunned the rest of the company, preferring to eat and drink alone. Yet when we took a prize he was always one of the first to board her and fought with skill and cold precision.

One day we found ourselves side by side mending the jib sail, which had got shot through in an attack. Mark's silence made me uncomfortable and finally I said, "You're a strange one, Mark Read. Why'd you join us?"

I thought he wasn't going to answer me, but at last the answer came gruffly, "It's one way of seeking my fortune and better pay than I got from the Dutch."

"Aren't you afraid of hanging?"

His eyes were blue today and suddenly they sparkled just as the sea was sparkling under the sun. "Aren't you?"

I shrugged. He shrugged in return, half-smiling at me. "I figure hanging's no great hardship. It it wasn't for hanging every fellow afloat would turn pirate until the seas were so infested the merchants would be afraid to venture out. Then we'd all starve."

"If we ever stand on the gallows I hope I'll stand beside you and take heart from your courage."

The eyes turned hard again as if a cloud had passed over them. "Better you should share the gallows with the captain since you share his cabin." The contempt in his tone was stinging.

I very nearly unlaced my shirt to reveal myself to him and ask, "And why should I not share it?" But I didn't. I bent over the sail burning with a shame that none of the other Brethren had ever been able to arouse. I resolved to leave Mark Read to himself.

Yet I could not. I wanted to show him I was not what he thought. I wanted his respect and I wanted him. I was like a bitch in heat and Jack did nothing to satisfy me.

Jack bored me these days. His once handsome face was bloated with drink. Often he was so sodden that his love-making was clumsy and he fell asleep in the middle of it. He reeked so of rum I used to leave the cabin at night to sleep on deck. He would waken, find me gone, and come searching for me. He would berate me so loudly it would rouse the crew and I always went back to the cabin with him rather than create an uglier scene.

I couldn't understand how the few months we had been separated could have wrought such changes. I wondered if I had ever been in love with him. I thought of all the time I had wasted ashore being lonely for him and longing for his return. I was like the two fishes each swimming in an opposite direction, just as Gillah had said. I still had affection for him because of the past we had shared, because he had brought Dove and Phibba to me—and made me pay for them with my emeralds. That bitter thought always interjected itself. Even today I am haunted by the loss of those emeralds. Perhaps my judges would have permitted me to wear them on the gallows. Perhaps they would have accepted them in payment for a pardon.

One night when Jack had stumbled into the cabin and passed out I went on deck and leaned over the side wishing I had the courage to drop into the sea. I couldn't go on like this. Every day my loathing for Jack increased. The alternative to drowning was to escape the next time we put ashore and take the pardon. God knew what would happen to me after that, but it didn't seem to matter. I began to imagine life ashore and various ways I could make a living. Nothing seemed practical except whoring and I had not yet fallen to that. What I needed was a man, but a decent man, like Mark Read.

So thinking of Mark Read I decided to find him. I knew he slept apart from the rest of the Brethren because Fenwick had told me.

I found him in the bow, well hidden from the rest of the deck. He looked so handsome sleeping there, one arm flung across his eyes to shut out the light of the stars that I could no longer resist my lust. I opened my shirt and unbound my breasts and let myself down beside him. He didn't stir as I touched him. Cautiously I unlaced his breeches. Still he didn't awaken.

I thought no one could sleep so soundly and I smiled. He knew what I was about and was only pretending. He had fancied me all along, which was why he was so bitter about my sharing Jack's cabin.

I kissed him and put his hand on my breast. I slid my own hand down into his breeches.

He awakened with a start and tried to push me away as if my flesh burned him. He struggled beneath me while I groped, puzzled. He half-pushed and I half-fell back from him and we stared at each other in the cold starlight.

"My God, lad, you have no parts!"

His eyes dropped to my bare breasts and I felt the blood rush to them under his gaze. "You—you're a *woman?*"

"Yes, but little good you'll do me, Mark Read. What happened? Was it Turks?" Tears gathered in my eyes thinking how he must have suffered, tears of disappointment for myself.

"Turks? Oh, I see your meaning. No. It wasn't Turks." Mark Read shook his head, his mouth twisted in a smile. Suddenly my perspective of vision shifted and I understood everything, his difference, his privacy, his contempt.

"You're a woman too!" He nodded. "My God! And I was trying to seduce you. But how—why—you're as mad as I am."

"I've been passing as a man for a long time. Until now I've never been found out." "He" gestured at my breasts. "You'd better cover yourself in case one of the company decides to stroll around the deck and look at the stars."

I was glad to do so. I was embarrassed at my behavior and at my blindness in not seeing through the disguise. You would think a woman could recognize another woman. "Who are you if you aren't Mark Read?"

"My name is Mary Read. It all began when I was a child."
I nodded. "The same with me."

"I hope not quite the same. My father was a seaman and
my mother had a rather—airy nature. I was born when my
father had been at sea too long. When he returned my mother
passed me off as the son she'd had by an earlier marriage. I
was a large child but my father couldn't have known much
about children or he wouldn't have been taken in. Perhaps
he did know and didn't care, though I'd rather not think
that. I was brought up as a boy and knew no other ways.
When my mother died my father put me aboard a frigate
as foot boy. As soon as I was old enough I left the ship and
enlisted as a cadet in the cavalry. I served under Marlborough
in Flanders."

"You *are* a brave one."

"I don't see that it matters how you die," Mary shrugged.
"After the campaign I married one of the troopers who had
been my comrade in arms. He was as surprised to find that
I was a woman as you were," Mary gave Mark Read's enig-
matic smile. "We opened a tavern in Breda and were happy."
She lay back and threw her arm across her eyes just as I had
found her. "He died."

Clouds blotted out the stars and there was a smell of rain
on the wind. I thought, it's getting on toward hurricane
season again, and remembered Stede.

"After that I enlisted in a foot regiment garrisoned in
Holland. But it was a dull life in peacetime. I decided to go
to the Indies. I signed on a Dutch ship as a common seaman.
The *Kingston* captured it and here I am."

"My life is dead calm compared to yours."

She leaned on her elbow and looked at me. For the first
time her eyes were friendly. "How did you come to be here?"

We lay side by side talking in low voices until night faded
into a gray, misty dawn. Suddenly a shadow fell across us
and Jack flung himself down on Mary, knife in hand. They
rolled over and over. Mary could pull neither her dirk nor

pistol and Jack was stabbing wildly, missing her, hacking the deck, ripping her shirt. He pinioned her under him, ready to slice her throat. I kicked his ribs, then threw myself on him and grabbed the arm that held the knife and sank my teeth in his wrist until I tasted blood. The knife clattered to the deck out of his reach. As he reached out to retrieve it Mary freed one arm and brought up a fist, which knocked him out.

Together we carried him to the cabin. The commotion had awakened the company and they blinked at us, holding the captain between us, his legs dragging, as we hauled him across the deck. I was sorry they had seen it and had a feeling it would make for trouble.

We threw Jack into his hammock and I bolted the door. He opened his eyes and began to thrash about but the two of us held him fast.

"You damned faithless bitch. I'll kill you and Read both."

"No, you won't. Listen, Jack. Mark Read is not what you think. He's a woman, just as I am."

Jack let out a string of oaths calling Mary and me liars and damning the days we were born. It was some time before he would listen, then he jeered at my having been duped.

The jeering amusement gave way to gloom. "The crew'll think I've been cuckolded. We'll have to tell them."

"And have her thrown off the ship? Oh, no. Rather they jeer at me. Mary—Mark can let on to them he wanted no part of me and set it right with you. I'll be meek and pout and suck up to you for a few days until it's forgot."

"You damn well will do that, anyway, you faithless baggage."

I held my temper with difficulty.

When Mary left us I said, "It's your own fault, Jack. If you weren't so soaked in drink I wouldn't have looked for another man. You're lucky I chose Mark. I wouldn't have any of those other swabs."

((198   ))

"No? You've strayed once, you'll stray again. A faithless bitch is what you are and what you've always been. Not only are you faithless, you're a castrater. You've robbed me of my manhood."

"The devil I have. It's drink's done that."

"I drink because of you. You won't stay ashore and be a wife like any other woman'd be glad to do. You try to run the ship to please you. You humiliated me at Coxen's Hole, taking over command and stealing the sloop."

"Would you rather have stayed there dead-drunk and been sunk by Spanish guns?"

"Hornigold was right when he called you a hellkite."

I yawned. I couldn't help myself. It added to his fury and he struck me. When I came to I was in the hammock and Jack was stroking my head and pleading forgiveness. Mary and I had talked all night. All I wanted was to sleep. So I forgave him and pulled him in beside me and fell asleep in his arms.

Mary did her work well, shrugging off the incident and saying she had squared things with Jack. Jack got sympathy and I got sly grins, what with my bruised chin and blackened eye. I turned them off with jests, saying Mark was a handsome fellow and you couldn't blame a body for trying, could you? Fenwick gave me a wink. He thought Mark had tumbled me and that it served Jack right.

For two days Jack didn't drink. Sobriety ruined his disposition. He snarled and cursed and behaved like a bastard generally, but in bed at night I had no complaints.

We were passing through warm, squally weather. When it wasn't raining the air was so humid we might as well have been trying to breathe underwater. We hadn't taken a prize in nearly three weeks. God knows where all the ships were. One of the former convicts accused us of being off course and that it was Jack's fault, due to drink. Jack jumped the man, which was strictly against Articles. No man is to strike another aboard ship. If the quartermaster can't settle the quarrel it has to be settled ashore with sword and pistol.

Jack had already broken Articles once by fighting Mary and again, striking me—though there were those who thought I deserved it. But this was too much.

Fenwick and Corner separated them and held them so they couldn't attack one another again. They hurled insults across the deck until they were out of breath and ideas. When they calmed down they agreed to go ashore on the first island we sighted and fight it out.

I told Jack he was a fool and should settle the matter by parley before he got himself shot or sliced to ribbons.

"You're right, Anne. Right as always. I was heading into foul weather all because that Newgate cutpurse thinks the sea's like a London Alley with a new victim every evening. It's being dry as a salt herring does it. If I'd had a corker in me I'd have laughed at the lubber and told him to stow it. Give me one rum, Anne, and I'll sip it slow as mother's milk while you go set things straight. You've a way of talking that'll make him understand."

I fixed things as well as I could with the fellow sneering at me.

"I've known his kind from way back, Andy. Take their drink away and they turn ugly. Give it back to them and they're no use. Only use he'll ever be now is to feed fish."

"You can belay that talk, Jeb."

But the fellow was right. I had heard Jack's promises before. He didn't stop with one rum. By nightfall Fenwick and Mary and I had to carry him to bed.

Later Mary and I leaned over the stern watching the wake boiling behind us. It was raining again but I was damned if I was going into that rumpot of a cabin and listen to Jack snore.

"How do I always get such rotten men?" It was unfair. I had rejected one good but dull one and lost Stede to the hangman. "It's enough to put me off the sex forever."

"We haven't had much luck, have we, Anne? But I'm still willing to try again."

"Then you'd better jump ship. You'll find nothing here but knaves and rascals."

"That's not true."

I looked at her quickly and she was smiling. "Who?"

"Robert Dousin."

"Who the devil's that?"

"The surgeon. He's different."

"Bones? I never knew he had a name. He's different all right. He wanted to put maggots in Fenwick's wound to eat out the putrefaction." I shuddered. "Do you really want him?" I couldn't believe it. I had worked alongside Bones and had never given him a thought, which is unusual for me with a man, but there was something repugnant about dealing with all that blood and fever. "Why? Why him?"

She got that dreamy-eyed look which had first attracted me to Mark Read. "Many reasons. First because he's good—"

I interrupted her by laughing. "That's a rum reason to want a man. Not that I'd expect you to want a bad one."

"He'd never treat a woman the way Jack treats you."

I shrugged. "Maybe I ask for it."

"And maybe Jack's a bully who thinks a woman is good for only one thing."

"Except when he wants me to hand out orders for him. All right, so Bones is good. There are all manner of fool reasons for falling love. I suppose that's as acceptable as any. But with a leech!"

"That's part of it. He's good and he's gentle because he is a leech, and I'm strong enough and bold enough for both of us."

"Sounds like you're reversing your roles, but I've done it myself. I held the reins with Bonny and I'm beginning to think I hold them with Jack, so who am I to object if you want a man who smells of someone else's sickness?"

She turned a cold blue gaze on me. "That's a damned

heartless thing to say. I think you said it because you're jealous."

"Maybe I did." I had never had a female friend before, having scorned my school mates in Charles Town. It was only now I was learning what I had missed, and it looked as if I were going to lose my friend to a man.

"I admire him for smelling of someone else's sickness, as you put it. Though he doesn't. He's clean, which is more than you can say for the rest of these stinking rogues. Look, Anne, so many good companions fell beside me in Flanders and died because there were too few leeches to mend them all, so many of them were crippled for life because the leeches sawed off their limbs or set them improperly or let them go rotten, so many died of fevers no one understood, so few people want to smell of someone else's sickness, that I think it's a grand thing what Robert does. My husband—and I loved him dearly as I told you—died because the leech was an ignorant fool. Robert is an expert bonesetter or half this crew would be peg-legged. He'd rather try to save a leg than saw it off. He knows that maggots will eat the putrefaction and that moldy biscuit will help to heal. He'll try things and I admire him and his skill."

"That's mighty doucey reasoning for a pirate as bold as you are and one who claims to have no fear of hanging."

"I'm not afraid to hang or die any other way, but what's that got to do with Robert?"

I shook my head. "Nothing, I suppose. If you want him, why don't you go to him? There he is, standing alone portside. Go, with my blessing."

"What shall I say?"

"Say? Don't you know how to be a coquette? No, I see you don't. Well, my girl, you can always reveal yourself to him, the same as I did to you, and I hope you'll have better luck than I did."

We laughed, then I gave her a push toward Bones.

It was past eight and the lights were doused. They had been hissing and spitting in the rain anyway. The men were sleeping below, out of the weather, and I pitied them in that sweathole. I got my hammock and slept under it instead of in it.

The weather cleared during the night. The moon wakened me, shining full in my face. I pulled my jacket over my head and was almost asleep again when someone touched my shoulder. I thought it was Jack again and jerked my jacket down to glare into Fenwick's face.

My first reaction was that he was going to kiss me because, of course, he knew I was a woman. I was trying to think of a nice way to rebuff him when he put his mouth to my ear and whispered, "Trouble's afoot."

He laid his fingers on his lips, rose to his feet, and tiptoed away.

I'd had a feeling that if Jack went on behaving as he did there'd be trouble. Now that it was here I wasn't prepared for it. I wished Fenwick hadn't been so mysterious. He had gone below again, and if there was trouble there, I preferred to stay away.

It was nearly dawn before I fell asleep. I awoke late, sweating under my jacket. It was a glorious morning. The sea was golden green and smooth as satin. It reminded me of the dress I had had long ago that had changed from green to gold as I moved.

I started the firebox. Dobbin came up with water and salt beef and dried onions and we threw them in to cook. Jack came out of the cabin, stretching and yawning, glowered at us, and went to the head.

I said, "Maybe we can catch some fish today and have a change. I'm sick of jerky stew."

Usually Dobbin was talkative but he merely grunted.

"Is there meal to make cakes?"

"Weevilly."

"Damn. We'd better sight a ship or find a port soon or we'll have sores."

"Tell *him* that." Dobbin spat in the direction of the head.

Jack deserved it. We'd been sailing around like a ghost ship because he thought that stupid Spanish frigate was after us. The one fishing boat we'd seen he had let go without taking it because all it would have was fishing gear instead of goods bound for the colonies. I wished I had the command. I'd change things.

It was obvious something was wrong when the men gathered for breakfast. Instead of crowding up to the firebox to fill their pannikins they waited until Jack came. Then one of the former convicts, Jeb Morrine, stepped forward and thrust a paper at Jack. "This here's for you."

Jack frowned at it and finally took it. His face turned dull red under its mahogany patina. He crumpled the paper and threw it from him. It rolled across the deck to my feet. I picked it up and smoothed it. It was a round robin and the only ones who hadn't signed were Fenwick, Mary, and Bones.

"Whereas," it read, "Captain Calico Jack Rackham spends most of his days in a Tipple, and whereas we haven't [*took* was crossed out] taken a Prize for many days, and whereas the Biscuit is Wormy, and all is Bungled, we want said Captain Calico Jack Rackham deposed."

"Deposed, is it?" Jack bellowed. "I'll depose the bloody lot of you."

Jeb Morrine was as oily as the sea in dead calm. He'd been a ripper in London. "Nah, Cap'n, you can't do that 'cause there's too many against you, don't you see? Most all has signed."

"I see most all has signed," Jack mimicked. "Why didn't you sign, Fenwick? Couldn't you make your mark?"

Fenwick took his pipe out of his mouth and blew a chain of smoke rings in Jack's direction.

Jeb answered for him. "Fenwick didn't sign because he's sweet on your boy."

Jack looked from me to Fenwick in disbelief. Fenwick, who had his back to the company, winked.

"Mark, why didn't you sign?"

"I'm satisfied with the way things are."

"You damned well should be."

"He's sweet on Andy, too, as you could see if you wasn't blind. Blind drunk, that is."

Corner said, "Hold your lousy tongue, Jeb."

"What about Bones?"

"A forced man should have no say in company matters," Bones said quietly.

"You might tell Timothy Davis that for me, Bones."

Timothy Davis looked as if he'd like to hide.

Jack stood there, hands on his hips, his eyes resting long and hard on each in turn. All the respect I once had for him came flooding back. He had grown paunchy, his eyes were bloodshot and swollen with drink, his hands trembled when he didn't have them resting on something, but he was still a handsome figure of a man and there was strength in him. He looked at them so long they began to be uncomfortable. Even Jeb Morrine seemed at a loss for words.

"So. You want me deposed. And who did you elect to take over as captain once you've deposed me, Jeb?"

Jeb hesitated and rolled his eyes at his comrades.

"Speak up!"

"Well, sir," Jeb looked as if he wished he could bite his tongue the instant he said "sir." "You see, Calico, we figured on Corner. He's a right man—"

"Corner? Richard Corner? My old friend Dick Corner? The man I trusted to steal the *Kingston?* My old shipmate who left with me when I left Vane? My old chum who's been in the sweet trade with me from the beginning? Corner's

((205))

going to replace me? Congratulations, Corner. I always knew you'd make captain one day if you didn't hang first. And you have a damned hanging look, Corner. Don't you ever dream of walking behind the Silver Oar up to the Hangman's tree?"

"You're talking too much, Jack."

"Is he, Corner? Seems to me it's the lot of you who've been talking too much. I always knew you had a hankering to be captain, but if you think I'd serve under the likes of you you're sunstruck."

"That's because you've a hankering to be captain yourself, Andrew Bonn. You keep Jack supplied with rum so you can hand out the orders. We ought've tipped you a round robin as well, but I've other plans for you."

"I've some plans myself, Corner, and one of them is to start by dueling with you."

"Mind what you're saying, Andy," Jack said. "If there's any dueling done I'll do it. Here's what I propose, gentlemen. I'm a weak man, gentlemen, and as you say in your round robin, I spend my days in a tipple. I can't duel all of you at once, so what I'll do is, I'll duel Corner. If I'm the better man, I'll duel you, Jeb. And I'll duel each of you, one by one, until every one of you god-bedamned swabs is lying in a pool of your own black blood." Jack's voice ended in a scream that made me shiver. "Agreed, Corner? AGREED?"

"Agreed, Jack."

"That's settled. There's a cay dead south of here—oh, yes, gentlemen, I may be in a tipple but I know where we are in these waters—and we should be there just past high noon. We'll put in there and Corner and I'll go ashore. Alone, gentlemen. I want no knives thrown in my back, Jeb. We'll fight like the gentlemen we are. And now I'm going to have my belly timber. I don't like fighting on an empty stomach."

They made way for him as he went to the caldron to fill

his pannikin. Fenwick and I followed, then Mary and Bones. We took our meal into the cabin. I went below and fetched beer. Jack ate silently, deliberately. At first we took our cue from him, then I could stand it no longer.

I said, "Why not let us pair off with them. It would be quicker."

"It would be a melee. I'm the one they want to depose."

"You'll tire before you've fought all of them," Mary said.

"I don't propose to fight all of them, Mark. If I can dispatch Corner I reckon the fight'll go out of the rest."

"It won't go out of that slimy Jeb Morrine," I said.

"Jeb Morrine doesn't know how to duel. All he knows is what he learned in the alleys of London. Cutpurse, rape, rip, and cudgel. Did you ever see him with a cutlass? He can't even lift one."

"He can throw a knife. I've seen him level many a man that way," Fenwick said sourly.

"Aye, John, he can throw a knife. But knife-throwing in a duel is against Articles."

"Him and his mates don't give sauce for Articles. Fact is, Jack, they aren't seamen and we ought never have let them sign on."

"They're shore hungry, are they? All right, I'll give 'em shore. I wouldn't want Jeb to be marooned without company. Six of them, aren't there? That little cay we're headed for should be real cozy for six, especially at high tide."

"You're damned confident," I said.

"Just you watch me!"

Breakfast done Jack took over the wheel. The company stayed clear of us and of each other. The conspirators weren't so chummy as you'd think. Even Corner wasn't exactly strutting. Not that he didn't look sure of himself, but he wasn't wearing his usual silly grin.

At noon the topmast called land-ho, but it was close to an hour before the string of low, sandy cays looked like land and not the rise and fall of distant water. The sea turned from grape blue to aquamarine to emerald green, and broke over rings of white coral. The cays were dazzlingly white under the high hot sun. The scrub palms tossed and rattled in the wind and a skein of birds rose to greet us, squawking as they circled the ship.

Everyone was silent as the rum was passed. Jeb and Dobbin rowed Corner ashore. Fenwick and I took Jack. At the last moment I insisted Bones should come along. The company agreed with surly nods.

We grounded the boats and the two men jumped ashore. We pushed off and rowed far enough away that Jeb couldn't use his knife.

Jack and Corner shook hands, then turned back to back. Fenwick counted off twenty paces. They whirled and fired. There were no hits. This surprised me as Jack was a prime marksman. Fenwick chuckled.

They whipped out their cutlasses and went for each other with awful fury. Back and forth, up and down the beach, stumbling in the soft sand and edging back to the firmer ground still wet from the tide, until the land was pocked and churned with their footsteps. The blades clashed like discordant tinny music. Their faces glistened with sweat. Jack began to breathe heavily. It seemed to me he was tiring. Corner was agile as a cat, leaping out of reach when Jack lunged at him, then dancing over for a side thrust. Jack fought more slowly now, though none the less deadly. He moved less, but stood in place parrying Corner's thrusts. Both men had minor cuts but seemed unaware of them.

I was sweating, too, and kept rubbing the palms of my hands on my breeches. Sweat trickled through my hair and down my neck. Midges circled, whining in our ears, settling in the corners of my eyes. My head ached with the glare of the sun, which crackled the water into thousands of sharp splinters of light. The boat bobbed up and down, and the sea spilled in.

On the *Mary Belle* the men sat on the bulwarks hanging their heels over the side or climbed the shrouds, the better to see. But except for the grunts of the two men and the rattle of their cutlasses, the sound of water and wind, there was silence.

"Corner's getting tired," Fenwick whispered.

"How can you tell?"

"His steps aren't so fancy now. D'you see what's happening? Jack's driving him inland, into the soft sand. It's harder to keep your footing there when you dance around the way Corner does. There he—GOES!"

Corner leaped backward, stumbled, kicked up a cloud of sand, and sprawled on his back. Jack was on him, his cutlass at Corner's throat, his foot on Corner's chest.

Jeb Morrine gave a howl of rage, stood up in the boat so it rocked dangerously, a silver flash of knife in his hand.

"Articles is Articles," Dobbin bawled and brought the edge of his hand up on Jeb's arm. The knife dropped and the boat took water as Jeb threw himself on Dobbin.

We heard the crack as Dobbin knocked Jeb's jaw. Jeb lurched back and Dobbin grabbed up the knife and flung it into the sea.

Jack seemed to be haranguing Corner, flicking the cutlass back and forth across his throat, barely scratching it, so there were only hair-thin lines of blood. Then he helped Corner to his feet and called for Bones to come ashore and treat him.

We rowed ashore and gave them rum. Jack rinsed his mouth, then spat it out. He picked up Corner's cutlass and called, "Come on Morrine, you're next."

"You'd better rest. You're tired. You're just too damned vain to admit it."

"I can't stop to rest, Andy. I've got to show these swabs. Anyhow, Jeb's no challenge."

"Why didn't you kill Corner?"

"Because he's a good man and been my mate too many years. Get back in the boat, Andy, and keep your mouth shut."

Any other time I wouldn't have let him talk like that, but this wasn't the time to act as if I weren't wholeheartedly with him.

Jeb flung an oath at Dobbin as he left the boat. He walked up the beach like the silent alley-lurker he had been, his eyes narrow with hate.

Jack flung him a pistol, which he caught, then, "Here's your hanger." Jack sent the cutlass flying toward him. Jeb started to grab it, then snatched back his hand as if he feared he could cut it. He hadn't the cunning to catch it by the hilt. His anger showed as he bent to pick up.

Dobbin counted to twenty. The men spun around on the last count. The pistols cracked and smoked. Jeb's face was black with powder. He swayed, took a step backward, crumpled.

Jack smiled at me and waved his pistol at the *Mary Belle*. "Bring on the next one, Dobbin."

"He's pushing his luck." But Fenwick shook his head at me.

"He knows what he's doing, so long as they keep sending the convicts. Now, if Harwood comes, that's different. He's a deadeye, Harwood is."

Some kind of palaver was taking place on board. Then Harwood made a trumpet of his hands and hallooed. "We want to speak to Corner."

Bones helped Corner to his feet. I hadn't realized his thigh was slashed as well as his arm until he hobbled down to the boat. He grinned at us as he passed.

Jack sat down on a hummock to rest.

"He ought to have his own cuts seen to."

"Wouldn't look good, Andy."

We waited, dripping with sweat, our mouths dry with thirst because the rum we had drunk had made us the thirstier. Corner was hauled aboard. After a while a convict slid down into the boat and Dobbin rowed him to the cay.

He was a short, lean, piggy-eyed man with quick, ratlike movements, and shiny stiff whiskers like a rat's. He had his own pistol and a hanger that he had shortened to suit his height. The end was cut off squarely and honed as thin as a razor. I had seen its work and I wet my lips and crossed myself, a thing I hadn't done since I had left home.

Jack's shot went wild. Ferret's (for that was all the name he seemed to have) singed Jack's shoulder, tearing away his shirt. The serpentine swung back and forth as he moved.

Fenwick grunted. "He needs something better than serpentine this day."

I thought Corner had done a dancing act. Ferret was like a terrier after a chained bear. It was terrible to watch. Jack was tired and out of condition, and had met more than his match. His movements showed it.

I'm still not sure how it happened, it was over so quickly. Jack was gasping for breath. He seemed to stop, stock-still, as if to rest. Ferret drove his blade straight for Jack's throat. As he lunged forward Jack lifted his cutlass over his head, using both hands, and brought it down cracking open Ferret's skull and severing his arm.

Aboard the *Mary Belle* there was an intake of breath so loud we could hear it. Then the company cheered. I vomited over the side of the boat.

Dobbin rowed Jack and Bones back. I was dizzy and half-blinded with the sun and water. Fenwick had to help me up the line.

I was out of my mind for three days with sunstroke. When I came to the mutiny was over. Jack was still captain and more popular than he had ever been.

The other four convicts had been marooned on the cay where the fight had taken place.

"I left them some rum to help them drown their sins," Jack said. "But they'll find damn little to eat."

CHAPTER

IX

JAMAICA

Our luck changed. We took a small interisland merchant sloop and a slave ship. We sold the slaves in Jamaica, which is the best slave market in the Caribbean. They fetched a whopping big price. I would have preferred to set them free but when I said so Jack asked, "Do you want another mutiny?"

Jack was all for going back to Coxen's Hole to spend the money. The truth was, he wanted to see Joanna. The company would have none of it.

"No prey, no pay, Jack, and we been without both too long."

He didn't insist.

Our crew was back to its original nine, plus Mary, Bones, and Timothy Davis. We were too few to go after big game. We would never have taken the slave ship if half its crew hadn't been sick with some fever they'd caught from the foul hold. They'll never learn to throw the dead overboard on a slave ship, but let them rot down there until the putrefaction kills off half their cargo and sickens half the crew.

As long as we were in the waters around Jamaica, we decided to stay, cruising the north and west coasts, until we had more crew. As soon as they could be replaced, Mary and Bones were going to leave us. Bones hoped to set up practice in Port Royal and take Mary as wife.

It sounded like a dull life to me.

"Won't you get bored being ashore, doing woman's work?"

"I did woman's work before when my husband and I had the inn. It's different when you love someone, Anne. There's contentment in caring for them."

"It sounds as bad as being becalmed. Pretty soon everyone gets edgy. I hated being at Coxen's Hole."

"You didn't have Jack with you."

"I did part of the time and it was just as bad or worse as when I was alone."

Mary's eyes narrowed. "Do you know what I think? I think you've never been in love."

"That's sauce," I said. "I have been but it didn't affect me the way its affecting you. With you it's like a sickness." Then I was sorry for my words and told her so. Everything was making me edgy these days.

We took one small craft, which yielded fifty rolls of tobacco and nine bags of pimiento worth about three hundred pounds. One schooner had ten slaves along with its regular cargo and fetched us a thousand pounds. We tried to take a schooner loaded with molasses and sugar but their guns were too heavy for us.

Mostly we took fishing boats with nets and tackle worth anywhere from twenty pounds to two hundred. We weren't geting rich, and no one had agreed to sign on with us. You'd have thought we were a plague ship.

Jack had started to drink again, and although there was

no trouble with the crew, I was disgusted. Those were lazy days with too much time for introspection. I looked back over my life calmly and coldly and realized I had not loved Jack any more than I had loved James Bonny. I had used them to escape from other men I had not loved. I told myself the only man I had loved was Hornigold, and a moment later, told myself I lied. I had not even loved him. The only man I had loved was my father—and perhaps Stede—but beyond that the truth was, I loved no one but myself.

Self-love soon becomes self-loathing, and once again I thought of throwing myself into the sea and letting it take me to the depths. ". . . Of his bones are coral made . . ." I hummed to myself. I had set that song to music once.

Mary tried to persuade me to leave the *Mary Belle* when she and Bones left. "You are my only friend, Anne. Someday there would be a man for you. A fine man like Robert."

A man like Bones would soon bore me. I had escaped one young leech. I didn't want another. As for living ashore— "No, Mary. No! It's inconceivable."

One evening as we rounded Point Negril a pink hailed us. Jack answered that we were English and invited the crew aboard for a bowl of punch.

They beached the pink and rowed over in their skiff. Nine in all and in the evening light reflecting off the water we saw the glint of cutlasses.

"By Lucifer," Jack said, "I think we've got ourselves a crew."

"We have if they lay down their arms before they lay them on us."

"We'll hoist the Roger."

"Pray some government boat doesn't see it."

"We've been here two months and haven't seen a government boat outside the harbor at Port Royal."

"You needn't think those fishermen haven't gone whining to the authorities about the loss of their gear."

The flag rippled in the breeze, blood red in the last rays of sunlight. The men from the pink waved their cutlasses and huzzahed.

"You see. Brethren." Jack gave me an icy look. "If you aren't trying to keep me from rum you're crying doom. Watch yourself or I'll take you back to Coxen's Hole and put you ashore."

Before I could sharpen my tongue on him he turned to welcome the men aboard. They were pirates right enough and had just disposed of some goods in Port Royal.

"The Brethren are as welcome there as rats," their captain said. "You must be the company that's angered them."

"We've been unwelcome at Port Royal for years. As long as we preyed on the Spaniards we were government's own angels, but as soon as we help ourselves to some damned planter's sugar, we're sons of Lucifer."

"I don't mean past times. They're carrying on about some sloop that's been raiding fishing vessels."

"That's us!" Corner slapped his thigh. "Bugger 'em. It's free waters."

"The governor has a search on for you."

"Good luck to 'em." Jack lifted his cup and drained it. We emptied the punch bowl and mixed another. We brought out the fiddles and drums and danced. By the time the second round of punch was drunk the dancers were stumbling more than they were dancing. Fenwick favored us with one of his favorite navy ballads,

. . . some pick bullets from the side
Some drive old oakum through each seam and rift   .

Dobbin mixed another bowl. Carty fell through a hatch and didn't reappear, but his snores rose like background accompaniment to Fenwick's song.

It was on toward ten o'clock and the entire company was

drunk when Harwood spied the running lights of another vessel standing straight for us.

The captain hailed us and Jack answered, "John Rackham from Cuba."

"Strike to the King of England's colors!"

"We'll strike no colors for you or anybody else!" Jack answered. "Get them, Harwood."

Harwood fired the swivel gun but it went wild. I had never known him to miss before, but it was dark and he was the worse for punch.

They gave us broadside followed by a volley of small shot, which carried away our boom. In no time the *Mary Belle* was a shambles. Even Jack, our brave captain, had gone below and was ordering Mary and me to join him.

"The devil I will," I yelled at him. "Come up here and fight, damn your rotten hides. They're going to board us."

Just then the ships ground together and sent me staggering. Mary and I laid out the first fellows who tried to board. Unfortunately we only maimed them, but it gave us time to reload.

Mary fired two shots into the hold to frighten the men into coming out to join us. All she succeeded in doing was winging Dobbin and killing one of our visitors. The men set up a howl like imps in Hell.

Even now, months later, I am still puzzled why they turned cowardly. Was it the rum, the surprise attack, or did they feel our luck had run out? To give Bones his just due, he came up and Mary ordered him back.

"Get below, damn it, Robert. You're no fighter. You'd be more apt to wing me than them. Below!"

"Fool!" I shouted at her. "We need every man we can get."

"Not him."

You understand this exchange was carried on in gasps and grunts amid the clatter of cutlasses and our dancing about as we retreated under the assault. It wasn't what you would call a conversation.

Mary and I fought alone as long as we could. I've been in some fierce fights but I've never been surrounded as I was then. Always before there'd been someone to draw off the man who came up on my flank or rear.

We were beaten and I knew it. I was dizzy with whirling from one man to the next. The cutlass seemed to weigh a ton. The government guns kept up a steady fire, splintering our mast so it swayed like a tree in a high wind, taking the sloop with it so half the time we were fighting up hill or toppling down. The deck ripped under our feet and often I stumbled over the debris and just missed falling.

Out of the corner of my eye I saw Mary holding off two men with her cutlass and pistol. Another came up behind her. She whipped around and thrust at him and drew blood but he didn't seem to notice. Any moment she would go down. I didn't want that. I had some wild idea that even if we were captured she might be spared and have a chance at happiness with Bones.

I cried for quarter and flung down my dirk and cutlass.

We were bound and thrown aboard the government sloop. Ours was towed, along with the pink. We made quite a flotilla when we sailed into Davis Cove at dawn.

It had been a silent voyage. I refused to speak to Jack. If I had I would have cursed him roundly.

Captain Barnet, a brisk, saucy fellow, sickeningly pleased with himself, handed us over to a militia officer, a Major James who was rather too damned saucy himself. He kept referring to us as rascals and assuring us it would do his heart good to see us hanged.

We rode in tumbrels, under guard, to the seat of government at Spanish Town. It was a hellish ride. They may call that a road in Jamaica. In Charles Town we wouldn't insult a donkey by driving him over it. My only satisfaction was that it was a steaming hot day and the guards had to walk, and frequently to put their shoulders to the tumbrels to heave them out when a wheel caught in a pothole. Sweat poured down their faces and one grumbled his feet were blistered. I hope they festered and he lost a foot.

When we reached Spanish Town we sat in the tumbrels in the square, stared at by the citizens, pelted with rotten fruit by the brats of the town. Another time I could have admired the buildings and the way the town was laid out. The houses reminded me of Charles Town with their walled gardens and piazzas, but the square was more imposing than anything Charles Town has.

All I could think of was my thirst, my aching head, the bonds biting into my wrists, and the awful need to relieve myself.

Mary had fainted, slumped against my shoulder. She was deathly pale and I hoped she wouldn't lose the child growing in her as she wanted it so much. I even prayed, though my judges may think I don't know how. I prayed, yes, as I had never prayed before. For Mary. It was the first time in years I had been concerned for anyone but myself.

At last Major James returned and snapped an order to his men and the drivers of the tumbrels. He didn't look saucy now, but annoyed. It seemed we were to be taken to the jail in Port Royal and I overheard him saying to his lieutenant he didn't know why the devil that hadn't been decided in the first place and spared his men the march. Barnet could damned well have taken them into the port by sloop.

"Yet, you just cock an ear, he'll claim all the credit and we'll get short shrift. They could have overpowered us and escaped, for all he cared when he handed them over."

I wanted to tell him that the way we were trussed we

couldn't have overpowered a louse in our hair.

"He'll hear about this from me if we lose one man from sunstroke, by ginger!"

I don't know who designed the jail at Port Royal. It may have been one of the old Spanish buildings that withstood the earthquakes. If so, it's a pity the earthquakes weren't stronger. I've heard about Spanish torture and this jail was one form of it.

The cells were too small and the company, plus that which had been visiting us when Barnet struck, were crammed in like smoked herring in a barrel. We sweated by day and shivered by night, puked at the stink between times, and upbraided one another for being cowardly whelps. Only Fenwick held his temper and Harwood his tongue. Harwood puffed away at his pipe, which through some mishap the guards had overlooked, and said not a word until the day he was tried. Then all he said was, "Not guilty," which still makes me laugh.

Our discomfort didn't last long. On the sixteenth we were tumbreled back to Spanish Town for trial. Sir Nicholas Lawes didn't look much like Jack had done that merry Christmas Day dressed in a jib sail and wig of green tendrils. But if our mock court had been as long-winded as that of our judges, our audience would have gone off in disgust.

Every sloop master, every member of a fishing crew, every owner of some worthless little pirogue we'd robbed, had his day of importance, testifying against us. They told some imaginative tales.

Then we were taken out and locked up while the court deliberated. They didn't pronounce sentence as Jack had done because it was their dinnertime, but they deliberated long enough to have had a banquet.

We were brought back. His Excellency, all solemn pomp,

announced, "The court has unanimously found you guilty of piracy, robbery, and felony, charged against you in said articles. Have any of you anything to say or offer why the sentence of death should not be passed upon you for said offenses?"

Timothy Davis said he had been forced and had only been awaiting liberation from our felonious hold upon him. Which is why the cur is strutting around the streets of Port Royal today.

Mary and Bones had had a furious whispered conversation the night before, and now Bones, too, pleaded that he had been forced. He told me later he had been willing to hang with the rest of the company but Mary wouldn't have it. She was a strong-willed woman and Bones was one of those men who likes his woman to do his thinking for him as long as it leaves him free to do his chosen work.

Then Mary and I stood, and I spoke for both of us.

"My lord, we plead our bellies."

My judges will remember that this caused such laughter that His Excellency threatened to order the court cleared. It was not only the counselors and witnesses against us who laughed. Our company guffawed the loudest of all.

The clerk said, "The court does not understand the plea."

"My lord, we are women and quick with child." The gasp gladdened my heart. "We pray that the Execution of Sentence may be stayed." I looked at Jack and nodded. "Yes, Jack, you've done it again."

One of the witnesses, a hysterical woman whose canoe we had robbed, spoke out of order and said she had known all along we were women by the largeness of our breasts. "Yet they swore and cursed and told their pimps to kill me to keep me from testifying should they be caught."

Which wasn't true. She was silenced. His Excellency said, "An inspection must be made to learn whether you are speaking the truth. A new trial will be held for you the twenty-eighth of November of this same year. Meanwhile, the jailer must lock you in cells away from the men."

The hysterical woman said loudly, "Humph, it's too late to lock the barn."

Corner swore at us all the way back to Port Royal, quoting Articles, and saying it was no wonder they'd had such ill luck with two women aboard.

"You knew it all along, Rackham, and you know the consequences. You deserve to die and I'm sorry I didn't dispatch you when we were dueling that day on the cay." Which was ridiculous. We all remembered it was Corner who was down. "I wish I could tie the noose for you myself."

Mary and I shared a cell that night and were more comfortable, if huddled together for warmth can be called comfort. A doctor and midwife examined us the next day and agreed that we were indeed women and pregnant.

Bones and Timothy Davis were freed. Bones came back later with fruit and beer and some decent bread for us.

On the eighteenth Jack, Corner, Davies, Howell, and Fetherston were hanged. Jack was allowed to speak to me before he was taken out. He was bleary-eyed and trembling and nothing like the handsome fellow who had courted me in Nassau. He took off his serpentine and started to hand it to me, but his hands shook so he dropped it. He could scarcely lean over to pick it up.

"They won't hang you, Anne, since you're pregnant."

"No, they'll hang me after the brat's born and it will be just as painful then as it would be now."

"At least our child will live. Put the serpentine around its neck for me, Anne."

"I will, Jack."

"I never thought the day would come when I'd be marching out behind the Silver Oar."

"It wouldn't have come if you'd been on deck fighting like a man instead of cowering below sodden with rum. We outnumbered them. You'd be at sea now instead of dying like a dog."

"Have you no kind word for me, Anne?"

"No."

"You always were a heartless bitch."

His body was crammed into an iron cage, far too small for such a big man, and was taken along with the bodies of Corner, Harwood, and Fenwick who were hanged the next day, to Gun Cay to warn others from evil. What is left of them hangs there still. I've grown so accustomed to the sight I scarcely pity them anymore.

Bones came every day. He was working with a surgeon. There was little money in it and what he earned he spent on luxuries for us.

Mary and I appeared in court again and were granted reprieves until after the babes were born. To kill us when we were quick with life would have been murder.

"By then," Bones said, "we can have the reprieves extended. We may live to grow old yet."

I didn't share his optimism. Mary had made a serious mistake during the trial. We had conducted our defense by explaining how we had fallen into piracy.

"But weren't you afraid of hanging?" one of the counselors demanded.

Mary shrugged just as she had done when I had asked her the same thing. "I risked being blown to bits on the battlefield of Flanders, I risked drowning or some other mishap when I signed on the Dutch ship, I risked hanging when I became a pirate. If we could choose, we'd all die in bed in our sleep having lived a rich, full life. But we cannot choose and a good hanging at least attracts a crowd."

For a sentimental woman she could be powerfully cold.

When the counselor turned to me I admitted I was afraid. "But as a spoiled young lady and my father's darling I had always escaped punishment. I thought capturing and hanging was something that happened to others, not to me."

Our trial and the fact that we were pregnant women created a sensation in Jamaica. People came to the jail to stare at us and sympathetic ladies brought us baskets of fruit. I suspected they envied us our adventurous lives.

One well-established matron in town whom I shall not name, as my judges know her, brought us knitting needles and wool to knit for the babes we carried.

She was astonished we didn't know how to knit.

Mary said, "I've been posing as a male all of my life and never had the chance to learn womanly things."

I said, "The child can go naked for all I care."

"I know you from the past, my poor misguided woman. My husband and I were in Charles Town on business and were entertained by your mother and father. You were just a child then and beautiful as an angel. You played the harpsichord and sang for us, then danced a little minuet with your father. At the trial when you said your name had been Cormac I recognized you at once."

I stared at her. "I don't remember you. But there were always so many guests." Why had she brought up the past?

"No. You were a child. You wouldn't remember. My husband was there to sell sugar to your father. A little deal to keep it from going to England for taxation, you understand."

"I understand. My father was full of those little deals and just as much of a thief and pirate as I am or your husband is. Pirates steal from shipping companies who can damned well afford it, and hang afterward. Your husband and my father steal from the King and the people by avoiding taxation, and go free to steal again."

((224   ))

Her mouth was an O of shock. "I am glad your mother is dead so she will never have to know you have grown to be a whore and a hussy."

"Thank you for the kind thought, madam. If you've spoken to my father recently he has probably told you that I killed my mother with my ways."

"Anne, hold your tongue."

"I can see pity is wasted on one like this. I shan't come again to be insulted by a slut."

After she left Mary turned on me. "You are a bitch, Anne. If you carry on like that they'll drag you out of your childbirth bed to string you up."

"Let them. I'm sick of the lot of them and I don't know why you aren't sick of them, too. There isn't a counselor sitting in judgment on us who hasn't his black mistress and half a dozen dusky children along with his white wife. There isn't one of them who doesn't drink, gamble, wench, and bilk his best friend if he can without being found out. What did we ever do? We seldom killed a man unless he asked for it. Almost never," I amended, remembering a lad I had carelessly slashed to bits. "We took our plunder and harmed no one but ourselves. Yet there they—" I jerked my head toward the window—"hang with those enormous crows tearing at their flesh. And here we sit in a stinking hole, losing our health and our teeth and any faith we ever had."

"Mine has been reborn," Mary said, looking pious as a parson.

"Bah, you make me puke, Mary. Here you sit growing paler and thinner by the day—" I stopped. I had flung out those words but now that I looked at Mary I saw they were true and I was afraid for her.

"It's natural, isn't it?"

"I don't know. All I did the first time was get fat. I've damned little chance to get fat on the swill they feed us."

"Robert thinks he can get our reprieves extended after the babies are born. He said there is much sympathy for us in the town."

"That's fine for you, but what would I do if I were reprieved? Turn harlot?"

"You could live with us. Damn it, Anne, there's more to life than robbing and murdering and wandering the seas. We're women, though you seem to have forgot it. Being in love is part of life. Bearing children is part of life. I want this child. What's wrong with you that you don't want yours?"

"Stop passing judgment on me, Mary. Lookee, I'm only twenty. There's a lifetime ahead of me. But little use it will be if I'm not free, even if I don't know what to do with freedom."

I spent my day pacing the cell. I wanted exercise and the feel of sun on my skin and clean salt wind in my lungs. When I hoisted myself up to the window and clung to the bars to look out what did I see? The slaves carrying the night's sewage down to dump in the harbor. Ships going off to sea. My old mates swinging in chains.

Small things marked the passage of time. In March Vane was brought in, tried, and joined Jack on the gibbet. The patch of sunlight in our cell moved with the season. The winds and rains and temperatures changed.

Mary's child was due in May. I often surprised her grimacing with pain and holding her sides or wetting her lips and leaning head head against the cold stones. There were days when she could not get out of bed but lay there alternatively shivering with cold or burning with fever. She vomited when she tried to eat and her bowels turned to water.

Bones pleaded with the guards to let him take her into custody. He was refused.

Her labor began a month early. The midwife did all that

she knew how to do, but what can be done for a woman with prison fever?

She was buried April 28 in unconsecrated ground outside the walls of St. Catherine's Church. With an escort of militia I was allowed to accompany her body. Bones and I stood there alone. The guards stood apart, picking their teeth, drolling with one another over some incident that had happened the night before. One of them pissed against the churchyard wall.

We covered the grave with flowers. It pleased Bones but to my eyes it made it only the more obscene in that barren, grassless plot of red earth where sun-cracked hummocks marked the graves of other dead not allowed within the churchyard walls. The flowers were already withering in the heat before we left the graveside.

Mary's death had one advantage for me. The Court of Justice realized that I, too, might die of prison fever and rob them of a hanging. I had two months yet to go and it was decided I should be allowed a walk, under guard, every day, and a special diet.

My guards thought it amusing to be parading, two before and two behind, and one on each side, of a pregnant female prisoner.

My favorite walk was along the harbor where I could watch the ships, but this took me past the gallows and the gibbet where Jack hung in his iron cage.

"Why do you want to walk there?" the guards would ask. "You like seeing your lover rotting? He's no good to you now. Everything he had in him, it went phfut! when the noose jerked."

I didn't answer them. Often I didn't even hear them when they spoke to me.

One morning when I was awaiting my guards a gentleman was ushered into my cell. He was a big man, as big as Jack had been, with a lean, muscular body and tanned skin that made his sun-bleached hair and blue eyes seem all the fairer and more piercing. He wore the clothes of a gentleman and had the hands of a gentleman but he had none of Stede's gentle reticence. His first words were, "Good God! This place stinks worse than I expected."

"So what are you doing here?"

"I'm Thomas Calderwood. I know you slightly. I once dined at your father's plantation."

"Jamaica must be populated with people who knew my father and dined at our plantation."

"Perhaps it seems so because we trouble ourselves to act in your behalf. Which is what I've done. Time's short and it seemed wise to act quickly and without consulting you. I've obtained permission to take you into my custody. It's called house arrest." He held up a hand to silence me as I was about to speak. "I have a house in the hills above Kingston. The air there will be better for your health, you will have better food, a maid to attend your wants, proper medical care—"

I interrupted. "Why? Why are you doing this?" Why couldn't he have done it while Mary was still alive? She might have been saved.

"Because I danced with you at your father's house. Because your friend died. Because this prison is a disgrace to humanity." He beat the wall with his fist."It should be torn down and the stones buried under twenty feet of earth."

"Lucifer's dog! You're a reformer!"

He cocked an eyebrow at me, quizzically. "And you've no liking for reformers? Don't concern yourself, madam, I won't try to reform you. I don't give a damn for pirates. I'm doing this out of respect and sympathy for your father—"

"I'm not sure father would be grateful."

"—And out of belated sympathy for your friend. We let Mary Read die here. That was *our* crime. There is a great deal of sympathy for you, Mistress—how am I to call you? Rackham? Bonny? Were you married to either of those fellows with whom you consorted?"

"I was married to James Bonny."

"I've heard he was something of a rogue himself. No matter. You have, as I said, well-wishers. Myself among them, though with reservations. Perhaps after the child is born we can obtain another reprieve."

"And what will I do with it?"

He gave a short laugh and his eyes sparkled. "You'll probably use it to go to the Devil. Come, madam, give me an answer. Will you go with me? I don't want to stay in this toad hole any longer than I must. I'll take prison fever myself and then what use would I be to you?"

His brusqueness amused me. I laughed and it felt strange. I hadn't laughed in a long time.

"Come," he said. "That's better. Laughter is curative. But it is not an answer, madam."

I thought of the sun and the smell of the sea and flowers, of a comfortable bed at night and decent food. "I accept your offer, Mr. Calderwood. I am ready to leave this toad hole whenever you are."

Mr. Calderwood puzzled me. Despite his offhand manner he was endlessly kind. He made every provision for my comfort. I could forget I was a prisoner except when I caught sight of the guards at the gate. The windows were without glass or bars. I was free to walk the garden paths, to read, to play the harpsichord—how stiff my fingers were at first!—to ask for anything for which I had a whim. I hadn't realized how much I had missed all those things, how hungry I had been for books, how delicious food could be, how comfortable a bed, how soft the feel of silken gowns, how refreshing a scented bath.

The evenings Calderwood was at home we dined together

by candlelight on the grassy terrace overlooking the harbor and the plains of Kingston. We talked, oh, how we talked! until the candles burned out and the moon set, talked of things I had long forgotten—philosophy, poetry, and politics; colonial expansions and rights of kings; history, the theater, everything.

Once he broke into the middle of a discussion to say, "Good God! What a waste to have put your mind to no better use than tarring ropes and scraping masts and caulking hulls. And a worse waste to have given your body to those damned rogues."

"I didn't give myself," I protested.

He reached and and tapped my great belly with his wine glass. "Don't lie to me, Anne. There was only one Immaculate Conception."

"I meant, I've never *given* myself to any man." Except, perhaps to Stede. "I took them as much as they took me."

He looked at me thoughtfully. "I'll wager you did. A pity you have a taste for trash."

Often he was away at parties and I would hear his carriage arrive toward dawn. I missed him when he was gone, though I wouldn't have told him so.

Several days a week he was at his sugar plantations. Those nights he did not come home at all. My maid told me, giggling, he had a mulatto woman there and as many children as fingers on my hand. "Eh, she beautiful, that one, slim like a palm tree."

It astonished me that I was jealous.

When my labor began he stayed with me like any anxious husband. He was the first to hold Pegeen in his arms.

Ten days after the birthing I was to appear in court for sentencing. There had been rain. Dark blue clouds blotted out the plain and the hills around me. I stood on the ledge of land where usually I could see Port Royal and Kingston, thinking I would probably never stand there again. A rainbow arced where the hills were hidden and ended far below—on the gibbets, if I could have seen them.

The guards hallooed someone and I heard a horse clopping into the grounds. I supposed it was nothing to do with me as it was not yet time for me to go. But I was wrong. It was Mr. Calderwood. He came up to me, his eyes sparkling and clasped my hands.

"Anne, you need not appear in court. You've been granted another reprieve."

I couldn't believe it. "For how long?"

"Three months."

"It's borrowed time."

"When it's run out, we'll borrow more."

We celebrated that night. We dined and drank and danced on the terrace. I taught him a hornpipe and he taught me a Jamaican dance. The servants smiled at us from the shadows, smiled when they refilled our wine glasses, clapped their hands together in soft applause.

When dawn set the cocks crowing and the servants yawning, he escorted me to my room. He took my hands and kissed the palms, then pressed them to my face. "Those damned rascals you chose to bed didn't know how fortunate they were."

I wondered if his mistress knew how fortunate she was.

A day or so later he said he must go to Spanish Town on business and wondered if I would like to go along.

"Why? To thank the governor for my reprieve?"

"To visit your friend's grave."

"Oh. Yes. I would like that, but I thought I was under house arrest."

He laid his finger on his lips. "It will be a secret between us."

We rode in a closed carriage so I saw nothing of Kingston.

((231   ))

When he let me out at the churchyard he said, "Do I have your promise that you will not run away?"

"I doubt I'd get far. Not everyone's so merciful as you."

"How true. They'd clap us both in the toad hole."

There were flowers on Mary's grave so I supposed Robert had been there. The earth had baked hard during the months since we had buried her. I had not been able to cry that day I had been so angry at the world and at the damned soldiers who had accompanied us. Bones had cried enough for both anyway. But I cried now. I wept as I had not wept since I was a child. I embraced the barren earth and regretted that I had told her she made me puke, that her love was like a sickness, that she was a fool. I talked to her as if she could hear and who's to say she did not?

Mr. Calderwood was thoughtfully quiet on the way home. Then I burst out, "My God, I almost wish I hadn't been reprieved!"

"Anne, there would have been reprieves for her too, if she had lived."

And so it's gone. Reprieve after reprieve. Three months, a fortnight, two months, one month. Sir Nicholas Lawes is reported to have said he was damned sick of everything to do with the Bonny female and wished to be shut of her. Even Governor Woodes Rogers had written to him from Carolina saying she had suffered enough.

"And Rogers once threatened to have her flogged. But he's in Carolina trying to raise money to keep his colony of rogues in New Providence solvent. No doubt the woman's father prevailed upon him. Hang her or let her go free, I say."

"Then why doesn't he say?" I asked Mr. Calderwood.

"We'll have one more try, Anne. A new petition—"

"Oh, God, not another!"

"Yes, you ungrateful female, a new one. Put down everything. Everything."

I have written far into the night, on the terrace, with the wind bending the flames of the candles so they smoke their glass chimneys. Mr. Calderwood is at my side, taking each sheet of foolscap from under my hands as I blot it. He laughs, shakes his head at me, and comments, "God knows, you don't deserve a reprieve, my dear. At least you'll provide Lawes with some entertainment."

"I am nearly finished. I have said everything."

"You have not said you have seen the error of your ways."

"Perhaps I haven't. How do I know I wouldn't do it all again?"

"You don't know it, and neither do I, damn it. But it would please the governor if you said so."

CHAPTER

FATHER

THEY HAVE HAD THE PETITION a fortnight and are still deliberating. I almost hope they refuse it. How long can I go on living day by day?

"Don't we all live day by day, Anne? How do I know that a slave on my plantation, harboring a grudge of which I'm unaware, won't knife me as I walk through the fields? How do I know my horse won't step into a pothole and throw me? How do I know some friend won't challenge me to a duel for some imagined slight and oblige me to fight. I'm no shot and a worse swordsman."

"Perhaps I should give you lessons."

"I wouldn't trust you with a weapon in your hand, woman. You'd kill me, loot the place, and be away to sea again like the rogue you are." He laughed. "You see how well I know you?"

It is all very well to jest but what will I do if I am reprieved? That is what I ask Robert—he has finally trained me not to call him Bones. He and Mr. Calderwood have become friends and with Mr. Calderwood as a patron, Robert is prospering.

The truth is, all this luxury is beginning to pall. I am lonely for the sea.

This morning I watched a three-masted schooner gliding into harbor and dropping anchor. She was so beautiful it wrung my heart. From here she looked no larger than the titchy skiff Clym had carved for me years ago, but I knew what she was like, every mast and rope and shroud and plank of her.

This evening when I had resigned myself to having dinner alone, for it was dark and Mr. Calderwood had not come home, I heard a carriage coming up the winding wooded road from town.

I do not go to greet him, though often I long to, so I continued to sit, watching the darkening sea. He called my name and came toward me with quick steps, through the garden. A gentleman was with him.

At first I didn't recognize him, then I flung myself into his arms and to my surprise, began to sob.

"There, beauty, there. It's not sobbing you should be doing, Annie, but laughing to see your old fool father. Or swearing at him as you were doing when last we saw one another."

"Father, do you forgive me?"

"Um, as to that, Annie, there's much to forgive. Setting fire to the house, marrying yourself to that sniveling panderer, robbing the warehouse strongbox, vanishing without a word, taking to piracy, and disgracing the name."

"It wasn't your name I disgraced. It was Bonny's."

"But 'tis well known who you are." He was older, his hair was white, and his face lined. Drink and sorrow had done that, not two years, three years, four years passage of time.

"How did you get here?"

"Mr. Calderwood sent for me. I came this morning on a schooner—"

"I saw it arrive. I never dreamed you were on it. What kept you so long? You should have been up here hours ago!"

"Well, as to that—" He looked at Mr. Calderwood.

"I'll leave you two. I think you have a great deal to say to one another."

"Don't go!" Father reached out as if to clutch him, but he went anyway.

"Well, beauty, the governor. That's what kept me so long. Sir Nicholas Lawes and your counselors and your petitioners, and the saints know who else. Between us, between Calderwood and me, we've done it. We've bought your pardon. You're free. God knows why. I read that long-winded petition of yours and I'm thinking you deserve to be hanging on the gallows with the rest of them. A fine sight to greet a man coming to the island for the first time. A lot of damned pirates hanging in chains and knowing one of them was my daughter's lover."

"I don't care what happens to me," I said, bitter because he had spoiled our reunion.

"You'd better be caring because it cost me dear. Do you think I'd be letting you hang? Do you think I could be walking the streets of Charles Town with my head held high, everyone knowing my daughter was hanged for a pirate? That I could not, beauty, not for a moment. Now I can go back and tell them, 'Ah, yes, 'tis pardoned Annie was. Proven innocent as a newborn lamb. 'Twas those bastards led her into evil ways and held her captive for their nefarious uses on their sloops. Aye, pardoned and married to a respectable Jamaican planter.'"

I laughed.

"Damn it, Annie, can you take nothing seriously?"

"It was the planter made me laugh."

The slaves had brought the hurricane lamps and wine and small salted cakes. I poured each of us a glass and kissed father as I handed him his.

"Don't be making up to me, Annie. I'm angry with you. Why do you never want a good man, a respectable man?"

"What man are you talking about?"

"Calderwood. Are you blind you can't see the man's in love with you?"

"Nonsense!"

"Why else would he save you and cosset you and buy reprieve after reprieve and send for me and pay a staggering sum so a damned bitch can go free? He wants to marry you. He told me so himself."

"He never told me so. Did he also tell you he has a black mistress and as many parti-colored brats as I have fingers on my hand?"

" 'Tis the custom in these parts, Annie. He'd put her aside when he had you."

"Would he? I doubt it. Maintaining your black mistress and her children is also the custom in these parts."

"What would it matter? You would have all this. He told me he has sent to Cuba for Dove and Phibba and the other child. They'll be arriving any day now. The man's besotted with you. You owe him something for all this."

"I want to go back to Charles Town with you."

Father was silent. In the candlelight a tear shone on his cheek. He sipped at his wine, then wiped his face with a flurry of handkerchief.

"No, Annie. I'm not taking you back. I've done my duty by you and that is that. I want no more part of you. I know the blackness of your soul as no one else knows it. I loved you and you broke my heart."

I fell to my knees sobbing with my head in his lap. He

stroked my hair and called me his darling beauty, but he would not relent.

There were no guards at the gates the next morning when he left so I knew I was truly free.

I watched the carriage rock down the hill, bending the foliage as it passed, hoping father would look back and wave, hoping he was weeping as I was weeping.

It rounded the bend and was out of sight and he had given no sign. I turned and found Mr. Calderwood standing beside me.

"He will forgive you in time, Anne. He was greatly taken with Pegeen. I wish he had stayed to see Joanna. Your slaves should be arriving with her any day now."

"They aren't my slaves. I freed Dove."

"I keep forgetting. We must have papers drawn up making it official."

I nodded. My head ached from crying. I wished he would leave me alone. I was terrified he was going to ask me to marry him.

He did.

"Father told me you wanted that and I didn't believe him. You're a fool. The society you move in may accept your mulatto mistress but they would never accept me. I would be as much of a prisoner as I am now—was. You would still be free."

"Not free, Anne. Your prisoner."

I was deeply touched. "It's true that in a way I love you, but—"

"I don't ask for an answer now, Anne. I will give you time."

The week has passed slowly, but time stretches out in this climate. I spend an hour watching a hummingbird feed or John Crow soaring in great sweeping circles, gradually dropping from the heights to the valley below me. I spend a morning watching the clouds form and change and sail away. I move with the shade in the afternoon, a book open on my lap. I watch the ships come and go and remember the days at sea and long for the freshening wind and the tilt of the deck. I await the fireflies in the evening and watch them until Mr. Calderwood comes. He is endlessly patient. He has not demanded an answer.

I do not mind the narrow solitude of my bed. Those appetites have not returned, thank God. Perhaps I shall never love again.

In my room I open my chest. There is the parasol I carried when I met Jack. There the ring with which I had been married to James. My dirk, my cutlass, my gold-inlaid pistol, a silver box with a lock of Mary's hair that Bones—Robert—cut off for me before she was buried, the green taffeta dress I wore for Hornigold, shredded now with salt air and age. There are the clothes I wore as Andrew Bonn. I bury my face in them and smell tar and tallow, the rum punch I spilled when we saw Barnet's sloop coming at us, the gunpowder, the sea.

The *Touchstone,* fifty-ton sloop, REGISTRY: Jamaica.
CARGO: two hundred hogshead sugar
DESTINATION: Spanish America
ROBERT ARCHIBALD, Master
SAMUEL GREGORY, Quartermaster
JOHN PATRIC AND RICHARD SADLER, Mariners
CREW: Silas Ade, Terance Appleby, Andrew Bonn . . .